RAVE RE...

"Tim Lebbon n... remember how ... ...ge bent can be."
—Jack Ketchum, bestselling author of *The Girl Next Door*

"Lebbon is quite simply the most exciting new name in horror in years."
—*SFX Magazine*

DESOLATION

"Lebbon's work is infused with the contemporary realism of Stephen King and the lyricism of Ray Bradbury."
—*Fangoria*

"Creative, intelligent, and absolutely enthralling... Utterly fresh and innovative, *Desolation* proves once again that Tim Lebbon is the Grand Master of Horror today."
—Horror Web

"Lebbon's imagination is one to be reckoned with... *Desolation* will keep you thinking to the very last page."
—The Horror Channel

FEARS UNNAMED

"Lebbon is a genuinely masterful writer...[with] fresh ideas, shimmering prose, and often terrifying scenarios."
—*Rue Morgue*

"This is a great collection to lose sleep for. Lebbon doesn't give you a chance to catch your breath. Incredible stories that take you to four different levels of fear and back again. Lebbon is one of the best new faces in horror, and you cannot ignore him!"
—Horror Web

MORE RAVES FOR TIM LEBBON!

FACE

"Intense and affecting, *Face* will seize and hold your attention from the opening paragraph to the end. A writer blessed with extraordinary gifts, Lebbon's chief talents lie in exploring the darker moments of everyday life…. A true disciple of the dark, Lebbon's imagery wrings true fear from his audience."

—*Hellnotes*

"Lebbon's novel will reward the careful reader with insights as well as gooseflesh."

—*Publishers Weekly*

"Lebbon draws the reader into this nightmare to experience the horror with his characters. [He] taps into our universal fear of the unknown, the unseen, keeping this reader looking over her shoulder to catch that slight movement of shadow glimpsed out of the corner of her eye."

—*CelebrityCafe.com*

THE NATURE OF BALANCE

"Beautifully written and mysterious, *The Nature of Balance* will put some readers in the mind of the great Arthur Machen. But with more blood and guts."

—Richard Laymon, bestselling author of *The Lake*

"Vibrant, exploding with imagery, Tim Lebbon takes you on a white-knuckle ride of uncompromising horror. This is storytelling at its best."

—Simon Clark, author of *The Tower*

"As fascinating as his plot is, it's the beauty of his prose that raises his work to a higher level."

—*Gauntlet*

IN THE PIT

The dead thing slithered toward him as he pulled, connected to the first headless body by the thick metal chain, and then another, smaller corpse followed it up. Tom stood and backed away, only partially realising that he still had a hold of the first body's mummified legs.

He was about to drop the legs, back away, *run* away, when he saw that the chain was wrapped around another corpse. This one still seemed to have its head attached. He pulled again and it popped free of the ground, wet and filthy and yet obviously whole. It was chained to the three headless corpses, the metal wrapped around its chest, under its armpits and between its legs, thoroughly entangled.

Tom faltered only for a second before moving slowly down into the pit again. The first skull stared at him as he reached over the two adult bodies, grabbed the child's skeleton and pulled it across to himself. The child was as light as a pillow, its body seemingly whole and yet dried out and desiccated. The only thing that gave it weight was the chain. Tom placed the corpse gently between the headless adults, clasped the chain and pulled. He lifted, grunting with the effort, tears and sweat blurring his vision as he tried to make out what was wrong with this thing's head, why it was shaped like that, why it was *turning*....

And then the tiny corpse reached out and grabbed Tom's arm.

Other *Leisure* books by Tim Lebbon:

DESOLATION
FEARS UNNAMED
FACE
THE NATURE OF BALANCE

BERSERK

TIM LEBBON

LEISURE BOOKS NEW YORK CITY

For Chris Golden

A LEISURE BOOK®

January 2006

Published by

Dorchester Publishing Co., Inc.
200 Madison Avenue
New York, NY 10016

ISBN 0-8439-5430-2

Printed in the United States of America.

Visit us on the web at www.dorchesterpub.com.

BERSERK

"Dead men tell no tales."

—Proverb

CHAPTER ONE

Ten years after Steven's death, Tom never thought that his son would change his life again.

Tom held dear every precious memory of Steven, especially those times that affected him so much that he believed they had altered his perception of things forever. His toddler son, pointing to the sky in wonder and gasping his first word: *Cloud!* Older, learning to ride his bike, Tom letting go and Steven only falling when he realised he was riding on his own. At thirteen he won a bronze swimming medal for his school in the national finals, and the photograph of the presentation showed a boy on the cusp of manhood: his expression delighted yet reserved, full of self-awareness. At seventeen Steven joined the army, and at nineteen he was accepted into the Parachute Regiment. Tom still had the photograph of his son wearing that red beret hanging above his fireplace at home. It made him proud. It made him sad. It was the last picture he took of Steven before he died.

Tom sat staring into a half-empty glass, listening to the bustle of the pub serving after-work pints and meals, wondering whether he should go home to Jo or stay for one more drink, and Steven suddenly popped into his mind. This often happened—he had been their only child, and his loss had stabbed them with a blade that time kept twisting—but mostly it was when Tom least expected it. He blinked tears into a blur, drained his drink and tried to imagine what Steven would be like now, were he still alive. After ten years in the Parachute Regiment he would have likely seen action, either in Eastern Europe or the Gulf. He would probably be married; he had always been one for the girls, even as a youngster.

Maybe Tom would be a grandparent.

"Hello, wherever you are," he muttered as he stood and walked to the bar. He often pictured the ghosts of those not yet born, shades of lives unlived, and sometimes he craved to be haunted by his own grandchildren. He hoped they would be proud, but he thought not.

"Same again, Tom?"

Tom had placed the glass on the bar with every intention of going home, but now he nodded and handed over a handful of change. Glass replenished, he returned to his table, but two men had taken his place. He considered asking whether he could join them, but the thought of entering into conversation with strangers did not appeal to him right now. Not when Steven was so fresh in his mind.

It's almost ten years. He sat in a window seat close to

his original table and sipped from his pint. *Ten years since he died. Jo has changed so much in that time. Gone from a lovely young mother into middle-age, barren of all but her hollow hobbies. And I still love her.* He drank again and closed his eyes, tears threatening. She loved him, too. It was strong, their bond, and passionate; perhaps the single positive outcome of Steven's death.

He wondered just how much *he* had changed.

The two men were talking quietly, yet Tom could not help overhearing some of their conversation. He had never been the sort who could shut out background noise, and even if he had no real interest in what was being said, the words still found their way in.

The men were talking about their time in the army. They looked around thirty. Steven's age, were he still alive.

Tom drank some more ale, already beginning to regret this third pint. Jo knew he stopped off for a beer on the way home every Friday. What she did not know was that he was invariably on his own. He had led her to believe that a few colleagues from the office went along, and that small white lie did not bother him greatly. There was no reason to make her think otherwise. She would only worry. And for Tom it was just a couple of quiet pints, during which time he could muse upon the week gone by and contemplate the weekend ahead. He sometimes chatted to the couple who owned the pub, and occasionally he entered into conversation with one or two of the regulars. But more often than not this was his own time. It was when he could really think about

3

whether or not he liked himself. The answers usually came in thick and fast, and that was why he was often home after just a couple of drinks, to immerse himself in life with his wife once again. Smother his thoughts. Bury the aching feeling that he should have done much, much more with a life so scarred by Steven's death.

". . . never knew what it was all about," one of the men said. The other nodded meaningfully and drank from his pint. He caught Tom's eye momentarily, then glanced away.

"Well, if he didn't know what they did there, he deserved it."

Tom turned to the side in an effort to hear more of the conversation, but somebody won jackpot on the fruit machine. The celebratory clunking of their ejected winnings drowned the bar for thirty seconds, and by then the two men were once again sitting in silence.

Tom looked around the pub and felt a familiar disquiet settling in. He spent only a couple of hours here each week, and yet sometimes it seemed more familiar than his own living room. Perhaps this was the only place he ever truly relaxed. He closed his eyes and sighed, and when he opened them somebody said, "Porton Down."

He looked at the two men. They were hunkered down over their drinks, leaning in close, but they were not catching each other's eyes. One was staring into his pint glass, the other had found a fascinating snag of lint on his jacket sleeve.

Porton Down! That's on Salisbury Plain where . . .
Where Steven was killed. "Training accident," they had
told Tom. When pressed, they gave a few more details,
and he had always wished that he had not asked. And
yet . . . there was that ever-present doubt. "Cover-up,"
Tom's own father had muttered at the funeral, but he
was long lost to Alzheimer's by then, and Tom did not
pursue the matter.

There came one of those rare moments of silence that
haunt bars waiting to manifest, a brief second or two
when conversations falter at the same time, the fruit machine falls silent between turns, the bar staff pause for a
drink or go to change a barrel, and the juke box takes a
breather between tracks. And into that silence—still so
quiet that probably only Tom could hear it—one of the
men whispered, "They kept monsters."

Later, Tom would spend some time musing on destiny,
and what cruel fate had deigned that he hear those
three whispered words. If he had gone home after his
second pint he would have never heard, and life would
have gone on, and perhaps he and Jo would have
grown old together, their love doing its best to fill the
void where Steven and his family could have been.

But by the time he thought that, he already knew the
monsters of which the man had spoken. And in the
face of their ferocity, regret had no place at all.

"Excuse me!"

Tom had watched the men finish their drinks, leave

the pub, glancing around as if their final comment hung in the air for all to hear. And it was the look in their eyes—scared, defensive—that made him put down his unfinished drink and follow them out.

"Excuse me!"

They were walking quickly, and he had to jog to catch up.

"Excuse me, gents. Hey!"

They paused and turned around. Neither of them looked very welcoming. This close, Tom realised how big they both were. He guessed that they were no longer in the army; one had long hair, the other sported a beer gut that testified to apathy and lack of exercise.

Tom came to a halt, panting, and wondered what the hell he was going to ask.

"Help you?" Long-Hair asked.

"Yes," Tom said, looking from one to the other. Beer-Gut seemed merely dismissive, as opposed to aggressive, so he concentrated on him. "I couldn't help overhearing some of what you were saying in there—"

"Ear-wigging, were you?" Long-Hair asked.

"No," Tom said. "But I heard you mention Porton Down. My son was killed on Salisbury Plain ten years ago, and I was just wondering . . ." *I won't mention their "monster" comment,* Tom thought. *That's what drove them out, the thought someone might have heard that word. Monster.*

"Sorry to hear that," Beer-Gut said, though he sounded indifferent.

6

"I was just wondering, if you were at Porton Down maybe—"

"We weren't there," Long-Hair said. "You must have misheard us."

"How long ago did you say he was killed?" Beer-Gut asked.

"Leave it!" his friend cut in, but Tom was quick with his answer.

"Ten years next month."

Beer-Gut's eyes widened slightly, he took his hands from his pockets, stood taller.

Long-Hair looked from his friend to Tom, then back again. "I said leave it!" he said, and he went for Tom. He grabbed his jacket and shoved him against the wall, not hard, but there was certainly nothing friendly in the gesture. His breath stank of fear. Tom had never smelled anything like it before, but he knew exactly what it was. This man was terrified. "We just came for a drink," he said. "We don't like people listening in on our conversation, and we don't want to be bothered by stuff we know nothing about."

"So you weren't there?" Tom asked, keeping his eye on Beer-Gut. The big man frowned and refused to meet his gaze.

"Where?" Long-Hair said. "And even if we were, didn't your son tell you anything about the Official Secrets Act? Now fuck off before I get angry." He let go of Tom and retreated, wringing his hands as if embarrassed at his show of aggression.

"If that wasn't you angry, I'd hate to piss you off,"

Tom said. But Long-Hair did not avert his gaze or apologise. He simply stared, and soon Tom was unnerved enough to back down. "Okay, I must have misheard," he said. "Sorry. I thought I heard you talking about monsters."

Beer-Gut turned and started walking away. Long-Hair smiled, shook his head. "Too much ale, old man," he said. Then he too turned away, and the two men left Tom standing alone. Neither of them looked back.

Too much ale, old man. And for every minute of his walk home, Tom wondered how true that statement could be.

"It's almost ten years, now," Jo said the following Monday morning at breakfast.

Tom nodded. He had just finished his cereal, and his thoughts kept returning to the two men from the pub. One of them aggressive, one of them quiet, but both uncomfortably aware of what he had been asking them. He had not been hearing things, and he had not imagined their comments in the pub. The palpable fear in their reaction made a mockery of their denial.

"You think we should mark the occasion somehow?" she said.

"How?"

She shrugged, twirling a strand of hair. She had always done this when thinking deeply, and Tom loved it. It gave him a glimpse of the vivacious woman he had known before their lives had been blown apart. "Maybe we could visit the Plain again."

They had gone to Salisbury Plain once since Steven's death, on its first anniversary. It was still a military firing range back then, and they had not been able to get anywhere near to where the accident had happened. They had to imagine from a distance; the RAF Tornado swooping in across the hills, unleashing the air-to-surface missile, its pilot pulling up when he realised his mistake. *He thought he was firing at a target vehicle*, they had been told, *not an actual troop carrier*. Steven was one of fifteen men killed. They had been returned to their families in sealed coffins with Union Jacks splayed across the lids, a yearly pension payment to the next-of-kin, and no real answers. *Accident*, they were told. *It was an accident*.

"We could," Tom said, "if you really want to."

Jo shrugged. "I'm not sure what I want."

"I'd like to go," Tom said. He nodded. The men's talk in the pub had reignited a deep-felt scepticism about what he and Jo had been told concerning their son's death. Much as Tom realised how ridiculous it was to link the two—the men's strange conversation could have nothing to do with Steven, not after so long—there was always that doubt in his mind to play on. Any small mention of military accidents, mistaken identity, friendly fire, always set his mind running again, turning over the few facts they had been given and creating whole new truths to fill in the gaping blanks.

The inquest had been long. The media had covered it intensively, and following the "misadventure" verdict, newspapers had run interviews with relatives and pressure groups. There had been several TV programmes about the incident, and two investigative journalists had spent a year trying to discover the "real truth." They had come away smug and victorious with what they had found: a few obscure facts about live weapons training policy, and a closet full of skeletons connected to the inquest's presiding officer's sexual preferences. But nothing concrete. After a year in which the fact of Steven's death had been hammered home to them each and every day, Tom and Jo knew little more than they had the day he died.

Tom had no faith in the inquest's findings, and even less in the papers and TV programmes that used it to promote their own sales and ratings. He had no doubt whatsoever that the story they were told was nowhere near the truth, but the glare in which the inquiry took place had swayed many people into believing that the real story was being fully uncovered. What was actually revealed at the end of that long, painful year was yet another skewed version of the same account. More names to blame, rules to change, heads to roll, many apologies made to hungry TV cameras and a public so used to being deceived that they no longer recognised the self-satisfied smiles of their deceivers.

Cover-up, Tom's father had whispered at the funeral.

Tom had always been angry, but the anger was tempered by a grief so all-consuming that he had barely known it himself. For that year he was a stranger living in his own body, existing purely to suffer the memories of his only son. He recalled many occasions that he had not thought about for years, random moments in time, as if his mind were searching for remnants of Steven. Everywhere he looked he saw his son riding a tricycle, kicking a football, leaving home at seventeen to join the army. It came to a point when Tom wished he could go a day without memories, but those were the times when loss hit him hardest. His anger, though rich and deep, was also useless. It would gain him nothing. And he knew that through it all, the most important thing was that he and Jo were there for each other.

He had never forgotten, nor forgiven, but in a way he supposed he had given in. And eventually life moved on.

They kept monsters.

"Yes," he said again, "I'd like to go. I think it would do us some good."

Jo lowered her head and looked down into her mug.

"Jo? You all right?"

She nodded, looked up at him with sad eyes. She rarely cried anymore. Somehow this look of wretchedness was worse. "I'm fine," she said. "It's only an anniversary. Not really a day different from any other."

"No, no different."

"I think about him every day anyway. It's just . . ." She trailed off, shook her head.

"We should mark the day," Tom said.

"Yes." Jo looked at him and smiled. "It's like a birthday, except this is Steven's deathday. Is that sick, Tom? You think people will think we're weird?"

Tom grasped her hand across the table and felt the stickiness of butter and jam between her fingers. "You think I give a flying fuck what people think?" he said.

Jo laughed. He liked that sound. It reminded him that they still had a life together, and sometimes he *needed* reminding.

"I'm going to work," he said. "I'll check out the Internet at lunchtime and see if I can find us a nice cottage somewhere nearby."

"I think just a weekend," Jo said. "Any longer may not be very nice."

"Just a weekend," Tom said. He stood and kissed his wife, hugged her, tickled her ear and stepped back as she aimed a slap at his arm. "See you later. Love you."

"Love you too," she said, already standing to prepare for work. "I'll be home a bit later tonight. I need to finish this design before the end of the week."

"I'll cook tea," Tom said. He smiled, and when Jo gave him a smile in return he saw the real, sad depth to her that no banter or play could ever hide.

That lunchtime at work, Tom booked a cottage on the edge of Salisbury Plain for the second weekend in October. It was a remote location, set just outside a little village, an old cottage with two bedrooms, a downstairs toilet, an open log fire and a cold room beneath the kitchen where occupants had once stored their meat and other perishables. It was a ten-minute walk from the nearest pub and restaurant, and a half-hour drive from the military areas of Salisbury Plain. If Steven's ghost haunted the Plain, they would be within shouting distance.

Tom often wondered about ghosts. *Steven is always with us,* Jo said, but she meant as a memory, the reality of him retained by their never letting his moment in life fade away. But when they were dead and gone, what then? Would their son become nothing more than a number in an army report, a photograph, an occasional thought for his surviving friends? And after that . . . nothing. How could someone so alive suddenly become so dead? Tom hated this way of thinking, yet he had always possessed a mind prone to exploring the more esoteric areas of life, and Steven's death encouraged that rather than lessened it. Some nights, napping on the settee next to Jo, he found himself wandering the moors, drifting above those dark acres of fern and grass, skipping across marshland, passing through occasional small woods where animals lived from year to year without ever seeing a human being. And occasionally, in the darkest moments, he saw Steven roaming the Plain, confused at his sudden death, crying . . . crying for his mother and father . . . because he was far too young to die.

Tom would open his eyes, stare at the familiar four walls of his home, and despair at the brief but intense sense of hopelessness that always followed.

It was a bad afternoon. He sat at his desk and stared out the window, occasionally shuffling papers or opening up new files on his computer to convince himself, at least, that he was working. Steven was there as always, but there was also the huge chasm of emptiness and regret that threatened to swallow Tom whole: regret at a life wasted behind a desk, watching his ambitions and drive rot beneath an assault of nine-to-five indifference; and the emptiness in his own mind, where once had dwelled such grand aspirations. He had always regarded his job as a means to an end, but he had never come close to achieving that end. He sat at his desk for five days each week crunching numbers and paying for his mortgage, forever mourning the career in music that continued to elude him. So many opportunities taken up and blown away, so many deals scuppered because of bad luck or his own stupidity. The fact that he had barely played a note since his son's death did little to quell his regrets.

In their third bedroom Tom's instruments sat on their stands, monuments to lost dreams. They had once been the means by which he hoped to make his mark on the world, but now they merely took up space and drew dust, all potential long since echoed away to nothing. These walls had heard wonderful music, but they gave none back. He would stand in that room sometimes and wonder whether he had changed anything at all. Had a bird heard him playing and changed its course? Had the molecular makeup of the house been subtly altered by the vibration of his double bass, the sweet serenade of his guitar? Was there, anywhere in the world, evidence of the talent he had squandered?

Sometimes he believe that the ghost of his music wandered the Plain with the lost spirit of his only son.

But today, with autumn sunlight making beauty from

dying leaves, there was something else on his mind. That doubt, risen from its uneasy grave. And the old anger at the lies they had been told, still tempered by grief, but no longer quashed by its intensity.

By the end of that afternoon, Tom needed to do something positive. He left work early and walked to the pub, hoping against hope, realising how foolish he was being, how naïve. And yet he was still not completely surprised to see Beer-Gut sitting at the same table he had shared with his friend that previous Friday, alone this time, pensive and scared.

"Can I get you a drink?"

"Oh shit, I didn't think you'd be here!" Beer-Gut stood at his table, wide-eyed. He looked toward the door as if planning an escape.

"But you came anyway?"

The big man shrugged. He was breathing fast, eyes averted, perhaps going over whatever he had to say in his head.

"Guilt's a weird thing, isn't it?"

"Look, don't fuck with me like that," the man said quietly, staring at Tom for a few seconds before looking away again.

"I'm so sorry," Tom said, shaking his head, meaning it. He offered his hand. "I'm Tom Roberts."

Beer-Gut shook his hand; sweaty palms, but a strong grip. "Nathan King." He sat back down.

"Pleased to meet you."

King did not echo the sentiment, and Tom realised

15

that this was probably the very last place he wanted to be right now. His whole manner projected nervousness and disquiet; the shifting eyes, tapping fingers, frequent sips from his glass.

"Let me get you a refill," Tom said. At the bar he took a few moments to compose himself, and he was suddenly hit by a cool, inexplicable terror. *I may discover something terrible now*, he thought. *Something I haven't known for ten years, and something it may be best I never know. Nothing will bring Steven back. We have a life, Jo and I. We deserve to live it in peace.* He paid for the drinks and carried them back to the table, and his deeper inner voice spoke up, the one that occasionally rose to see past the bullshit. *Truth deserves a chance*, it said.

Tom sat down opposite Nathan King, and prepared to have his life changed again.

It took King several minutes to begin speaking.

The two men sat there silently, letting life wash by in the swish of coats and the waft of end-of-the-day body odour. Tom watched the barmaid smiling at each customer and making them all think they were special, dropping her tips into a glass behind the bar. He listened to the bland pop song whispering from the juke box. He smelled the sharp tang of fatty burgers and chips cooking in the kitchen, a haze of smoke blurring that end of the big room. In one corner an elderly couple sat next to each other without speaking, the contact of their arms communication enough. The man was drinking stout, the woman wine, and Tom wondered how many children and grandchildren they had. People lit cigarettes, laughed, coughed, drank, stared, and none of them were aware of the tension between him and King.

At last King finished the pint Tom had bought for him, placed the glass carefully on the table, sat back and sighed. "I didn't know your son," he said.

Tom frowned, his expression question enough.

"But though I never met him, I'm not here to waste your time. You don't need to know anything about me, but to decide if what I know is of use to you, *I* need to know about *you*. And your son. And how he was killed."

Tom sat back in his chair, feeling a peculiar release now that Nathan had initiated conversation. *Maybe I will hear things I don't really want to,* he thought, *and maybe they'll change my life. But if so, then that's only right.*

"I've always suspected the story the army gave us was false," Tom said, watching King for any reaction. There was none—he was stony-faced—and Tom realised that he wanted the whole story. Whatever King had to reveal demanded that, at least.

So he continued. It was the first time in years he had spoken in such depth about his son's death.

"They said he was in a training exercise on Salisbury Plain, involving the army and RAF. It was Steven's first major exercise since joining up, and he told us how much he was looking forward to it. Who wouldn't? He was still a kid really, and playing war games for real was exciting as hell for him. He didn't know what it would involve other than having to spend three weeks on the Plain, though he did say he'd be out of contact for that time. He told us not to worry. Of course he did. He was young, indestructible, and it was us that had become more aware of death as time crept on. Having children does that to you. He was dreaming of the parachute drop, the march across the moors, the camaraderie, the triumph of achieving their objective for the day, the smoke and noise and the excitement of knowing that there was nothing *really* there to do them harm. We were thinking about failed chutes, tanks sinking in the marshes, live rounds when blanks should be used . . . we were doing our parenting bit, for every day of those three weeks. But I was still thrilled for Steven. He was achieving an ambition he'd had since before he was a teenager. Making a life for himself. I've never really done that, though I've tried, and the fact that my son was doing it . . . I think I was living vicariously through him. Relishing his success, reveling in the joy he felt, because it was something I rarely experienced myself."

Tom took a swig of beer, looked around the bar at the people who all meant nothing to him, and space closed in. He and King could have been sitting anywhere. "You see what I'm trying to say, Nathan? About how much I loved my son? I loved him so much I could live through him, and there wasn't an ounce of jealousy in me. I really, really loved him." He broke off, swallowed hard, waiting for his stinging eyes to clear.

"My parents were never bothered what I did, so long as I left home," King said. "You must have been a good dad."

"I hope Steven thought that way," Tom said, nodding. "I hope he did. Anyway . . . the exercise. It was a long three weeks for my wife and me. We knew he said he'd be out of contact, but still we waited for the phone to ring, or someone to knock on the door. It's crazy, but you never stop worrying about your children, even when they're adults. There's always something of the child to them in your eyes. Do you now what I mean? Do you have children?" Tom knew the answer even as he asked, and Nathan shook his head.

"Haven't found the right woman yet," King said.

"Good luck to you. Steven left his girlfriend when he joined up, and as far as I know, there was nothing serious for the last years of his life. I guess he was living it up, a man in uniform enjoying the attention. Something else I never did . . . never played the field. Sounds mad, but that's another thing I'm glad he did. Had fun."

"So what happened?" King asked, a note of impatience creeping in.

"The accident." Tom drained his beer. Through the bottom of his glass the bar seemed even farther away, as if he could close his eyes and wish himself home. "They waited until the end of the exercise to tell us. It happened during the second week apparently, but they waited another week until they called, and by then . . . by then his body was already being shipped to us. How fucking cold, you know? Icy cold. Even the officer's voice on the phone was hard, however much he tried to project sympathy."

"He was probably scared," King said.

"Scared of telling us?"

King glanced away, shrugged. "Go on."

"They said Steven had been in an armoured troop carrier, out on its own, traveling across the Plain. There were fifteen men in there, including the driver, and they'd just stopped beside a copse of trees when a Tornado fired a missile at them. The pilot thought they were one of the targets set up across the Plain for the RAF to practise bombing. They killed everyone, all fifteen men. And that's it, that's all they said. Apart from sorry. As if sorry is ever any good!" Tom grabbed his glass, realised it was empty, and when he looked across at King he squeezed hard, feeling the *click* of a crack beneath his fingers. "What is it?"

King had turned pale, and was staring down at his hands in his lap. There was sweat on his upper lip. When he looked up, Tom thought he was going to leave.

"What?" Tom asked again.

"Tom, I'm going to get another drink," he said, and when he picked up his glass his hand was shaking.

For the couple of minutes King was away Tom's mind ran riot, trying to imagine who he may be and what secrets he had to reveal. Was he a survivor? Did he know that lies had been told, and if so what they were? Was he the pilot that had fired the missile? Who, what, when, where . . . ?

Tom closed his eyes to try and calm himself, prepare for whatever revelation may come. *I won't tell Jo*, he thought, surprising himself with his own conviction. *If it doesn't change anything, I won't tell her. She's suffered enough.*

King placed another pint in front of him, sat down and leaned forward, elbows on his knees. He rushed his words, as if afraid that they would dry up. "Tom, your son wasn't killed in that accident. That never happened. Fifteen men died, but they died at Porton Down, not on Salisbury Plain."

"Porton Down," Tom said, guts clenching, skin running cold. "The chemical and biological research place. Steven was involved there?"

"No," King said, sighing and looking down at his feet. "He was there on a trial period as a guard, that's all. But wasn't involved in that exercise on the Plain." He stayed that way for several seconds, tensed with some inner turmoil. When he looked up again, his eyes had gone hard. "I've said too much already," he said.

"Don't you fucking dare!" Tom hissed, leaning in so that their faces were a head apart. "Don't you even *think* about starting this and not finishing it! Do you know what I've been through since it happened? The doubt, the suspicion? And now you've told me everything we thought is wrong, you can't just fuck off without telling me *how* wrong!"

"I could be shot for this," King said, and Tom thought there was little exaggeration in his comment.

"Then why are you here now?"

The big man shrugged and leaned back in his chair. "Maybe sharing my nightmares will lessen them."

"You think I don't have nightmares?" Tom asked.

"No," King said, "you don't." And the look in his eyes was cold and terrified.

"So . . . ?" Tom asked, and he thought, *maybe he* should *leave, maybe he* shouldn't *tell me.*

"So . . . there was an accident at Porton Down. Your son and those others were there, and they were killed. And the army whitewashed it. Made it into something it wasn't. Hushed it up. Believe me, they're good at that kind of thing."

"What sort of accident?"

King looked into his beer. "Something escaped."

"So what did I bury?" Tom asked, suddenly certain that the coffin he and Jo had wept over had been filled with nothing to do with them.

"Sod from the marshes. They buried the dead on the Plain. They didn't want the infection to spread."

"What sort of infection? Plague? What?"

"A plague of sorts," King said. He finished his drink in two gulps, looked around, twitchy. Tom realised that he would be leaving soon, and there was nothing Tom could do to stop him. King already knew he had said too much. But this was still a story without an ending, and Tom could not live with this mystery anymore.

"How do you know all this?" Tom asked.

"I was at Porton Down too," King said. "I had to bury the bodies."

Bury the bodies. Tom closed his eyes and tried not to

imagine his son's rotten body, flopping around in the bucket of a JCB with a younger Nathan King at the controls.

"Where's my son's grave?" he asked, eyes still closed.

"Tom, you'll never—"

"Where is my son's grave? Nathan, I need to tell you something. I've mourned for ten years, and I'll mourn until the day I die. What you told me bears up what I've always believed: that we were lied to. But I don't see what I can do about it, other than visit my son one last time. I've spent too long crying over an empty grave." *But there is more I can do*, he thought, *so much more. But not here and not now . . . I have to think first. Make plans.*

"Don't go looking," King said, standing. "I saw the bodies. And I know the truth."

"What truth?" Tom asked, and then the comment he had heard the previous day came back to him just as King spoke.

"They kept monsters there," he said. And before Tom could hit him with any more questions King had left the pub and disappeared into the night.

Something escaped, the ex-army man had said. *A plague of sorts. They kept monsters there. . . .*

Tom sat at the table for a long time, staring into the murk of the pub and seeing so much farther—to the moors, to Salisbury Plain. Though he saw *something* there, its true form was blurred by lies.

But now that the seed of truth had been planted, Tom needed to see it bloom.

CHAPTER TWO

When Tom and Jo left home for their journey to Wiltshire, it felt as though they were going for more than a long weekend. Tom checked that the doors and windows were locked, unplugged the TV and stereo, closed all the internal doors . . . and he felt as though he should be laying white dust sheets over the furniture. *Only three days*, he thought, taking one last look around the living room, noticing some of it instead of just seeing it. The picture of them on their wedding day, with such a promising future evident in their happy smiles. And Steven, photographed at his passing out parade, with that same potential future reflected in his eyes. *Nobody expects catastrophe*, Tom thought. *Everyone knows it's coming at some point, but nobody expects it. We just can't live like that. But that makes it so much harder when it arrives.*

Tom wiped the dust from Steven's picture and smiled, and a peculiar thought came to him unbidden. *Coming to see you, son.*

"Tom?" Jo stood behind him, watching him stroke the picture frame.

"I'm coming now, babe."

"We're doing the right thing, aren't we? You don't think this will just dig it all up again?"

Tom winced at her choice of words. "Jo, we've agreed that we'll go, and I think it's the right thing to do. Really. It'll be good to get away, anyway. Steven will be on our minds, but it'll be a break for us, too. A break from everything."

"Some things you can't escape from," she said.

He nodded, hugged her. "Let's go."

Jo hugged him back, and as Tom looked around the room he held on hard to his wife.

They were silent for most of the journey. Jo made occasional comments—pointing out a hovering sparrow hawk, an air balloon, asking Tom whether he wanted some mints—and Tom answered briefly, with a yes or a no, or sometimes with a nod or a shake of the head. It was not because he did not wish to talk, nor even because he knew that Jo really only wanted to sit there and think about the coming weekend. His silence was borne mainly of frustration.

In his back pocket sat the envelope he had found shoved beneath a wiper blade when he had been loading the car. He had not yet had a chance to open it without Jo seeing. And he had a feeling—a *certainty*—that whatever it contained he would not want to share with her.

He must have waited outside the pub, followed me home.

"Shouldn't be long now," Jo said. Tom nodded.

Couldn't finish the story face to face, and now it's there in my back pocket, more hints at the truth.

"It's been a long time since we were down this way."

Tom was certain the envelope was from Nathan King. Anything else would be a huge coincidence, and a cruel one.

The miles swept by and Jo nodded off, the envelope burned in Tom's trouser pocket. *Read me, read me.* He even began to reach around to delve into his pocket, but the car drifted into the next lane and the blare of a lorry's horn startled him back to reality.

"Shit," Tom muttered, heart pummeling him for his stupidity.

"You want me to drive the rest of the way?"

"No, no, I'm fine. Fine."

Don't feel fine. Feel fucked.

Motorway filtered down to dual carriageway, then they turned onto an A-road, and then B-roads led through startlingly beautiful countryside to the village where they were staying.

Not far from here, Tom thought. *Not far from here at all.*

After a few minutes they pulled up in the driveway to their holiday cottage.

"You check out the box in the shed where they said they'd leave the keys," Tom said. "I'll start unloading the car."

As soon as Jo's back was turned Tom pulled out the envelope, and though there was no writing in the clear window, Tom's name had been scrawled across the front in red ink. Whoever had written the name had pushed so hard that the pen had torn the paper, like a cut in pale flesh. He ripped it open, glanced at Jo disappearing around the side of the cottage, and pulled out the sheet of folded paper.

It was a map, an enlarged OS section of part of Salisbury Plain. And near the centre, away from any distinguishing features, sat a small, neat X. It was marked in red. There was nothing else, but no explanation was needed.

"X marks the spot," Tom whispered, and then he heard Jo's footsteps in the gravel behind him, and he crumpled the map and envelope in his hand.

"Lovely cottage," he said, even though this was the first time he had even glanced at it.

"Don't break your back unloading the car, will you?"

Tom smacked Jo's butt as she walked by, delighted at her giggle, already wondering how he could get away on his own for a few hours.

After unloading the car, they had a look around the cottage together. It was small, cosy and very countrified, with plates lining walls, dried twigs stacked on windowsills and arranged in old china pots, and dozens of landscape prints by local artists gracing the walls upstairs. The bath was an old cast-iron freestanding type, great chunky pipes standing proud of the floor at one end like the exposed arteries of the house. The toilet would not have looked out of place in a museum. The air was musty with age, and although Tom spotted air fresheners secreted in several places upstairs and down, he thought they were fighting a losing battle. This house was old—maybe three hundred years—and it would take more than a few modern chemicals to purge the tang of its history from the air. It had stood for a long time, and it had a right to project its age. He breathed in deeply and enjoyed the aroma, smiling at Jo when she gave him a quizzical look.

From the kitchen, a low door revealed an impossibly narrow staircase that led down to the cold room. Jo declined Tom's offer to investigate, but he had always been one for exploring hidden places. It was that idea of never quite knowing what he would find; an old painting in the attic, a forgotten master; a half-buried chest in a seaside cave, the padlock a rusted remnant from centuries before. He never had found anything of value, but that did not deter him. In fact it encouraged him to explore further, because really it was the mystery that lured him. If he ever did find something other than darkness and empty spaces, the mystery would be dissipated, and perhaps he would change.

The staircase was narrow and twisted in a tight half-spiral, so that even moving down sideways Tom's shoulders and gut touched the walls. He would be filthy when he came back up, but the cool, damp darkness below was irresistible.

"What's down there?" Jo called. She was standing aside from the doorway, allowing as much light as possible to enter.

"Spiders," Tom called. "Big ones. Huge. *Unnaturally* huge! Oh my *God!*"

"What?"

Tom chuckled and the sound carried up and down. Above, it elicited a muttered curse from Jo; below, it echoed for a second, overlapping itself and turning into a groan. Tom took out his car keys and pressed the button on the tiny torch that hung on the keyring. Its makers' claims that it could be seen from a mile away were instantly vapourised when the beam barely managed to fight back the dark more than a couple of feet.

Thick dark, Tom thought, *like it hasn't been disturbed for ages.*

At the bottom of the narrow stairs he found himself in a tiny room with a low ceiling and bare stone walls. The walls had been whitewashed at some time in the distant past, but moisture had bled through and shed the paint onto the floor. His torch lit the room just enough for him to see that there was nothing down there, other than a few shelves and a damp floor that looked prone to flooding. No sign of an electric light, and no indication that the room had been used for decades.

It was cold. Bitterly cold. He wondered if everywhere underground was like this.

"Anything?" Jo called. Her voice was muffled, even though the staircase only took a half-turn.

"It's horrible!" Tom called back, putting on his best horror movie voice.

"Well retreat from the horror and help me in the bedroom."

"That's an offer I can't refuse."

Jo laughed. "Maybe after dinner if you're lucky."

"If *you're* lucky!"

He started up the staircase, knees straining from the unnatural angle at which he had to climb. He thought of the people who had actually used this place to store their meat and perishables, wondered how they had lived, whether they had shared the same banter as he and Jo. Perhaps the cottage was haunted. At least a ghost tickling his foot in the night would take his mind off Steven, and that map, and the fact that Nathan King for some reason wanted him to find the grave.

Or did he? Maybe the red cross was a red herring. Perhaps King was just a cruel man, taking pleasure in Tom's desperation and loss.

"You're filthy!" Jo said. "Oh for God's sake, you and your bloody exploring."

"Want to wash me off in the bath?"

"Stop being a frisky old sod and carry our suitcase upstairs, will you?" She smiled at him, one side of her mouth rising in a look that spoke of years of love and familiarity. Sometimes Tom thought they knew each other too well—that Steven's death had left an irreparable hole in their lives that they tried to fill with more of themselves—but he found endless comfort in their strong relationship. Many people turned to God, but he had to look no farther than his wife.

Upstairs, Tom and Jo unpacked their suitcase, hung

their clothes, pulled back the bedclothes to let them air, and all the while Tom was aware of the map in his back pocket. It felt heavier than a piece of paper. He kept touching the pocket, slipping his finger inside to make sure it was still there. If Jo found it he had no idea what he would tell her. Not the truth, for sure: *Jo, I think this is where Steven is really buried.* Oh no. That way lay madness. But lying to his wife was not something that came naturally, and he was sure that whatever happened, she would see through his lie to the terrible truth beneath.

"What shall we do for dinner?" Jo asked.

Tom looked at her blankly for a few seconds, trying to haul his thoughts back from their buried son. "Dinner?"

"You eat it," she said. "Here, or in the local pub?"

"Oh, er . . ." Tom shook his head. "The pub, I think."

"You sure? I could cook the steak we brought."

There'll be people in the pub, he thought. *Noise, bustle, spaces I can stare into without Jo wondering why.* "Let's have that tomorrow," he said. "Come on, it'll be nice to eat out our first night here."

"Alright, but you're not allowed to choose steak. That chance has gone, mister." She pecked him on the cheek and went into the bathroom.

Tom clunked downstairs, making a noise so that Jo did not think he was sneaking around. He snorted, shook his head and sat on the flowery settee in the living room. *Damn it, I'm not sneaking about all fucking weekend!* But he took the map from his pocket, coughing as he opened it to mask the sound of paper crinkling, and spread it on his knee. There was little to reveal its location on the Plain other than the coordinates, and for that he would have to buy a larger scale OS map. There were no villages, farms or settlements, no major roads, and no names that he could see to identify any particular area. All the map displayed were the contour lines of gentle hills, a couple of stone mounds, and a meandering stream at the bottom edge. That and the red cross. *How dare they bury my Steven in no place at all*, he thought, the sentiment raw and sore in his eyes. He wiped away the first tears, sniffed, stood and walked to the kitchen. In one of the food boxes he had packed a bottle of Jameson's, and he spun the top off and took a long, luxurious swig from the bottle.

Jo said he drank too much. But then she barely drank at all, so she did not understand the pleasure he derived from it. That was his excuse, anyway, and his stock answer when she brought it up, though sometimes he thought his drinking had more to do with drowning pain than promoting pleasure.

He took another swig, put the top back on, and closed his eyes as the whiskey burned its way into his stomach. Upstairs he heard the toilet flush and the tap turned on, the water hammer in the pipes actually seeming to set the house shaking on its foundations.

"Tom!" Jo called.

"Okay, I hear it!" he shouted. "Probably the ghost trying to get out of the pipes."

Jo was silent. Tom knew he could take this ghost thing too far; she claimed not to believe in them, yet they terrified her. Perhaps the mention of ghosts only brought Steven to mind.

The local pub was surprisingly accommodating to visitors. It had a smattering of locals—they gathered at one end of the bar, playing darts or sitting protectively around their pints of local brew—but there was still an honest welcome from the staff, and a friendliness that put Tom immediately at ease. The landlady recommended a pint of local beer for him, and she let him try a half before he committed to buying some, which he did. She gave Jo her first glass of wine on the house, and when Tom said they'd like to eat she showed them to a comfortable, private table in an alcove close to the front door. Its window looked out onto the village street, and past the houses opposite they could make out the rolling hills of Salisbury Plain in the dusk. Tom glanced that way, saw Jo do the same, and then they both concentrated on the inside of the pub.

Tom had left the map back at the cottage, hidden in the book he had brought to read this weekend. His pocket felt empty without it, as if he had left purpose behind.

They ordered food, and while waiting they indulged in one of their own private games; spotting peculiar-looking people, giving them a name, then building a background around them. The old farmer at the end of the bar, sporting sideburns the size of small rabbits, became Major Crisis of the Indian Expeditionary Force, here on leave and making the most of British beer brewing. Whenever he spoke he spat at those around him, and Tom had to bury his face in his hands when Jo muttered, "Machine gun effect."

There was a huge open fireplace but the fire remained unlit. Tom imagined it would be very cosy here in the winter, with flames roaring in the hearth and hail pummeling the windows. Perhaps they would have a lock-in after eleven o'clock, allowing the locals to remain here lest the wind blow them away. The landlady would cook them bacon sandwiches throughout the night, and if any beer barrel needed changing one of the regulars would volunteer, sparse payment for their use of the pub as a shelter against the elements.

And maybe Steven had drunk here once.

Tom sighed and took a drink. Jo spotted his instant mood change but ignored it. He thanked her silently, smiled, and made a joke about the young family that had just come in. They had a daughter and son, both under five, and the parents looked hassled and strained. The children stared around the pub wide-eyed, marking places for forthcoming expeditions and items to investigate as soon as their parents turned their backs.

He might have grandchildren that age, if Steven hadn't been killed.

Tom tipped his beer, and as he was looking into the bottom of the glass King's face came back at him, pale and haunted by what he had seen. He had obviously wanted to tell Tom everything, and yet from that first moment in the pub he had seemed reticent about speaking. He had let out a few details, but everything he said inspired a dozen more questions. And then he had left the map.

Why? What could Nathan King gain from revealing any of this? Unless it really was as he said: *Maybe sharing my nightmares will lessen them.*

"Do you remember how he used to like vampires and werewolves?" Jo said. Neither of them ever had to say who they were talking about.

"And not just when he was a kid," Tom said, smiling. "There was always something going on with him. He always liked to think about things differently."

"Just like his father," Jo said, smiling. "I never understood the fascination." She was moving her wineglass around in small circles, setting the wine swirling, staring into its centre as if seeing the past in there. "Stuff like that always seems so nasty."

"I think maybe that *is* the fascination," Tom said. "Finding nastier things than anything you'll meet in the world. Reading about them. Facing them."

"Still, there's nicer things to read about and watch."

Like war, and death, and murder, Tom thought, but he said nothing.

"I wonder if he'd still be into all that stuff if he were still with us," she said, setting the glass down and watching the wine settle. She looked up at Tom, eyebrows raised.

"The person he would have been is someone we'll never know," Tom said. "Ten years is a long time."

"A stranger," Jo said sadly, and she turned and looked out the window. A street lamp reflected in her eyes, catching the moisture of threatening tears.

"Don't cry," Tom said. His wife looked back at him, and then their food came to save them.

They ate in silence, enjoying each other's company and the fact that there was not always the need for conversation. Tom often saw couples sitting in pubs or restaurants, not conversing, uncomfortable, obviously having nothing to say to each other. He and Jo had never been like that; their silence was merely another form of conversation. It said, *I'm alright, I'm content, I love that you're here next to me.* A big part of their being together was their ability to be on their own.

Later, Tom sipped some single malt while Jo had one more glass of wine. They had finished their meal and moved their chairs so that they both sat behind the table, looking into the pub. They watched the young couple struggle through a noisy dinner, bickering with their children and each other, leaving when the little boy began crying and refused to stop, whatever the parents offered him. Major Crisis remained at the end of the bar, slumping farther and farther down in his seat the more he drank. He was a quiet drunk, his moist eyes blinking slowly and heavily.

Tom began to feel tired, worn out by the journey here, but also troubled by the map and Nathan King's comments. Such a weight on his shoulders, unshared. Such a burden to carry, secret from his wife. And that lie by omission caused a form of mental exhaustion. For the first time in years there was something between them, blocking the total contact their minds enjoyed and demanded, and it was something that Tom had brought on himself. If only he had been able to take things as they were, accept whatever reality made life most comfortable. But he had never been one to shy away from truths hidden in the dark. Just as he liked to explore derelict houses or dingy basements, so he could never resist delving into mysteries secreted away in hidden corners of reality.

Somewhere not too far away from where they now sat, Steven may be buried. However disturbing that was—however wrong that made everything feel—it was something that Tom could never simply ignore for the sake of a quiet life.

But he would spare Jo that knowledge for as long as he could. Forever, perhaps.

Next morning, fate dealt Tom a powerful hand. Jo woke up with stomach cramps and reached the bathroom just in time to vomit. Tom went to her, held her, wiped her mouth, wanting to shy away from the stink but too concerned to do so. After a few more dry heaves she staggered back to bed, muttering about gone-off food or too much wine, and Tom sat beside her, stroking her hair.

"You think maybe this is all too much?" he asked.

"I don't think so, really, love," she said. "I wanted to come here, for us as much as Steven. I enjoyed our time together last night. I feel a little sad, and I'll have a weep this weekend, but I'm glad we came."

"You look glad," he said, pleased when she offered a weak smile.

"I feel bloody awful." She closed her eyes and sighed as Tom stroked her cheek.

A few minutes later, when Jo was almost asleep, Tom leaned down and whispered to her. "Do you mind if I go out?"

She shook her head. "No, go, go, leave me to sleep, I'll be fine," she mumbled, tiredness distorting her words.

Tom kissed her forehead, pleased to feel no fever there. It was bad food or too much wine, as she said. He would have never left her if she were truly ill, but now . . .

He picked up his book containing the map, closed the bedroom door quietly behind him, and hurried downstairs to gather his things. Food for lunch, money, walking boots, and a shovel he took from the lean-to shed behind the cottage.

I'll not be digging anything up. That's just fucking crazy. I'm not doing any digging. Of course I'm not.

But he put the shovel in the car boot anyway, glancing up to make sure Jo was not watching from the window. He closed the door and stood there for a while, listening to the sounds of the world waking up. Birds chirped, fallen leaves rustled, but his breathing was loudest.

As he drove away from the cottage he felt unreality settling around him. Part of it was being away from Jo, he supposed, and part of it was the map in his back pocket once again. But there was also a sense of foreboding, hanging over him like thunderclouds on the dawn horizon.

Did I really just put a shovel in the car boot?

He smiled and shook his head. But he could not dispel the sense of danger that accompanied him as he drove away, nor the feeling that his life was changing by the second.

He picked up a hiker's map at the post office on the outskirts of the village. It was an expanded Ordnance Survey map, with rights of way and footpaths added to enable walkers to find their way across the Plain. It also had a boxed key to one side, where local areas of interest were listed and coordinated with the map. As he sat in the car, the village behind him and the expanse of Salisbury Plain ahead, Tom felt the full desolation of that wild place opening up before him.

It was a beautiful autumn day. The sky was clear. The leaves remaining on trees were gold, orange and yellow, still clinging to branches but almost ready to fall; beauty in death. A mile from the village he pulled up on the grass verge, looked around to make sure he was totally alone and took out Nathan King's map.

It only took a couple of minutes to locate the area on the new OS map. The scales were different, but the coordinates were accurate, and Tom stared down at the point of his search. It was nowhere. There were no villages nearby, no farms, no signs of habitation or humanity whatsoever. Such a cold place to die. Such an empty place to be buried. He closed his eyes and saw Steven as a toddler, running through the local woods and swishing at fern heads with a stick, laughing back at Tom when he growled and clawed his hand and threatened to give chase.

"It's not fair," Tom said, not quite sure what he was referring to. All of it, perhaps. Life. "It's not fair."

It took half an hour to drive across the Plain toward the red X on King's map. A mile or so away from that place the road veered to the south, bounded on the left by a bank topped with a security fence. Warning signs were placed at regular intervals:

WARNING

NO ACCESS

M.O.D. PROPERTY

LIVE FIRING ZONE

"Fuck." Tom pulled over onto the side of the road and stared at the fence. It was tall, anti-climb, and though it showed signs of age it still seemed sturdy and intimidating.

So close! He checked the map again, trying to imagine what this fence and the bank it stood upon hid. He left the car and climbed, grasping at shrubs and clumps of thick grass for purchase. It was steep, obviously meant to deter the curious. Perhaps he was being observed even now.

He paused, looked over his shoulder, confirmed that

he was alone. He could see no security cameras lining the fence. There were no other cars out here, and no sign at all that there was anyone other than him on the moor this morning. Yet the feeling of being watched lingered, and Tom put it down to guilt.

At the top of the bank he knelt and looked between the metal fence uprights.

There was nothing out of the ordinary about the landscape beyond. Wilder than the area he had just driven through, perhaps, but only because he could see no roads or tracks in there. There were no buildings, no artificial earthworks, and no sign of any activity.

Out there, that's where Steven may be buried, he thought. *That bush on the hillock over there, perhaps its roots are in his skeleton. Or over there, that spread of heather, like a bruise on the land, maybe that was planted to cover the mass grave.*

He wondered how close he was to Porton Down. He had not been able to find it on the OS map, but that was hardly surprising. Though everyone knew of its existence, a chemical and biological warfare research establishment was hardly a place that the military would want advertised.

They kept monsters there.

Tom shivered. The wilderness was getting to him already. He loved the countryside, but only the version he was familiar with, where he would meet neighbours walking their dogs or kids damming a stream, all of it recognisible and safe. This was a truly wild place. He could imagine the big cats of legend prowling the Plain, and at night, when there was only moonlight and mist, the ghosts would have it to themselves.

He glanced at his watch. He'd been away from Jo for under an hour, but already she felt far away.

"So how the hell do I get in there?" he said, leaning against the fence, shoving, feeling absolutely no give whatsoever. There was another sign farther along, and he walked along the top of the bank to read it:

NO ACCESS

AREA PATROLLED BY SECURITY GUARDS

"Well, if there are guards patrolling, there aren't any live firing exercises."

He tried to picture this place crawling with military hardware, aircraft swooping low across the Plain, unleashing awesome firepower against target vehicles and vehicles they only believed to be targets. But that version of Steven's death was rapidly dwindling in Tom's mind, fading like an old photograph, replaced already by the mystery planted by his brief talk with Nathan King. Life had become complicated again, and here he was trying to exacerbate that confusion.

Whatever he found in there, he knew that it would not give him easy answers.

Tom walked the fence. He chose to go south, simply because the geography of the land hid the fence in that direction, swallowing it with a small wood. He remained on top of the manmade bank of earth, holding onto the fence here and there when it became too narrow, glancing left again and again, wondering whether at any moment he was looking directly at Steven's grave. He had brought the shovel and a bag of food from the car, and the exertion was making him sweat.

He had no idea what he would say if he was stopped. The shovel was hardly easy to explain. *And just why the hell am I bringing it? It's not as if I'm going to dig up a mass grave, even if there is one.* But he shoved the thought aside, hid it away, aware that it was there but happy for now to ignore it.

The height of the bank slowly lessened, leaving the fence sitting on the natural levels of the Plain. Not far beyond that it wended its way into a small woodland, edging left and right between trees, and it was here that Tom found his way in. The fence had been erected years ago, and even though the trees had been here for much longer, they continued to grow. Roots had sprained the metal, twisted the foundations of some of the posts, and one section of the fence had been so badly warped that there was a crawl space beneath it, scoured clean of vegetation by whom- or whatever used it.

Badgers, he thought. *Foxes. Wild cats.*

Tom sat on a fallen tree, opened the bag of food and ate a sandwich whilst staring at the depression beneath the fence. This was where he would cross a line. Until now he was only investigating around the edges of what King had told him, circling the myth, trying to draw from it whatever facts he could without getting too close. Now, if he crawled beneath this security fence, he would be grabbing hold of the story and interrogating it. Action, not words. And with the trepidation that idea brought came that same old feeling; the conviction that he should be leaving this alone.

Nothing he did could bring Steven back.

"But he's my son," Tom said. The sound of his voice in such silence surprised him. He finished the sandwich and tied a knot in the bag.

The fence was cold. The trees whispered above him, though there was no breeze at ground level.

As Tom crawled on his stomach, the base of the fence scratched at his back on the way through. *Now this has marked me*, he thought, and he pulled himself up into the restricted area.

Emerging from the woods on the other side, Tom felt completely exposed. He hung back by the trees for a while, looking across the Plain and up at the sky, trying to spot whoever may be watching him. A pair of buzzards circled high up, uncontained by fences and restricted areas. They would see him walking across the landscape, watch as he found the place marked on the map, and whatever he revealed would be made open to them as well.

Soon, Jo would start to wonder where he was.

Tom stepped away from the trees and set off across the moor.

He had always enjoyed the moors, his love stemming from the many camping holidays he and his parents had taken on Bodmin. The spring of the ground underfoot, the smell of heather and tall ferns whipped aside by a stick, the thrill of exploration as he and his brother ventured into old surface mines, the wonder of every new pile of ancient rocks or hollows in the ground that contained a sheep's skeleton, a bird's nest, or simply a shadow promising more secrets to come. He adored the smell of the place, and the feel of a wild breeze on his face, and the humbling sense that the moor itself was a living entity. It had secrets, that was for sure. As he grew older he had become used to what he knew—the safe countryside where he lived, no risks, no dangers, no sense of true wilderness—but now, walking across Salisbury Plain, he felt charged with the raw energy and mystery of this place. He felt *good*.

He paused and took out King's map. The red cross drew his eye, but he looked at the surrounding area, almost featureless and without any point of reference. From the walker's map he had bought, he guessed that he was now at the bottom right corner of King's map. The stream would be farther on, hidden somewhere ahead of him by the lay of the land. The red cross was almost central, and by converting scales he guessed that he had maybe half a mile to walk before he was in the vicinity of the grave.

"Oh shit." The full import of what he was doing suddenly hit him. His knees felt weak, his stomach rolled and his balls tingled with fear. What if he was caught? What would he say? How could the truth possibly help him, when it had always been the army keeping the truth for itself?

Tom knew that there was only one way to confront

his doubt and fears; he moved on. He counted his paces. There was little to see on the small map, so the only way he could approximate his location was by estimating how far he had come from the fence. He crossed the small stream, and that at least gave him a point of reference. When he had come over half a mile into the military zone he paused, looked around, consulted the small map again, ran his fingertips over the indent of the red cross, and saw something that would change his life forever.

At first he thought it was a small rock buried in the ground, its matte surface pitted by years of frost and sunshine. There was a hint of yellow to it, and one edge was badly cracked, a thin line of moss growing there. As he moved closer a feeling of dread came down, sending a chill through him even though the autumn sun fought to hold it back.

It can't be.

Tom closed the map, crumpled the piece of paper, leaned on the shovel as he eased himself to the ground. Kneeling, he was that much closer to the object. He reached out to touch it, but one of the buzzards called out high above. He sat back on his heels and looked up. The bird was circling him, and if he was not so scared he would have laughed at the outrageous symbolism of this.

He leaned forward and touched the buried object, and it was not a rock.

Something happened then, a momentary realisation that this was the point at which he could change his future. Jo would be wondering where he was. She had been sick, he had been away for a couple of hours already, and that provoked a cool sense of guilt. She would be sitting up in bed reading, perhaps having made herself a cup of tea, and after each paragraph her eyes would flit to the bedside clock, then back again. Soon she would check the time after every line, and then perhaps she would not be able to read at all. He should go to her. He should leave this place—where he really had no right to be—and forget everything that Nathan King had told him. Perhaps he had been drunk. Or maybe he and his friend had simply decided that it would be fun to mess with Tom, fuck with his mind.

He reached out again to touch the thing buried in the ground.

He should leave.

And as his fingers skimmed what he already knew to be a buried bone, he actually felt the world shifting around him. Whatever safety net he had been living with was ripped away, leaving the bare landscape of stark truths ready to pull him down and tear him to ribbons. Preconceptions of what was right and wrong, true or false, were suddenly questioned again. He had never truly believed most of what he had been told about Steven's death, but he realised with a jolt that he had never imagined his own idea of the story. Perhaps it would have been too terrible. Now, everything he knew could be a lie. There was no safety in the world anymore. He was in his mid-fifties, and his childhood was at an end.

Tom stroked his finger across the pitted surface. *I could be touching my son right now.* There was a definite curve to the bone. A skull. He came to the crack and, using his thumbnail, scraped out the moss. Then he moved his fingers down to where the skull entered the ground, pushed, found that he could slip his fingers in quite easily. He worked them deeper, feeling the coolness of damp soil on one side and the smooth, slick skull on the other. He pulled, tugged, and his hand came free with a clump of earth attached. Tom dug again, using both hands this time, amazed at how easily the soil moved. He pulled away an area of heather around the buried skull, lifting soil as it came, and soon he had built a small pile of the purple-flowered shrub. He sat back panting, glanced down at his hands, realised how filthy he was already and how worried Jo might be, but he went back to work at the ground around the skull, the depression deepening with every handful of earth he removed.

Tom suddenly remembered the shovel and the going became easier. He threw the soil behind him, not wishing to pile it up in case he had to move it again. He placed the shovel, stood on it, pressed down, bent and heaved up another load. He took care not to work too close to the skull so he would not damage it. That could be Steven down there . . . or maybe there were more, the remains of fifteen men buried deep after being killed by whatever had escaped from Porton Down.

Tom paused and looked at his hands, the mud beneath his nails, the muck already ground into the creases between his fingers. Whatever they had died from could still be here. Plague? Some dreadful chemical warfare agent? It could be eating into him right now, entering his bloodstream and revelling in this unexpected new victim. He closed his eyes. He felt no different, other than the fact that he was digging up a secret mass grave close to a biological warfare establishment.

He laughed out loud, fell to his knees and held his stomach. The shovel dropped and landed in the hole he had created, clanking against the top of the skull, and Tom's laughter turned to tears. Tears for himself, for Jo, for Steven buried somewhere beneath him. He could turn and leave, accept the truth now that the lie was revealed, get on with his life; or he could carry on digging. He had come this far.

My son's corpse? Do I really want to see that? His skeleton, his skull, whatever is left of his skin? He looked up at the rising sun, squinting, seeing no answers there.

"It's madness," he said, and the sound of his own voice startled him into action. He picked up the shovel and worked around the skull.

A few minutes later he revealed the first eye socket. Tom backed away and slid around the hole to work at the back of the skull. He had no wish to be watched. He knelt and used his hands again, and minutes later they tangled in a chain. Tom cursed as he felt the metal pinch his finger, but then he tugged gently at the chain around the skeleton's neck, bringing the dog tags up into the sun for the first time in a decade. He did not question why they were still there, why they had not been removed, the panic that this suggested in the men who had buried the bodies. He *could* not. Because here, at last, was a name.

His heart thumped as he spat on the metal and cleaned away the muck. He scraped with his thumbnail, revealing the letters and numbers, sobbing as he did so. Tears blurred his vision and he wiped them away, smearing mud across his face.

Gareth Morgan. This was not his son.

Tom kept digging around the skeleton, not so careful now that he knew it was not Steven. He was sweating, his clothes stuck to his body with sweat and grime, and his heart was hammering from the exertion. He thought of Jo again and how worried and afraid she would be right now, but this was for her as well, this truth he was uncovering out here on the Plain. But could he tell her? Even if he found Steven's corpse would he be able to tell her? That was something he would have to overcome should the situation arise.

Bastards! Anger filtered in past the shock. *The bastards, killed our sons and lied to us about it!* The significance of this weighed heavy, and the implications of what he was doing suddenly felt so much more serious. If he was captured doing this—uncovering a scandal that could very well explode the heart of the British government—what would be done? Would he simply be added to the hole before it was filled in again?

He stood, looked around, saw the buzzards still circling high overhead, then carried on digging.

Around the remains of the stranger called Gareth

Morgan the soil suddenly became loose, and Tom stumbled as it fell into a hollow with a rush. As his foot sank in, he dropped the shovel and spread his arms, falling onto his rump beside the skull. *Mass grave*, he thought, and then the smell hit him. Wet rot, decay, age, not the smell of the recently dead but the stench of time. He leaned back and pulled his foot free, rolling across the disturbed ground away from the new hole and the smell drifting up from it. He closed his eyes and buried his face in heather, breathing in the muddy freshness of it, trying to clear the smell of his son's death from his lungs.

"Oh for fuck's sake," Tom said, suddenly sobbing into the ground. He had no idea what he was doing. His hands clawed, fingers dug in, as if afraid that he would fall off the world if he loosened his grip. And wasn't he doing that already? So much had changed in the last hour that he would not be surprised to open his eyes and find the world spinning the opposite way. Smelling the honest peaty smell of the ground beneath him, he wished that he had never overheard those two men in the pub.

But he had. And King had given him the map, and now here he was. Looking for his dead son.

Tom crawled back to the skeleton—revealed to its chest now that the soil around it had tumbled into a hollow—and stared down at what he had done. There were other bones visible down there, touched by sunlight for the first time in years. The corpses must have been piled in together, covered over with a layer of soil and heathers, and as their flesh rotted away beneath the ground it left hollows behind, dark wet spaces filled with nothing but the gas of decay and the undying echoes of their violent deaths. The skeleton called Gareth Morgan still wore the remnants of a uniform, and shreds of leathery skin clung to its bones, moist and browned by the damp soil. Beneath it a tangle of bones and clothing, skin and hair, marked where other bodies had found their final resting place.

"Oh God," Tom muttered, reaching down into the dark. "Oh God, oh God . . ." He could taste decay on his tongue, sweet yet vile. He wondered whether each body smelled different in decomposition, and if so which smell was his son.

But death was the great equaliser. Personality had no part in rot. Humour or seriousness held no truck with the processes of bacteria and decay. Steven was long gone from here, yet Tom had never felt so close.

He slid on the wet soil and moved forward, his outstretched arm sinking deeper into the void. He cried out in alarm but came to a stop, his hand closing around a clammy bone. He pulled gently but there was no give. The shovel was under his stomach, and he eased it out and used the blade to shift more of the soil above the grave. It took little effort now, and by kneeling up he found he could simply push the heather to one side like a carpet, revealing the horrors of what lay beneath.

Sunlight struck the bones. Subtle autumn heat ate away the coolness of their decade-long rest. The buzzards cried out and drifted away, perhaps sensing death even from such a height. Tom knelt among the rotted corpses of so many men and looked up, welcoming the sun on his face and the sense of his skin stretching and burning. "Jo," he said, but she did not answer him. "Steven." Still no answer. Tears dripped from his chin and disappeared among the bodies, perhaps cleaning small spots on his son's bones.

Shaking his head, his whole body shivering, fear and shock and rage combining to draw his mind back from what he was doing, Tom bent over and reached back into the grave.

For just a few seconds the madness of this reached down and clasped Tom's hand. It was his wife holding him, whispering into his ear, telling him to let go because they still had each other, and no matter how Steven had died it was only the living that really mattered now. But Tom let go of her hand and held onto what he was doing. His belief that perhaps he and Jo had too much of each other reared up again, a selfish justification. And as Jo's voice faded away, and the touch of her hand seemed more remote than at any time in his life, Tom turned back to his work.

Richard Parker. That was not his son. He dropped the dog tags and stared at the skull of the body he had uncovered, its crew cut of auburn hair so colourful against the stretched grey skin of its face. Here lay a million stories Tom would never know, other than the lie of Richard Parker's violent death.

He shoved the skeleton aside and delved deeper. He encountered tangles of bones and clothing, and mud-caked hair brushed his hand as he quickly withdrew.

There were too many. He would have to start moving the bodies, sorting them, until he found Steven.

He's not here.

Tom shook his head. Where had that idea come from?

He crawled back and prepared to grab hold of the first skeleton, Gareth Morgan, Mr. and Mrs. Morgan's son, another soldier whose family had buried a coffin filled with rocks or earth or something else they would never know. He wondered whether this boy's family had doubts about the story as well, and whether they had entertained the idea of travelling to Salisbury Plain to honour their son on the tenth anniversary of his death.

Tom looked back toward the fence, half-expecting to see other fathers coming at him with shovels at the ready. But he was still alone.

Gareth Morgan grinned at him. His skull was almost bare of skin, but there was a hint of a moustache still clinging beneath the hollow of his nose. Tom reached out and grasped the skeleton's ribs, heaved, and cried out in surprise as it sprang from the ground with a brief sucking noise. He tumbled forward and threw it ahead of him. It landed with a thump and its arms spread above its head, as if relishing the sudden feel of sunlight on its wet bones. *So light,* Tom thought, and he realised he had been thinking of it as a man.

Its spine was snapped, several ribs broken off, and

one thigh bone was splintered and holed. Another violent death.

Tom moved back into the hole and dragged out Richard Parker, hands beneath the skeleton's armpits, its legs dragging, heavy with wet clothing and the mummified remnants of muscle and skin. He pulled it across to lay next to Gareth Morgan, and the skeletons' arms seemed to entwine, friends together again.

Back at the hole, Tom went deeper. He pulled out more bodies—some of them rotted down to the bone, some still hanging on to a leathery layer of skin or dried brown flesh—investigated the dog tags, moved the bodies to one side, going deeper still, breathing hard and trying not to pay any attention to his heart as it pummelled at his chest, demanding that he rest, cease, stop this insanity.

It was hot. He could blame his madness on the heat, perhaps.

Tom looked at his muddied hands, felt his forehead, spat in his hand and checked his saliva for blood. No disease had taken him. No chemical warfare agent had turned his insides to mush. Perhaps whatever had killed these men had been released to the air, only to bide its time before striking again. Perhaps it would wipe out the world. Right then, the only thing that mattered for Tom was the image he had built in his mind: Steven's dog tags, muddied and cold, resting in his hands.

Leigh Joslin, Anthony Williams, Stuart Cook . . . none of these were his son. Jason Collins, Kenny Godden, Adrian Herbert . . . all strangers, all the dead sons of other families. Eight now, and there were more down there, he could see the mess of their bones and skulls and clothing, muddy and damp, he could smell their sweet smell of decay, taste the wrongness of this in the air.

Tom caught sight of the dead men laid out in a row and looked away, unable to believe what he had done. Joslin's head had slumped from its mounting atop its spine. Herbert was missing an arm. Godden's ribs had been smashed, as if something had tried to get inside. Such violence, such death.

The next body he grabbed still wore hair, and dried flesh sunk in between its bones, and its eyes were pale yellow orbs nesting in its skull. Its strange, misshapen skull. Tom frowned and leaned in closer, edging to one side to allow more sunlight to enter the depression in the ground. The soldier's skull seemed elongated, jaw distended, and his teeth must have risen from their roots because they looked too large for the head. His brow was heavy, nose cavity bulging out over the mouth in a canine aspect.

"What the hell . . . ?" Tom whispered. There was a bullet hole in the back of the skull. Perhaps that accounted for the distortion.

He reached out and grabbed the body's legs, trying to ignore the feel of cold leathery flesh beneath his hands, clammy with moisture. He pulled. The body shifted a few inches toward him then stopped, held fast by something he could not see.

The skull had remained exactly where it was.

"Fuck!" Tom moved sideways to another skeleton, dragging it up the small slope to the expanding pile laid out on the heather above. He checked the dog tag, discarded it—another stranger—and went back for more.

Jo grabbed his hand again. She squeezed tighter and Tom cried out, a wretched exhalation of despair. He looked up at the sky and it was pure, clean, unsullied by death. But though he saw blue, and heard Jo whispering her love for him, he could still feel the slickness of the grave between his fingers.

Have I changed? he thought. *Have I changed so much?*

He rubbed his fingers together and let Jo go.

"It's all for you," Tom said, and he looked down again. The strange skull stared at him with its shrunken eyes. The unnatural distance between it and its departed body gave the whole tableau a surreal aspect, and Tom almost pushed the body back close to the head . . . but its limbs were too long, the ribs too narrow, and why was he doing this? Why was he playing games with himself?

"Steven!" he shouted, and as he dug down again . . .

He's not here.

Tom wondered when that sensation of being watched had amplified without him really noticing. The buzzards were gone, but the skin of his neck was tingling, set in motion by a gaze he could not pin down.

The weird skull grinned at him through lips shrunken back from the jaws.

"You're dead," he said, pulling at another skeleton, not Steven, then another, also not Steven.

And that was it. Eleven bodies excavated and spread across the heather, eleven sets of dog tags, and none of them were his son. There had supposedly been fifteen killed; perhaps Steven and the other three missing had been buried elsewhere, or incinerated, or . . .

Why leave the dog tags? Too dangerous? Too much risk of infection?

Down in the pit, though, there were more. Behind the body he could not move he saw the glint of more bones. He reached underneath and his hands touched something cold, heavy. He tugged the corpse again and heard the chink of metal on metal. He pulled harder and another body slipped from the mud, this one also headless and as deformed as the first. Its skull—left behind—also had a bullet hole behind one ear.

I'm not seeing this, he thought, *I've been digging up fucking corpses and now it's getting to me, it's hot, Jo is worried, I'm crying and my tears are distorting everything, I'm just not seeing this!*

The dead thing slithered toward him as he pulled, connected to the first headless body by the thick metal chain, and then another, smaller corpse followed it up. Tom stood and backed away, only partially realising that he still had a hold of the first body's mummified legs. He brought the dead things with him, two headless adults and what could only have been a child, also headless, its skull lost somewhere in that rank pit.

He was about to drop the legs, back away, *run away*, when he saw that the chain was wrapped around another bundle, another corpse. This one still seemed to have its head attached. He pulled again and it popped free of the ground, wet and filthy and yet obviously whole. It was chained to the three headless corpses, the metal wrapped around its chest, under its armpits and between its legs, thoroughly entangled, and Tom wondered why anyone would need to bury a dead person like this.

He faltered only for a second before moving slowly down into the pit again. These bodies were more whole than any of the others he had brought out, mummified rather than rotted, perhaps because they had been buried deeper in the peaty ground. The first skull stared at him as he reached over the two adult bodies, grabbed the headless child's skeleton and pulled it across to himself. He was crying, and moaning, and there was a strange keening sound that took him many seconds to realise actually came from him. The child was as light as a pillow, its body seemingly whole and yet dried out, desiccated. The only thing that gave it weight was the chain. Tom placed the corpse gently between the headless adults, clasped the chain and pulled. He lifted, grunting with the effort, tears and sweat blurring his vision as he tried to make out what was wrong with this thing's head, why it was shaped like that, why it was *turning . . .*

And then the tiny corpse reached out and grabbed Tom's arm.

CHAPTER THREE

"What did you tell him?"

"I've already told!"

"I don't believe you."

"Then why bother asking me again, Cole?"

Cole stared down at Nathan King, tied into a chair with his own torn-up clothes. The idiot was still trying to play with him, string him along, and Cole did not have time for that. Not now. His purpose, stalled for a decade, was moving again. The last thing he wanted to be doing was beating information out of his friend, this useless ex-grunt. "You're wasting my time," he said.

King shook his head. "For God's sake, I told—" Cole's fist connected with his chin and flipped his head back and to the side.

King gasped, spat blood, and Cole stepped back so that he did not get splashed. "Think about what you're going to say to me next," Cole said. "Daz told me you went back to the pub to meet Tom Roberts. There's only one reason you'd have done that, and we both know what that is. So, for the last time . . . what did you tell him?" He massaged his knuckles and turned away.

King's flat was small and untidy. There were grubby hand marks around the light switches, cobwebs in the ceiling corners, and used fast food containers piled up beside the only armchair. Food was trodden into the carpet. Beer cans were crushed and thrown into one corner of the kitchen. He lived like an animal. Cole did not want to be here—he felt dirtied just breathing the air—but he needed more from King. More than just, "I told him it wasn't like the army said." In one way he was glad that King had spilled the beans at last, but he needed to know which beans and what flavour. It would do Cole no good at all storming blindly into the countryside in search of phantoms he had lost a decade ago.

"Cole . . ." King spat several times and a tooth tumbled from his mouth. "Fuck's sake, Cole, you knocked my tooth out! I don't see you for ten years, then you turn up and knock out my tooth? What's the point of that, eh?" He stared at the bloodied molar stuck on his thigh, shaking his head, and his whole body shivered.

Cole looked at the pathetic man strapped into the timber kitchen chair, and shame bled into his anger. "Sorry, Nath," he said. "Really mate, I'm sorry. But more than being sorry, I need to know exactly what you said to the old guy about his son. *Exactly. Everything.* He's left his house with his wife and I need to know why he's suddenly gone. I can guess *where* he's gone, that's no problem, because it's ten years ago this weekend. But

Nath . . . I don't want to go down there blind and deaf, mate. I need to know how much you told him. I need to know *everything* he knows. And I'll hit you again if you continue to piss me around."

King hung his head, blood dripping into his lap. Tears followed, and the big man sucked back a sob. "Cole, it just came out," he said. "Steven Roberts was his son—remember Steve?—and the guy looked so sad, you know? So desperate for the truth. I thought it might help him to know. And I told him where to look."

"The grave?" Cole went cold. *We left her chained up, wanting her to suffer, wanting her to be alive down there forever . . . "I'll meet you again," she said . . .* "Holy shit, Nath."

"I didn't tell him anything about—"

Cole hit him again, and there was real feeling behind this one. "You twat! Why the hell would you do something like that. Does he know? Does he know about *her?*"

King shook his head, blood and saliva swaying from his chin. "Of course not," he said, tired and sad and scared. "You think I'd have told him about them? I don't even know all about them, or understand what I *do* know. And I don't want to think about them but I do, every night, I dream and scream and sometimes I think sharing the fear will reduce it, you know? But if you think I told him all that, you're mad."

"I am mad," Cole said. "Mad that they got away."

"The ones that got away . . ." King shook his head. "They're long, long gone mate."

Cole sat on the armchair and stared at King. He had been a good soldier ten years ago, and someone Cole could have trusted with his life. Now he was a fat shit, living like a pig, sitting in the chair and spilling his guts after a couple of punches. He stank. He had no respect for himself anymore, and no sense of responsibility about the secrets he knew.

"Did you tell him his son isn't buried there?"

King raised his head and stared at Cole, and Cole thought, *Oh shit, he doesn't know, he really doesn't know.*

"What are you on about?"

"They didn't all die, Nath. Some of them were taken away."

King stared over his shoulder at a past he had been trying to forget forever. "Poor bastards."

"Now you realise why I want to know exactly what you told him." But the words suddenly felt hollow in Cole's mouth, because really there was little point in going on. He knew as much as King could reveal—Tom Roberts had gone down to the Plain to look for the grave of his son—and the most important thing he had to do now was to follow Roberts, stop him, and if necessary silence him. Roberts knew too much already. The slightest risk of him opening the grave . . . that could not be allowed to happen. Not now. Not after so long, when most of the people who knew about the berserkers were dead, or mad.

"I showed him where to find the grave, and that's all. But Cole, you mean they took some of the guys with them? Who? Where? Why?"

"Where is what I've spent the last ten years trying to find out," Cole said. "And I think you know why."

King bowed his head. "Poor bastards," he said again.

Cole stood to leave. "Nath, you live like a pig. What happened to you? Why did you go this way? You could have sorted yourself out, got a decent job in security. Worked abroad, maybe. Why this?" He gestured at the filthy living room, encapsulating the whole of King's life with one wave of his hand.

"Seeing what I saw . . ." King said, but he shook his head and looked down at his bound arms and legs. "You leaving me like this?"

Cole put his hand on King's shoulder and squeezed. His old comrade. His old friend. "No," he said, and as King's shoulders relaxed Cole grabbed him around the head and broke his neck.

Outside Nathan King's second-floor flat, Cole stood for a while and held onto the landing balustrade. He was shaking. His hands were clawed, cramped, and his shoulders ached. He had not killed anyone for six years; he had *never* killed a friend. He closed his eyes and breathed in deeply, taking strange comfort in the city smells after leaving the reeking flat. Exhaust fumes and the stench of stale fat from fast food restaurants were preferable to the stench of King's decline. Memories flashed by, images of King and him ten years ago, young and brash and indestructible.

Working at Porton Down had been a much sought after secondment. The food and accommodations had been good, the security work interesting, and the local ladies had always been interested in men clothed in uniforms and secrecy. Days on the base were spent patrolling the perimeter, fixing fences, handling the dogs, guarding the gates and occasionally doing over reporters who made it their mission to "reveal breaches in security." Evenings were spent at local pubs and clubs, spreading wild tales without actually saying anything, and letting the local girls work off their fascination in the backseats of cars or on the moor behind the pubs. Cole, King and the others had revelled in the assignment. They were reliable men, good soldiers—that was why they had been chosen—but they were also more than aware that they had landed a cushy number. They worked hard at the security of the base, always aware that a true breach would likely result in them being sent back to their regiments, and put a lot of energy into their leisure time, too. The base had a good gym and ample countryside for running; they kept fit. They banked their extra wages. Rarely, if ever, did they question what was going on at the camp. They all knew of the facility's history, but they were army through and through. They understood the need for deterrent and retaliation, and none of them had any time for the occasional protestors who camped at the main gates, waving their placards and demanding the safe return of a bunch of bunnies or puppies.

Three months after starting there, he and King had witnessed the return of the berserkers from Iraq.

Cole opened his eyes and stared out across the park

opposite the flat. A young mother was pushing a pram along a path, a toddler running beside her, aiming for the playground. The toddler, a little girl, ran on ahead, jumping onto the roundabout and waiting impatiently for her mother to begin pushing. The baby squealed in its pram as it watched its sister having so much fun. The mother, tall, red-headed and attractive, pressed the pram's brakes and pushed the roundabout, bending to kiss her daughter every time she spun by. The little girl giggled and the mother smiled.

They don't have a clue, Cole thought. He had just killed his friend for them. For their safety. For the little girl's future. That's what all this was about. After six years spent living in one bed-sit after another, drawing the meagre army pension they had awarded him after letting him go, picking up crappy, menial jobs as he watched for signs of the berserkers' reemergence, it had all come to this. He was convinced that he was doing right, and yet sometimes he had to remind himself, to reinforce his conviction.

Because Cole was not a bad man. Cole was a *good* man.

He had left the army six years ago, three months before killing Sandra Francis. They had refused to let him pursue the escapees, saying that they were gone and that was that. *Gone back to wherever they came from,* the brass told him. *They'll not worry us now.* But he had never forgotten the wagon that rolled in one June morning under cover of darkness, ROBINSON FRESH FOODS painted across its sides. The sounds he had heard from within had stayed with him forever. And later, seeing those things as they brought them out, his view of the world had changed in seconds.

The woman in the park reminded him of the scientist, Sandra. She had been attractive, her red hair hiding a stunning intellect behind Barbie doll looks. And that had been Cole's mistake. He had been a bigot, believing that it would be easy to persuade the truth from her.

What did you do to the girl?

I can't tell you.

What makes her special?

I can't tell you.

You have to—

No, I don't.

What was in the syringe? Did you help them, did you make them immune to the silver?

I can't tell you.

Did you help them escape?

A silence, long and loaded. And Francis never shifted her gaze from Cole's eyes.

You did. You did! Why? You have to tell me. Really, you do, because I need to know, and I'll find out one way or the other.

Then it's the other.

More talking, more pleading, but however tightly he'd tied her to the chair and however much he had threatened, Cole could not bring himself to torture her. And really, looking back on it, he believed that nothing would have made her talk.

Because she was scared.

Please, tell me or—

Or you'll shoot me?

And perhaps that had been *her* mistake: not believing that he would.

Cole marked this as the point when he had grown up. Leaving the army had turned his purpose into a private crusade. His shoulders had bowed under the weight of guilt and responsibility, and he spent many waking hours convincing himself that he was doing everything right. There were no voices, no jealous gods giving him their time, but there *was* God, present at every twist and turn of his life and listening to his fears and hopes. He knew what Cole was doing, and He knew why, but that did not make the remorse and doubt any less difficult to bear.

Cole let go of the balustrade and smiled as the woman glanced across at him. She smiled back, then went back to playing with her children.

I'm doing all this for them, he thought, patching any holes in his conviction. He had just killed a friend. He shook his head to dislodge the memory and it slipped down through the grates in his mind, under the skein of reality he had created over the past ten years, finding itself prisoner with so many other memories, ideals and discarded morals that he worked so hard to keep subdued. That false vision of reality kept them all hidden away. The memory would come back, he knew that, and would haunt him forever, just as the memory of Sandra Francis' death haunted his dreams. But even as Cole walked along the landing and down the external staircase, Nathan King became a man he had once served with at Porton Down, a fun friend, a good soldier. He was a million miles and ten years away from that corpse already cooling in the filthy flat.

Cole climbed into his Jeep. Salisbury Plain was about two hours away. He could be there by dusk.

For a long time, Tom could not move.

The corpse of the child still lay where he had found it, wrapped in chains and virtually buried in filth. It had been a girl; he could see her long hair (*and hear her voice, that was a girl's voice*), and she wore the rotten remnants of a dress. It may have been pink once, but burial had bled all colour to a uniform brown. Between the chains he could still make out the patterned stitching on the chest, flowers and butterflies and everything a little girl would love. It was a long dress, sleeveless, something for the summer, not this cool autumn day. Her leathery skin seemed unconcerned by the freshness in the air. Her face (*it should be looking the other way, not at me, it shouldn't have turned to me*) was a mummified mask of wrinkles, a dead young girl with an old woman's skin. The creases around her eyes and the corners of her mouth were deep, home to muck and tiny, squirming white things. Her mouth hung open, filled with mud. Her eye sockets were moist, dark, and not totally empty. The eyes sat like creamy yellowed eggs, waiting to birth something unknowable.

Her hand still touched his arm. He remained motionless, staring at the places where her fingers squeezed, the slight indentations in his skin, hairs pressed down, redness around where her fingers touched him because she *was* squeezing him.

Tom gasped, realising he had not breathed for many seconds. A breath shushed across the Plain, shifting grasses and setting a spread of nearby ferns whispering secrets. He could not take his eyes from the girl.

"That's not squeezing me, it's just touching me," he said, staring down at the hand. He raised his other hand, ready to lift her mummified arm and set it down across her chest. "I shifted her . . . she moved . . . her arm lifted and fell, all because I shifted her, all down to gravity . . ." He breathed hard between each phrase, trying to force away the dizziness that blurred the edges of his senses, determined to ignore the feeling that the corpse was about to move again. Every instant held the potential of another squeeze, another touch.

But her fingers are pressing—

Tom pulled away and the little girl's nails scratched his skin.

"No!"

The girl's body settled back into the mud, the chains holding her tight. They clinked as she shifted slightly—

Gravity, it's gravity.

Then a small slick thing slipped from a hole in her shoulder and scurried across her body.

Tom crawled backward out of the grave, pushing with his feet, pulling with his hands. There was no sign of Steven down there, not exposed at least, and he could not go back in to go deeper, he just could not. Jo would be frantic by now—it was mid-afternoon already and the sun was dipping to the west, ready to kiss the horizon and invite in the dark—and he suddenly realised just how many hours he had lost here. His shoulders and arms ached from the exertion, and his heart galloped hard.

"Oh Jesus God fucking hell," he moaned, closing his eyes and trying to understand what he had done. It was a moment of reason in madness, clarity in confusion, but the moment was chased away. He felt it leave, lifting its legs and sprinting from his consciousness as a strange voice forced its way inside.

Are you Mister Wolf?

Tom's eyes snapped open. The child's corpse was shifting. He could not see actual movement, but the sinking sun reflecting from the moisture on its body was wavering, the reflections stretching up and down, left and right, repeating their rhythmic movements. As if the body were breathing.

No . . . no, not Mister Wolf.

Tom was shaking, his eyes watering. He wondered whether it was that giving the corpse an illusion of movement.

"No," he moaned, filthy hands pressed to his face as if to squeeze out the truth. "No, no, no." He scrambled to his feet and backed away. His heels tangled in the outstretched legs of one of the excavated skeletons, and as he tumbled backward the voice came again, an invader in his own mind.

Don't leave me again, Daddy, not after so long! It was

wretched, this voice, and pathetic, and altogether terrifying.

Tom fell back into a skeleton's embrace. The impact shook its arms and they clanked against him. Bones cracked and crumbled. He screamed. It was a full, loud screech that hurt his throat, and the sound and pain brought him briefly up from the dark depths of disbelief that were pulling him down, drowning him. He found his footing again and backed away, treading carefully this time so that he was not tripped, stretching his legs back over the bodies he had dug up and laid out to view. He kept his eyes on what he could see of the corpse wrapped in chains. He could not really think about the chains, not yet. That was for later. Their reason for being there, their intention . . . that was for much later, when he was away from here and crying in Jo's arms, begging her to go home, continue their life, accept the lie and try to find their way with Steven's memory intact and unsullied.

Please . . . , the voice said in his head, and Tom screamed again. *So cold . . . so alone . . . I hurt.* It was the accent that terrified Tom the most. The words were bad enough, and their implications, but the accent was one he could not place, a smooth-flowing speech that he was sure he had never heard before. If he was imagining this voice, he could have never invented something he did not know.

"This is real," he said, and though she did not speak, he knew that somewhere in his mind the dead girl smiled.

* * *

Tom backed farther away, knelt in the heather and stared at the open grave. The bodies he had brought out were catching the setting sun. He could smell their decay, even this far away. Perhaps they would rot faster now that they were uncovered. Some were skeletons, others had traces of skin and flesh . . . and the little girl, with her wrinkled skin and those ping-pong ball eyes loose in their sockets . . .

Even from where he was now he could see her hand, resting across her chest and ready to grab again. "Tendons tightening," he whispered, "and muscles contracting, out of the cold ground at last, just something natural that's making her fingers move like that." He looked down at the scratch marks on his arm. *Almost as if she didn't want me to go.*

Those words, that accent, the idea that she was not as dead as the others. "That chain."

Steven, the voice said, and although he jumped, Tom did not stand and run. He should have. Any sane thought would have told him to run as fast as he could. But sanity seemed to be setting with the sun, inviting in its own breed of darkness.

"My dead son," he whispered to the air.

Not dead, Daddy.

"I'm not your daddy."

There were tears, the unmistakeable sound of sobbing inside his head. *I know*, the voice whispered at last, *I just wanted to say it again.*

"Not dead?"

You didn't find him, his skelington?

"No." She said skeleton like a kid, with a "g" in there. *I wouldn't have made that up, would I? If I were imagining all this?*

Then he's not dead. He's . . . gone.

"Gone where?"

Silence, loaded with potential. He could feel something in his mind, a presence remaining, hanging quietly back.

"I'm not talking to you," Tom said, shaking his head and standing.

Please—

"No, I don't mean I don't want to, I just mean I'm *not*. I *can't* be. This isn't happening." Tom turned to leave. He would abandon everything he had done for the sake of his mind; losing it would not help Jo, not on this anniversary of Steven's death. And he *was* dead. His son was dead. Thinking any other way would drive Tom mad. He smiled, almost laughed, wondering how true madness compared to what was happening to him now.

He pinched the back of his hand until his nails drew blood, then wondered what germs would invade his bloodstream from the muck on his skin.

"I'm going home," he said, setting out for the hole beneath the fence.

Not that way! Bad man, nasty man, big bad Wolf!

"I'm not hearing this."

This way, another way, please Daddy!

"I'm not your—"

He's come to kill you and—

74

"You can't know this."

A loaded silence again, filled with a promise of something incredible. *I know so much more,* the little girl said. And though she still sounded scared and panicked, her words held power and control beneath the surface.

"I'm leaving." But even as Tom set off across the Plain, he heard the distant sound of a car engine from beyond the artificial boundary bank.

That's him, the voice said, quieter and more controlled. *He's a bad man. Very bad. He has only death in his head.*

"And you have life?"

No, freedom. I don't want to be here anymore, Daddy! Please come and get me, pick me up, hold me and hug me and I'll tell you where to take us to be safe. The man's coming now! I can feel him. Mister Wolf!

Tom heard the engine's tone change as the vehicle came to a stop. It rumbled on for a moment and then cut out. He strained to hear the car door opening and closing, but it was too far away. *I could be doing this to myself,* he thought, *making this up to try to cover what I've done.* He looked down at his filthy hands and clothes, tainted with soil from a grave. The back of his hand still bled. The blood was startlingly red against the mud drying across his pale skin. Autumn colours.

What would he tell Jo?

I'll help you find Steven, the little girl said. *My name is Natasha.*

"How do you know my son's name?"

It's at the front of your mind. And Jo, as well.

"My wife." *In my mind . . . so what else does she see, know of me?*

Please, take me out of here, out of the hole. Come and take me, and I'll show you what happened here. I can, you know. My real Daddy told me how. If you touch me I can show you, even though I'm . . .

"What?" Tom asked, scanning the fence for any signs of movement. "What are you? Dead? Dead and wrapped in chains?"

Wrapped in chains because I'm not dead, the little girl's voice said.

"Not dead?" Tom turned and looked back at the dark hole in the ground, the fragmented bodies arranged beside it.

Please, I'm very scared. And lonely. Take me, hold me, and I'll show you everything. And if you believe, I'll try to help you find Steven. Please!

"Why would you do that?" He was talking to the air, the Plain, the sinking sun, and yet already he was certain he would receive an answer. Tom felt peculiarly comfortable with his newfound madness. Perhaps acceptance was insanity in its purest form.

Because my Daddy loved me, and I think you love Steven the same way.

"Where is your Daddy?"

Daddy! the voice shrieked, and Tom winced as if he had been punched. *Daddy is here! With me! He's here in these chains, and Mummy and my little brother, all dead now, with—*

"With their heads cut off."

Natasha was silent for a few seconds, and Tom heard her sobbing again. *They wanted me to be alive. Down here, alive, with all the crawling things.* She sounded so vulnerable, so small, such a child.

"They?"

There's time to tell . . . but not too much. Not now. No time now!

Tom looked back over his shoulder at the mound, the small wood where he had found the crawl space beneath the fence, and he wondered how he could explain this new madness to Jo. He had always been the strong one, the one to comfort her when tears came and memories shadowed the present. Now, covered in mud and with the stench of old corpses on his skin, how could he possibly explain?

In the dusky light he saw someone climbing the fence.

It's him! Mister Wolf! Help me, please, don't let him put me back in!

Tom tried to imagine being buried alive, thrown down into the pit with all those bodies, surrounded by dead family. But the thought that galvanised him into action was the certainty that if he were discovered, he would never get away from here. He had uncovered a horrendous crime, a monstrous lie. Madness or no madness, he had to flee.

And whether Natasha was real or a made-up presence in his mind, she was about to take control.

* * *

Cole parked a hundred feet behind the other car. He remained in his Jeep for a few minutes, lights off, scanning the surrounding area for any signs that he was being observed. He kept reminding himself that this was a fifty-five-year-old office worker he was following, but caution had always been his way. It had saved his life more than once and now, so close to this place, his hackles were up.

He had not been here for ten years.

He stepped from the Jeep, shut the door quietly and rested one hand on the pistol in his pocket. Day was slipping into dusk, and he wanted to investigate Roberts' car before full darkness fell. This was a bad time of day to be sneaking around with one hand on his .45 . . . but yet again, he reminded himself of who he was following. Roberts was hardly going to be perched on a hillside with the cross-hairs of a .30-30 centred on the back of Cole's head.

Still . . .

Glancing left and right, Cole quickly made his way to the parked car. He approached from the passenger side, keeping well away from the vehicle, closing in only when he was certain it was empty. He tried the door. Roberts had left the car unlocked. Other things on his mind.

Yeah, his dead son.

Cole shook his head. There was no time for pity.

He climbed the bank and stood at the security fence, staring out across the Plain. Although he had not been here since that fateful day ten years before, he could still remember every detail about this place, every point of reference that would lead him to where the bodies were buried. To his right lay the small wood, to his left in the distance a slight hill that was already merging with the darkness, and in front of him, somewhere past the fence, would be the rock shaped like a rugby ball standing on end. He sniffed the air and remembered the scent of the moors, closed his eyes briefly and heard the familiar silence. Even the feel of the place on his skin and in his guts was something he still understood so well; that gravity, that sense of the raw power of nature sleeping here. He was back, and it felt as though he had never been away, as if every day of the intervening ten years had been wiped from existence. God knew he had lived that day in his nightmares enough times to make it last forever.

"God help me now," he muttered. "God help us all." He scanned the Plain, zeroing in on the approximate location of the grave . . . and there was movement. He looked to the side of the shape and saw it stand and walk, though whether it was toward or away from him he could not tell.

Now, suddenly, dusk would become his friend.

He set about climbing the unclimbable fence. Roberts had got in somehow—cut through the steel, found a hole—but Cole had no time to search for his point of ingress. He wanted this to be quick and easy, no long chase across the moors, just a brief sprint and a bullet to the back of the head. Though the prospect of killing again filled him with a sense of emptiness, it would not be the first time he had buried people out here.

Cole had spent a lot of his youth climbing mountains. Now he used techniques he had learned years ago to brace himself against the gap between two fence uprights—toes and fingers pulling and pushing in opposite directions, ankles and wrists burning, fingers and toes cramping—and slowly, gritting his teeth, he moved higher. Once he was within reach of the curved rails heading the fence he swung one foot up and hooked it behind a rail, pulling himself up and over. He dropped down on the other side and rolled, bringing the pistol out of his pocket and kneeling in one movement.

This low down he could see Roberts' shadow against the horizon. If he kept low enough he would be able to approach in this way, ensuring that he himself was not seen until the last moment. If Cole was very lucky— and very quiet—he would be able to shoot the guy without him even knowing what had happened. That would be best for both of them.

Then, away from here as fast as fucking possible. Even this close to the grave Cole's skin was crawling.

Can she get out? he thought. But no, of course not, not after so long. She'd be dead down there. Or if not dead, close enough. *But she's still there. Still so close. And those others, their heads gone, but did we really know what we were doing? Did we?*

"Fuck it!" Cole muttered. Bent low, he hurried toward Roberts.

He moved quickly across the Plain, passing the rock shaped like a rugby ball, not needing it now because he could still see the movement of his target. In maybe five minutes he would come close enough to risk a shot, but between now and then he had to keep his eye on Roberts. There was still an hour until the sunlight bled away completely—and tonight, with no cloud cover, there would be moon and starlight—but once he lost that shadow it would be difficult to find again. The need to get away from here was pressing on him already, trying to turn him and urge him back to the road. Every step he took closer to the grave felt heavier, as if he were running into air growing thicker by the second.

And he remained alert for any whispers in his mind.

Of them all, Natasha had been the one most adept at touching minds. Just a touch, a feel, a nudge, never anything more, but enough to know that she was there. Her psychic fingers were vile. It was like opening your mind to a sewer exhaust.

Even if she is still alive, she won't know we're here.

In his mind, in the underground where he relegated those memories he was desperate to forget, something stirred. He ran through the streets above, dodging from idea to idea as he neared the central hub of his consciousness, that place where his whole life converged and found meaning. His concentration was complete, and the manhole covers and tunnel entrances were well sealed by his determination to do what was right. Each day he prayed to God, and each night when he slept the memories leaked out. Another prayer on waking usually put them back down. But now there were signs of life down there, an echo awoken from distant memory, a voice that stalked the tunnels and dark places, barely a whisper as yet but growing, growing, each echo from mossy walls or crumbling brick ceilings increasing rather than diminishing its strength.

Eventually he heard the words: *What's the time, Mister Wolf?*

"Fuck, fuck, fuck," Cole whispered as he ran. He knew that he should be utterly silent, that he was acting like an amateur. But there was something he had to cover up, a rising sound inside him that needed camouflaging. Was that her, actually talking in his mind, or had he imagined it? So he whispered while he ran, and his underground sang louder with the voice that he had prayed he would never hear again.

The smell told Cole that he was nearing the grave. It was damp, rich, a cloying sweetness, the stench of old rot and buried secrets laid bare. He knelt down, sniffed again, then started to breathe through his mouth. The whole area felt corrupt. The water soaking into the knee of his jeans could be infused with chemicals from their rotten bodies, and the air was rich with their stench. He was breathing in gases from their exposed corpses. Even the deepening darkness was slick and greasy.

He's opened the grave!

He had never expected it of him. He hadn't even thought that Roberts would find the grave's location; it had been chosen because it was away from any real point of reference, just another nowhere in a Plain of many such nowheres. But Cole now knew that this had already gone much further than he could have guessed, and for the first time since killing King he felt anger at him, not pity.

Stupid fuck! What was it with him? Why the hell start talking after so long?

Cole wanted so much to turn and run, but his whole life was centred on this place and what had happened here. He had always hoped and prayed that he would never have cause to return. He had never picked up the trail of the escaped berserkers, but he had tried continuously, never giving in. Not like the army. Their shunning of their responsibilities had been the main reason for his leaving and pursuing the escapees on his own. He was not unrealistic, or even superior, but he saw himself as the army's conscience. The fact that he was the only person who knew of his mission did not concern him in the least.

Perhaps one day when this was all over, he would write his memoirs. Get some people into trouble, topple a government. Perhaps one day.

Cole took in a huge breath and, letting it out slowly, stood and ran toward the grave. He remained bent low, the .45 held tight in both hands, finger resting against the trigger guard. His footfalls were gentle and soft on the springy ground, yet to his ears he sounded like a crippled bull. As he neared where he judged the grave to be—and as the smells grew stronger, the sense of foreboding richer and slick as blood—the voice burst up from his mental underground, echoing through his head and driving him to his knees.

Too late Mister Wolf! You can huff and puff, but I'm not home anymore!

Cole hissed and cursed, fell to his knees, trying desperately not to cry out. So loud! So powerful! He lowered the gun and realised only then what he was kneeling beside.

The first body was close enough to touch. It wore the remnants of military fatigues, and he could just see the glint of its exposed and cleaned dog tags. There were others next to it, laid out in a long, uneven line, on their sides or fronts or backs, limbs missing here and there, heads shorn from necks . . . and he had known these men. He reached out and touched the cool, slick skull of the body closest to him. *Rich?* he thought. *Gareth? Jos?* He had hoped to never see them again.

The girl had shouted at him, mocked him—*And so strong, so alive!*—but it could easily be a ruse to send him away.

He had to know for sure. He plucked a penlight from his pocket and flicked it on, playing the beam quickly across the bodies closest to him. He stood and walked the line, counting as he went, and when he came to the grave he jumped down into the hollow and kicked amongst the scattered bones and clothing. He knew whose remains he was rooting amongst now, and he bore them no respect. He kicked and stamped, glad to crush their deformities beneath his heels.

The girl was not here. Cole shook his head, moaning. No chains, no bones, no sign of her at all.

One skull stared up at him, distended jaw hanging open as if preparing to laugh.

"I see your daddy," he said, "and I'm going to give him another one." Whether or not the girl sensed his words, Cole thoroughly enjoyed putting a bullet through the empty skull. It exploded into a shower of brittle bone. Nothing moist in there now, nothing preserved. Only in *her*. Of all the stupid things to do . . .

He climbed from the hole and set off in pursuit.

Cole had been the one to insist that the berserker girl Natasha should be alive when they buried her.

They had shot down the father and son with silver bullets, held their thrashing bodies while others cut off their heads with chain saws, and the little girl had stood and watched and cried just like a normal child. They all knew her by then—knew what she was—but still some of the soldiers had shown signs of pity. One of them even moved toward her, swinging his SA80 onto his shoulder and holding out his hands to pick her up. Natasha raised her head and stared at him with red-rimmed eyes, and it was Cole who saw the grin beneath the tears. She opened her mouth to say thank you, and to bite, and Cole put a silver bullet in her shoulder.

She fell back into the heather, thrashing, clawing at herself as silver burned into her flesh. Her tears turned to screams. The man standing before her seemed frozen to the spot, and Cole had to grab him and spin him around, shouting into his face to bring him to his senses.

"King! Don't let her get to you! Not now, not after all this! The others have got away, and we've been told to see to these, and that's what we're going to do."

"But—" King said.

"No buts. *No* fucking buts! We should have buried these things long before now, and you know it!" Still the girl was screeching, like a wounded pig awaiting the coup de grace. But Cole suddenly knew that he would not be the one to deliver it, and neither would any of the other men there. There was something better they could do for the little bitch. Something much more effective. More poetic.

They wrapped her in chains and secured them to the corpses of her parents and brother. It took six men to push the tangled bundle of living and dead into the hole they had dug. The three severed heads were thrown in after them, and Cole himself went down to make sure the chains were secure.

"Hey, Mister Wolf!" the girl shouted, and Cole winced at the fury in her voice.

"What is it Natasha?" he said.

"Please let me out, Mister Wolf! Please . . . I promise I'll be good." Her voice was suddenly weak, slurred, the silver acting as acid in her veins.

"Good like your friends? Good like Sophia and Lane?"

"That was them, not us! My mummy and daddy never did anything like that, never. We always just did what we were told."

"Is that all you did, Natasha?"

"Well . . ." her voice trailed off, sly and cool. "Well, maybe when we were taken away, sometimes we enjoyed ourselves a little . . . But never anything bad *here*." She was slurring again, doing the little girl act and adding her own pain to make it more realistic.

"I have my orders," Cole said, starting to climb from the hole.

"Kill me!" Natasha pleaded, quieter. "A silver bullet in the head. My mummy . . . Daddy . . . my brother Peter, my little baby brother! Why did you do that to them? Please let me be with them. *Please* Mister Wolf!"

Cole stood on the lip of the hole and glared at his men. They were terrified, enraged, pumped up by the day of violence. They had all seen so much—blood spilled, friends killed, chaos visiting the normally ordered atmosphere of Porton Down and polluting it forever—that they seemed to be dazed, stunned by the sudden visitation by death that none of them had ever dreamed they would witness. The autumn sun blazed down as if to burn the sights from their minds, but they would always remember this, all of them. They looked at Cole as if he could offer them answers.

He looked at the bodies piled in the back of the wagon. Men he had known, men who had been his friends. Flesh ripped from their bones. Bones chewed and broken. Skulls crushed. And not a bullet hole or knife wound among them.

He turned back to the grave and looked down into Natasha's pleading, pained eyes. She was as ugly and obscene as she had always been, and the tears inspired no pity in Cole. No pity at all. They only fueled the hatred that had been growing in him for years.

"You will be with them, Natasha. Always."

"Fuck you, Mister Wolf!" The words were shocking coming from such a young girl, such rage in a child's voice. But of course, Cole knew that she was no ordinary girl. She was a monster.

"Bury them," he said.

"I'll see you again," Natasha whispered as Cole turned and walked away. The words were a knife in his back, a promise that would haunt him forever.

As his men piled in the broken bodies of their friends and comrades, it took a long time for Natasha's screams to fade away to nothing.

Sometimes, years later, when he woke up sweating and shaking and feeling malevolent memories scurrying back into the underground depths of his mind, Cole wondered whether Natasha was still screaming, and what the mud tasted like in her mouth, and whether she would ever fall completely silent.

CHAPTER FOUR

Tom ducked down when he heard the single gunshot, dropping the body and falling to his hands and knees.

Shooting at me!

He turned and tried to see back the way he had come. But though he could still make out land from sky, it was now too dusky to discern any true detail on the landscape. Perhaps if it were daylight the grave would still be in sight from here; maybe the contours of the land had already hidden it away. Either way, the gun had sounded too far away to be firing at him.

Not that he had ever been shot at before.

He almost laughed, but it came out as a sob. *What if he finds me and kills me? What will happen to Jo then? What will people think of me, found out here with a bullet in my skull and a dead little girl in my arms?*

They wouldn't find us, the girl's voice muttered in his mind. *Mister Wolf would put us back in the hole with my mummy and daddy and brother.*

Tom gathered up the body once again, trying to pile the chains on top so that he could lift them all as one. They were heavy, and he did not think he would be able to move very far like this. Even as a young man he would have found it difficult. Now, older, having spent an afternoon digging and pulling out corpse after corpse from that hole, he was almost at the end of his reserves.

Not far to go, Natasha said.

"Stop it," Tom whined, "just stop talking in my head."

The girl fell silent and Tom was glad, though he could still feel her in there. Quiet, still, but waiting. Her presence was like a hollow in his mind that he had never noticed before, a place begging to be filled.

He was panting from exertion now, bent low with his burden. He had the feeling that without the chains the girl would have been incredibly light, but there seemed to be no way to separate her from the bindings right now. He could not do the same to her as he had done to her family.

Break us away, she had said. Tom had paused, uncertain, but Natasha insisted. *I've been here for a long time, and they've been dead here with me. Break them away. They won't feel it anymore.* Stamping, kicking, bending to grab bones and pull them from the twists of chain, tugging, snapping, until he could lift the chains clear of the other bodies and wrap them around Natasha . . .

As Tom left the hole, the little girl had exuded a deep sadness. He supposed it was a form of letting go. But he knew from experience that this would never be complete.

"I know how you're feeling," he whispered as he struggled onward. Though Natasha did not answer, he felt her listening. "I lost my son. And even though I don't think he was in that hole, he's still been lost to us for ten years."

My family are lost and dead.

"I don't know what you are. You pretend to know about Steven, but you can't. You've been down there . . . so you say. How can you know?"

We'll talk more later, Natasha said. *But if Mister Wolf catches us, time will stop. For both of us. I'm very scared.*

"I am too." Tom was not sure whether it was the answer the little girl wanted—*Little girl? She's a dead fucking bundle, a bag of bones, and it's your own madness driving you to do this*—but it was all he could give her right now. The truth. He was scared, and confused, and close to exhaustion.

Tom ran. Not because of that gunshot or the shadow of the man he had seen climbing the unclimbable fence, but because of the seed of hope that had been planted. The hope that Steven may yet be alive. Small and unlikely though this seed was, it fueled whatever madness had taken him and drove him on.

Here, the voice of the girl said. *Behind this rock. Climb up and wait on top.*

"You see it?"

I see through you. But now I'm cold . . . I'm cold! She sounded pained, tired and distant, and in Tom's mind her voice was very small, the echo of a child from far away.

"What is it?"

The bullet . . . still in me . . .

"What bullet?" The voice drifted away, and Tom felt something leave his mind.

He closed his eyes. He felt so alone, so cold and alone and abandoned, even though it had been his own choice to come out here into the wild. Now it was dark and Jo would be panicking. It was a sensitive time for both of them, and all sorts of thoughts would be running through her mind. She would have called the police, but they would probably not begin looking for Tom for some time. He seemed to remember from all the TV police shows he'd seen that an adult was not a missing person until they had been gone for three days, or five, or some other statutory time. He'd been away from Jo for maybe ten hours. Her panic would be hot and deep; he was her rock, and she was his. They held each other up. Had he now driven something between them that could never be removed?

He looked down at the shape at his feet, the mummified girl wrapped in chains, and the unreality of this bit at him again. He had come out here to look for Steven's grave—and yes, to dig it up, he supposed that had always been his intention. And now he was lost on the Plain, trying to hide from a man with a gun, and he had a child's body at his feet. Not a normal child, either. She was misshapen, mummified . . . and after so long, still *there*. A ghost? A monster? A vampire? Tom believed in none of them—not even ghosts, not even after

Steven—but there was *something* happening in his head.

"I'm going mad," he whispered at the dark, but there was still the body. He could reach out and touch her leathery skin, feel the cool chains retaining the coldness of the grave. However mad he may be, he still owned his senses. The slickness of the metal, the smell of the pit, the sound of the nighttime breeze wandering across the Plain, carrying with it the echoes of ages—Footsteps?

Tom picked up the girl and hurried around the rock she had pointed out. His heart thumped, and the pursuing man would surely hear that, so he breathed again, opening his mouth slightly and breathing light and shallow.

Silence, but for the breeze. Tom eased himself up onto the rock and hunkered down low, suddenly realising that he would be offering his silhouette to anyone who cared to look. And if Mister Wolf caught them he would put Natasha back into the ground with her family, and probably take off her head to ensure that she was dead.

Tom almost laughed. *Take her head off?* This was madness, pure and simple. He ached to feel the heat of Jo's breast as he cried into her chest, the soothing hush of her voice, her hand stroking his head as she calmed him down and forgave him his madness, as she would always forgive everything. He stared into the growing dark and whispered for his wife. . . .

And then the footsteps came again, a few seconds of rapid padding before they stopped. Tom turned his head slowly to look the way he had come, and he saw a shadow kneeling beside a clump of ferns.

He'll see me. He'll look up and see me, and I'll feel the bullet before I hear the gunshot.

But Mister Wolf did not see. Instead he stood, hurried over to the large rock and knelt almost directly below Tom.

Tom raised himself onto his elbows and looked down. He saw the top of Mister Wolf's head, and the glint of metal in his hand. And without thinking, he knew what he had to do.

Natasha! But the girl remained silent. *Sorry, Natasha.* And then Tom shoved her body, chains and all, over the edge of the rock.

He heard a grunt from below, and then a longer groan.

Wolf wolf wolf wolf wolf! Natasha cried, and Tom winced at the terror in that little girl's voice. He stood and shuffled to the edge, trying to gauge the distance to the ground. He could make out the sprawled figure of Mister Wolf, and beside him the twisted shape of the body and chains. He jumped, landing beside the man, falling back and cracking his head against the rock. Even as Tom cried out in pain he heard another groan, a long, low sound that must mean that Mister Wolf was hurt, if not unconscious.

The gun! Tom thought. He remained leaning against the rock, feeling a dampness on the back of his head as blood seeped from his skull.

You're bleeding! Natasha said.

"It's not too bad," Tom said, and he thought, *How does she know?* It felt like a lot of blood, and in his madness would he really feel the pain? Even if his skull was cracked would his sudden lunacy let him know about that? He thought not. And yet in the same instant, he decided that it did not matter.

He pushed himself away from the rock. A breeze swept in across the moors and his back felt cold, sweat and blood cooling and sending a chill through his shoulders. He closed his eyes, remained on his feet, shook the dizziness away. When Mister Wolf groaned again Tom stepped forward. He had no idea what he was doing. Here was a soldier, a killer, armed and ready to shoot, and Tom was tackling him. He had never done anything like this in his life. The nearest he had come to any sort of trouble was helping a young lad being mugged outside a town centre pub in Newport, and even then the cowardly assailants had run off with a shouted "Fuck you" over their shoulders. Now he was standing over a prone man, looking for a gun.

He laughed. He could not help it. The sound was frightening in the darkness; the sound of a madman. But it also comforted Tom because it was a real voice, not a whisper in his head—*Lots of blood!*—and not the wild sound of the Plain at night, when anything could be abroad.

He stepped over the shadow of the fallen man, waiting for a hand to close around his ankle to trip him. But Mister Wolf groaned again, and Tom felt a smile in his head.

"He's not dead," Tom said.

Kill him, Natasha said. She still sounded weak and distant, and behind the words there was a vulnerability that was almost hypnotic.

"No!"

If you don't, Daddy, he'll wake up and—

"I'm not your daddy! And I'm not killing anyone."

Tom bent down beside the man and felt across the ground. His hand soon closed around the greasy metal of the pistol, still clasped in Mister Wolf's hand. He prised his fingers away from the stock. Even in unconsciousness the man held tight.

Kill him, Daddy.

"Shut up."

Natasha's voice withdrew from Tom's mind, and again that sense of loneliness washed over him. His head had started to ache from the impact. Blood ran cool down his neck and between his shoulder blades. As he stood with the gun in his hands, dizziness assailed him once more and he staggered back to the rock for support.

The gun was surprisingly heavy and cool, so cold that it felt slick to the touch. Tom weighed the weapon, resting it in his splayed hand and moving it slightly to get the feel of it. He could see very little, and he thought that keeping hold of it in the dark would be dangerous. He'd likely shoot himself in the foot. He had no idea about safety catches, how to hold or fire it, so he swung back, threw the gun and held his breath until he heard a dull thump somewhere out on the Plain. With any luck it would have buried itself in the muck. He thought that the chance of this man—whoever he was—finding it upon waking was very remote.

The possibility suddenly hit him that this may well be Nathan King lying before him. Tom knelt and rested his hand lightly on the back of the man's head. It came away sticky with blood, and there was slight movement as the man breathed and twitched in unconsciousness. He moved down and felt beneath the torso. This man was heavily built and felt fit, not fat like King.

Whoever it was, he could wake at any moment.

Tom knew what he had to do. He felt his way to where Natasha and her chains had fallen after knocking out the man—*She won't be there, she never was there, it's all in my messed-up mind!*—and there she was, hard and alien beneath his fingertips. How could there be anything alive about her? But such questions, Tom knew, avoided the obvious facts about the last couple of hours. The mad part of him snickered at his denial, and the old Tom, who had come here ten hours earlier searching for a simple truth about his lost son, was suddenly someone from history. It was months ago that he had left his wife, come out here and found the impossibilities that had driven him mad.

There's no corpse wrapped in chains, he thought, gathering the metal loops onto Natasha's chest and stomach and lifting her, *and if even if there were, she wouldn't be talking to me in my head, a ten-year-dead girl talking in my fucking head!* As he started back in the direction of the grave and perimeter fence he waited for that tingling feeling in his mind, the one that would warn him that the dead girl was about to speak again. But for now there was only silence. Carrying his madness in his arms, Tom walked across the dark moor.

He knew when he was nearing the pit. He could smell the stench of the grave.

The weight in Tom's arms was becoming unbearable, but he knew that if he set the girl and chains down now, he may never make it to the car. He would lie here all night, cold, damp from dew, and he may well die of exposure, adding his own fresh corpse to the body count this Plain had already notched over the years. Either that or Mister Wolf would regain consciousness, find him lying here and throttle him. So he walked on, willing his legs to move another step, drawing cool breath into his burning lungs, doing his best to ignore the pain in his arms. The muscles in his shoulders ached. If only he could get rid of the chains! *Then I could carry her forever.*

He passed the open grave, and the bodies spread out across the heather and grass. Whatever Natasha was thinking this close to her dead family, she kept to herself. Tom was glad. Her voice was that of a young child, and yet it was so totally *wrong* that he relished this silent time. Perhaps later she would speak again and he could begin asking questions. But for now he had only one aim in mind: make it back to the cottage. There he would hide the body in the room below the kitchen and try to comfort Jo, come up with a story, a lie. He had lied to his wife before and he had not liked it then. But sometimes lies are uttered in the most benevolent of voices. To protect. To insulate loved ones from insane truth. Some lies are created for love.

He walked in a straight line when he could, hoping to reach the fence and then eventually the crawl space beneath. He stumbled, either on rocks or the twisted stems of ferns or old heathers, and a couple of times he fell, dropping Natasha and landing on his face on the damp ground. Each impact hurt the back of his head more than anything else, and he gingerly explored the wound there, wondering whether he'd done worse damage than he had at first thought. It felt tender and soft, but if he winced against the pain he could press hard enough to feel the skull. There was no give to it, and that at least was a good sign. But he also knew that he had lost of a lot of blood; he could feel it cold across his back and shoulders.

At least the blood could aid his lie to Jo. A story was already forming in his mind.

He walked more slowly after the second tumble, partly through fear of falling again, but mostly from sheer exhaustion. He had excavated a mass grave, fled across a moor with a corpse wrapped in chains, attacked a man trying to kill him, and now he was making his way back through the dark to potential safety. Maybe this would be a standard night's training for a young soldier, but not for someone in their fifties, someone who had let fitness take a second ranking in his life, below food and drink and frequent bouts of self-indulgent misery. Events carried him on, even though he knew this was madness. Perhaps, he thought, he had never even left home.

He saw the fence from some distance away, glinting in the moonlight. Stars glimmered more powerfully than he ever saw back home. Here there was no light pollution to distort and lessen the stars' impact, no stain of humanity on the skies, and ten thousand sources of ancient light were hazed across the heavens. Grateful though he was, Tom felt even more lost in time than ever.

He turned left and began to follow the fence toward the wood. He was not sure how far he had come, but even if he had neared the fence where Mister Wolf had climbed over, the wood would only be a few hundred yards farther on. He could make that distance. He *had* to. His arms were growing numb now, and his shoulders sang with pins and needles, circulation rebelling against the strain being put on his muscles. His legs were aching as well, and with every step his knees were becoming more rubbery, less certain of their soundness. If his legs buckled beneath him now it would be over, he would fall and not be able to get up again until he'd had a rest. And however long that lasted, it would be too long.

That feeling in his mind again, the sense of another consciousness, and Natasha said, *Keep going.*

"I'm not sure I can," he said.

You can, Daddy. Just think of me . . . think . . . aim your thoughts down . . .

Tom looked at the shadow in his arms, but soon realised she did not mean that at all. The contact in his mind lulled him, whispered words that he did not understand but which had a calming quality all their own. If it was a lullaby, it spoke of little that he knew. If it was something else—*a spell? a hex?*—then he was glad for it to work. The pain in his muscles grew distant without lessening, and the growing agony in his knees became more remote than his toes, so far away that it could not belong to him. He looked in and down, and Natasha's presence was palpable.

Tom walked on. He kept the fence-topped bank to his right, moving away from it only where there were clumps of trees or heavy shrubbery barring the way. It may have been minutes or an hour later when he came to the small wood. He plunged straight in, unafraid of the dark—*not while she's here with me, in me, guiding me and comforting me*—but cautious with his footing. He could so easily slip on a rock or step into a small hole, and *snap* would go his leg or *pop* would go his knee. Natasha's calming thoughts could do little to prevent his bones from breaking.

When he came to the crawl space beneath the fence he became dizzy, swaying on his feet, skin suddenly cold with fresh sweat. He knelt and lay the bundle of bones and chains on the ground, then fell onto his hands and knees, retching, but bringing up nothing but bile. He realised that he had not eaten or drunk anything for hours. He was dehydrated, hungry, and terrified.

"So can you stop me from being thirsty?" he asked, shaking his head at the idea that he was talking to himself.

We have to go, Natasha whispered, cool psychic fingers stroking across the insides of his mind. They were exploring there—he suddenly realised that, wondered why he had not felt it before—touching places that were dark to him, hidden ideas and memories long-since consigned to the past.

"What are you—?"

We have to go, Daddy! Mister Wolf is up, the bad man is awake, and he'll be coming for us already!

"I threw his gun," Tom gasped. The nausea had given way to an intense tiredness. Reality was more distant than ever. The only thing that kept him awake was the dead girl's voice in his head.

He's a killer. He'll have more than one.

"Don't call me Daddy," Tom said. Natasha did not answer, and he pushed her across the ground toward the fence. The chains caught on ferns and trailing stems, and he pushed harder, hands flat against the firmness of her mummified skin. He dug in his toes, shoved, kicked, and eventually the body and chains slid down into the crawl space, sliding against the slick soil and passing underneath the fence. Tom followed, one hand held out ahead of him to push Natasha through. It took only a few seconds to struggle to the other side and he stood immediately, picked up the bundle and stumbled back to the road.

The girl was silent, and her presence had retreated from his mind. He thought that maybe she was asleep, or whatever it is dead things do. He wanted to continue questioning her about Steven, but there would be plenty of time later. For now he was content to struggle through his exhaustion, welcome the madness that enveloped him—*I'm at home in bed, the doctor's there, I'm drugged up, I'm dreaming, tasting and smelling and knowing things that can't be real, but dreaming nonetheless*—and make his way back to his car.

When Tom arrived at the vehicle he saw Mister Wolf's Jeep parked a hundred yards farther along the road. Too tired to think straight, he did not even consider trying to disable it, perhaps by slashing the tires or ripping wires or pipes from the engine. It was simply there, ready to follow him, and that was how he perceived it.

Later, the possibility of that missed chance would haunt him. It could so easily have changed the heartache that was to follow. And later still, he would begin to wonder exactly where the dead child Natasha had been at that moment, when everything could have changed.

Tom put the body in the boot, collapsed into his car and drove away.

* * *

Cole lay in the darkened streets of his mind, mugged, attacked, unconscious, and the voice was coming from very far away.

Fuck you, Mister Wolf.

He twitched, feeling the damp ground beneath him. The voice echoed throughout the subterranean world of his mind, filling that space but only leaking out from a few badly sealed openings. Manholes that did not sit quite straight in their frames, perhaps. Old, rotted doors opening onto unused basements, which themselves held steel doors rusted open, leading down into darker places where forgotten memories and old guilt dwelled. She was calling him from far away, but still he heard.

We're leaving now, Wolf-boy. You stupid shit. Call yourself a soldier?

Cole shifted, and the whole substructure of his mind moved with him. It flexed to allow the words entry and then clamped shut behind them. If he entertained those echoes they would become true. He could hear, but he did not have to listen.

And there was something else behind the words. A slippery intent, an unwanted invitation. Burying her voice away could not hide the way in which the words were spoken. Mocking. Scathing. Even deep in unconsciousness Cole knew that he had to follow the girl, and he knew that she knew.

He slowly began to surface. The cool pavement beneath him changed into the soft damp ground of the Plain. The dark building beside him turned into the rock from which Roberts had ambushed him, dropping the girl wrapped in chains on his head. As his unconscious underground receded and hid itself away, Cole heard the voice again, dulled by distance instead of the divisions of his mind.

Goodbye! Goodbye, fucker!

Cole pushed himself up onto his hands and knees. The world swayed and threatened to tip him off. His head ached like a bastard, and there was a patch of dried blood above his ear, tight in his hair and crackling as he flexed his scalp. He touched it, feeling around the edges for any telltale softness. Painful, sore, and he would have a headache for days, but he thought he had escaped lightly.

Escaped.

"Little bitch!" he said. "Oh shit, how could I have been so stupid!"

The Plain was utterly silent at night. Even the occasional breeze gave little more than a sigh, and any animals were stealthily hunting for food. Cole cursed, winced at the thud of pain in his head, and heard a car starting up in the direction of the road.

Roberts. And he had Natasha with him, and they were leaving. Natasha—a berserker as mad and vicious as any—was leaving Salisbury Plain for the first time in ten years. And Cole knew where she would be going. She would take Roberts, lure him ever onward until she had what she wanted: her kin around her, and a chance to live again.

He did not waste any time looking for his gun. He

had another in the Jeep and time, suddenly, was something that had taken solid control of his life. He stood, swayed, but urgency drove his pain down and fear gave balance.

"I'm coming for you, you little bitch," he said to the dark. Nothing answered, but Cole had a sense that his words were heard. They were heard very well indeed.

CHAPTER FIVE

After half an hour of driving Tom had to pull over. He had begun to shake and he could not stop. He tried breathing deeply, but that only made his breath stutter, which in turn encouraged his shaking even more. He turned off the engine and reclined his seat, crossing his hands in his lap, hoping that he would calm down soon enough. The shaking was exhausting.

He was alone. Already he was wondering what he had put into the car boot. A dead girl wrapped in chains? Really? Or perhaps only a bundle of twigs and grass?

Natasha was silent on the matter. Tom's mind jumped and danced with his body, slipping from belief to disbelief, terror to confusion. It skitted from reality to madness as well, though Tom did not know which was which. His feet knocked against the pedals and his hands jumped in his lap, knuckles rattling against the door on one side and the gear level on the other. He groaned, begged for it to end, but nobody was listening.

It took ten minutes for the shaking to die down. He supposed it could be shock. However much he tried to deny what had happened, he had grave dirt beneath his fingernails. And whenever he doubted he had heard a voice in his mind, the memory returned of the way it felt when Natasha was there. The intrusion was gentle yet definite, and when she withdrew . . . he felt so alone. Abandoned. Like a body buried alive, destined to spend eternity underground with only the true dead for company.

He suddenly remembered the man who had been chasing him, Mister Wolf, and he knew that the chase was still on. Tom had been *shot* at tonight! That in itself was almost beyond belief.

He started the car and pulled away. He was still shaking, but it was little more than a hangover shake now. He was used to those.

The headlights carved a tunnel of light through the darkness, throwing back occasional reflections from pairs of eyes hiding away in the hedgerows. *Road kill*, Tom thought, and the word sent a shiver through him.

His thoughts turned to Jo and Steven. Everything happening now was all because of his love for them. Natasha's suggestion that Steven could still be alive pounded at his mind, rivaling the pain from the back of his head. It drove him on. The possibility had, he supposed, enabled him to do what he had just done. He had come to the Plain hoping to find out where Steven was buried, and instead he had been told that he may not be dead at all. How trustworthy his source, he could not tell, whether it really was a living-dead girl from out of the ground, or his own mad hallucination. But the idea was all that concerned him for now. Exploring it would come later, when he arrived back at the cottage and opened the car boot. If he found Natasha in there, he could ask her the dozens of questions presenting themselves to him right now. If there was nothing but a pile of twigs, then he would have to question himself.

"She's real," he said, and from the boot came a single, distant thought in confirmation: *Yes.* Tom looked at his filthy hands on the steering wheel, felt the ache in his arms and shoulders, and from that moment on he was never in any doubt.

Acceptance was easy. Understanding could come later.

It took Cole three attempts to climb back over the fence. His fingers kept slipping on the dew-speckled metal, and he was still weak and dizzy from the blow to his head. It was the thought of what Roberts had taken with him that drove Cole on. He recalled her mockery from ten years ago; even when he was burying her in a hole in the ground there was mockery. Because she *knew* she was superior. She knew that was why she was being buried, hidden away, put down deep where she could be forgotten. And even though the future for her had offered only pain and suffering, she had taken comfort in that knowledge. Begged for him to kill her, yes, but with a smugness that ensured he had not.

And now, after so long in the ground, her voice and its impact was louder than ever. Whereas before she had been able to touch, now she could shout. And beyond that, Cole thought, there could be even more. That time in the ground must have bled her senses and bloated that strange ability all berserkers had to touch with their minds.

He could not let her go. She was mad. She was a berserker. And soon, now that she was back in the world, she would want to feed again.

"Coming to get you," Cole muttered, sliding his hands up the fence posts one at a time, pushing against his weight with his feet, sliding them up, hands, feet. "Coming to get you, you little monster, freak, nightmare. Hear me? Do you hear me now, do you know my thoughts?" He thought she did not—she must have been too far away already—but it pleased him to think them. Fear had always been a good motivator. Add hatred to the pot and the brew is ferocious indeed.

Cole feared and hated Natasha in equal measures. To service both emotions, he had to kill her.

Hands, feet, more muttering and cursing into the night, and now he could see the top of the fence, curved over and sharp. Difficult to negotiate at dusk with all his senses about him; now, at night, his head still spinning, it would be almost impossible.

"Go over now, or find where Roberts got in," Cole muttered. His arms and legs were already starting to shake from the tremendous strain, and sweat soaked his skin. He swung one leg up and caught it quickly over an upright. He slipped and a curve of metal sliced at his jeans, tearing them and scratching the skin beneath.

He had no choice. If he tried to find the way Roberts had come through, he would lose him—and Natasha—forever.

Cole snatched at the curl of a fence upright, feeling the keen edge slice his palm. He scrambled over, trying his best to avoid more cuts, but in his tiredness made mistakes. He fell down on the other side, landing heavily on his back, neck bent to save his head from another impact. The wind was knocked from him, and seconds that seemed liked minutes passed before he hauled in a huge breath. The movement brought pain with it—from his gashed hand, cuts on both legs, bruised back and still-bleeding head—but Cole shut it all out. He stood, scampered down the bank and ran to the Jeep, ignoring the pouty feel of the flesh of his shin. He hauled open the door, bloody hand slipping on chrome. The clasp of the storage compartment beneath the driver's seat passed through his fingers several times, and he had to wipe his hand across his jacket to clear the blood before he could get a firm grip. The .45 felt heavy, cool, good in his palm, calming the pain. He released the magazine, check that it was fully loaded, clicked it back in and dropped the pistol onto the passenger seat.

"Now let's find out where you're going on holiday," he said, smiling as the Jeep grumbled to a start. He tried to convince himself that the smile was because he was in action again. But behind all that lay an intense relief that he was heading away from the Plain. The Plain and that terrible grave, uncovered now, evidence of a past atrocity laid bare to the moon's timeless gaze. He pulled away, and the more distance he put between himself and the pit, the better he felt. Calmer. More assured.

He tried not to think of what might lie ahead. If he had let his mind probe the future—if he had known what was to come, or even guessed half of it—he may well have eaten a bullet there and then.

In the darkness, with everything that had happened weighing down and distracting him, Tom lost his way. The landscape looked totally different at night. The road signs read the same, but behind them the darkness skewed direction, and any sense of where he was or where he was heading soon vanished. Regardless, he drove on, trying to maintain the same direction because he knew that the man would be coming. *Mister Wolf*, Natasha had called him, a little girl expressing little girl's fears. In her voice he had heard true fear, but something else as well, something he could not quite place. Something wrong.

He came to a T-junction, and both ways were villages whose names he did not recognise. He chose left because it felt closer to the direction he should be travelling. The road soon curved to the right and straightened, and Tom pressed his foot down, trying to put as mush distance as possible between himself and the pit he had opened in the ground. *Opened a can of worms now*, he thought, and that inspired images of squirming things in the meaty wetness of a corpse.

The landscape became more hilly, trees and hedges bordering fields, mostly bare and stubbled after the harvest. Tom wondered briefly what else may lie hidden beneath the surface of the world around here, just waiting to be discovered. What other secrets did Porton Down own? He had read tales of disease and radioactive elements being released so that scientists could chart their progress across the British Isles. Perhaps even now, Tom's skin was aglow with radioactivity, changing, cells mutating and readying themselves for the cancer they would eventually welcome. Or maybe, after unearthing so much horror, he was a carrier for some bizarre bug or chemical, a trace of which had been buried along with those it had killed. A chemical conjuror of nightmares, perhaps, turning his brain to mush even as he tried to escape with a bundle of twigs and rags.

But no, none of that fit. Everything King had told him felt right, and Natasha seemed to be the proof of that. The living proof? He was still unsure. She spoke to him, but she was cold and hard, a mummified *thing*. She had mentioned the bullet still within her—the silver bullet . . .

"Oh for fuck's sake!" Tom slammed on the car's brakes and the vehicle slowed to a halt across the road. He had seen no other traffic since leaving the Plain, and a collision was the least of his worries right now. He turned and grabbed the map book from the backseat, switching on the interior light. If Mister Wolf were closing in, Tom would present him with a fine target. But there was nothing else for it. He was completely lost, and he had to find his way back to the cottage.

And what then? Flee with Jo, letting the maybe-dead Natasha guide them with silent words in his head?

"Cross that one when we come to it," he said, flipping the pages of the atlas. He found the hamlet where they were staying, the area of the Plain he had just come from, and eventually he located the village he was now heading toward. Not that far out of his way, he was pleased to see. Lost and found again. He grunted, closed the book and moved off.

Maybe half an hour and he would be back at the cottage. Then he would have some explaining to do.

Natasha remained silent for the whole journey. There was no feeling that she was probing at his mind, no sense that she was about to speak at all, and Tom wondered again at that bullet still inside her, and how his moving her had shaken it loose. What a cruel, ridiculous irony that would be: unearthing a ten-year-old corpse that spoke to him in his head and told him that his son could actually still be alive, only to have it die on him because he had moved it. How he would laugh at the Fates that planted *that* one on him. He tried to speak to her in his mind and out loud, but there was no hint of a response, and he soon felt foolish doing so. *Not as if anyone's watching*, he thought. But after tonight, he would never feel certain of that again.

It took twenty minutes to drive to the cottage, not

half an hour. A whole slew of possible scenarios hit him as he approached the corner and turned into the driveway. The police are inside, comforting Jo and liaising with the station, passing on news of the search under way on the Plain. Tom pulls up in his car—only twelve hours late—and whatever apology he offers, he cannot hide the filth on his clothes, the mud beneath his fingernails, the blood in his hair. And just then the officers receive a call about a mass grave turned out on Salisbury Plain and one of them goes to search the car, glances into the backseat, approaches the boot . . .

Or perhaps there is no one there and Jo is sitting up alone, nursing yet another cup of hot sweet tea as she awaits his return. She is angry and scared and afraid of being alone, very afraid, she has always told him that, and in a way he thinks it is Steven's death that brought her own mortality screaming down upon her. And Tom's as well, because it is his death she fears the most. *I never want to be left alone*, she often tells him, and in that statement are implications that they refuse to discuss. But he often thinks to himself that she never will be alone, because if anything happens to him she will ensure that she follows soon after. So she is there, staring at the door and waiting for it to open, and at the back of her mind is that growing shadow of suicide. . . .

Or maybe Mister Wolf is there already, somehow knowing where to wait for Tom. And perhaps Jo is lying dead in the kitchen, her blood staining the flagstones black and the look on her face something Tom will never see. Because Mister Wolf is a hunter, a killer, and as soon as he has Tom in his sights he will shoot. Natasha will find her death at last. And Steven, wherever he may be . . .

But there was no vehicle in the driveway, and the cottage lights blazed, and even before Tom had stopped the car Jo was out of the house and flinging herself at his door, hauling on the handle and leaning in as he applied the parking brake, hugging him, hitting him, cursing at him and screaming how much she loved him, how worried she had been, and never once did she ask where he had been or why he had returned so late.

"Jo," Tom said, tears coursing a surprising hot streak across his cheeks. "Are you feeling better?" *We need to move*, he thought, but here was his beloved wife. He had made her like this, and he owed her this moment.

"I was so worried!" she screamed into his neck, unable or unwilling to lift her head and lose contact with him. Tom felt her voice pressing against his skin, finding his flesh and bones whole and reveling in that, screaming again. She moved back slightly then, her apparition of her husband now made flesh, and Tom's heart broke at the sight of her face.

She must have been crying for a long time. Her eyes were puffy and red, her face swollen and sore from the tears. Her mouth was turned down at the corners, as if the weight of her fears had been acting on her with a terrible gravity. She was still wearing the nightclothes he had left her in, and they were rumpled and creased, smelling vaguely of must and fear. *I can smell the fear on my wife*, Tom thought, and fresh tears came to his eyes.

For a while, he forgot about the thing in the boot.

"I'm so sorry Jo," he said, reaching out and hugging her back to him. She shifted position so that she was sitting on his lap in the car, bent low, her head resting on his shoulder so that her hot face pressed against his neck and cheek once again. "I love you honey, really, I'm so sorry if I frightened you. Time ran away with me, just left me. And I got lost on the way home, and I didn't know what to do, I had no idea what I was doing!"

"You smell," she said, "mud and earth. You stink. You're filthy! Oh Tom, I was so terrified that you'd never come back!"

Tom's idea about lying to his wife—about the car having a puncture, and him knocking himself out changing it—had fled the moment he saw her. In truth he had no wish to lie to her about anything, not anymore. And with that certainty came a sense of excitement at what he had to tell her next. *Steven*, he would say, *Jo, I really think he might still be alive*. But he did not have the chance to speak. Jo hugged him tight, squeezing the air from him, keening like a dog welcoming home its long-lost owner. And Natasha, so silent for the whole journey, chose that moment to make herself known again.

Daddy! she said. *He's coming! Mister Wolf is coming!*

Tom glanced past Jo's head at the rearview mirror and saw that Natasha was mistaken. Whether or not she could have spoken up earlier was something he did not think about until much later, but right then all he knew was that she was wrong. Mister Wolf was not coming; he was already here.

The Jeep was parked in the drive entrance, blocking any hope of escape out onto the road.

He's here to hurt me, Daddy!

The driver's door was opening.

Please don't let him hurt me . . . it hurts so much already!

And as Tom opened his mouth to speak to his wife for the last time, the shooting began.

To begin with, Cole was aimless. He drove simply because he had to drive. Sitting in his Jeep waiting for inspiration to hit would have felt even more useless than just driving for the sake of it. So he powered along country lanes, taking lefts, rights, or heading straight on at junctions, trying to imagine which way Roberts had come. He slowed down and turned his lights off intermittently, looking for signs of other car headlights in the countryside around him. There was nothing.

He drove fast, because slow would have felt even more hopeless.

Blood was pooling in his boot, squelching at every gear change. His jeans rubbed at the gash on his calf, and each contact was like the touch of a white-hot iron. He needed stitches, he knew, but they would have to wait. What were causing him more problems were the cuts on his hands, the sliced left palm especially. They smeared the steering wheel with blood, and every time he changed gear his hand slid around the gear stick, threatening to slip off. He wiped his hands on his jeans and jacket, but that only aggravated the wounds and encouraged the bleeding.

I've really hurt myself, he thought. *Done some real damage.*

He drove on. At a T-junction he turned left without thinking, simply because there was nothing else to do. And inside, he searched for Natasha.

She would not be out in the open, in those parts of his mind that he knew so well. She would be *below*. Down in the dark, hidden away, rooting around like the devious little bitch she was. So he hunted for her, running through the familiar streets of his consciousness, heading off down alleys he did not recognise. There was graffiti on walls, but he could not read it. Letters swam in and out of focus. He thought they were a language he did not know, speaking of things he could not understand. As much as this disturbed him, Cole was used to it. He often felt like a stranger in his own mind, and like everything else that was wrong with life, he attributed it to Porton Down.

He sought further, deeper, inviting Natasha in even though he hated the sense of her in his head. Especially this Natasha, newly risen from the ground with a shout instead of a whisper.

"How does the air feel on your skin, monster?" he said. "Are you lonely without the bones of your kin to keep you warm, vampire?" Like all berserkers she despised the word vampire, he knew, but it was more out of vanity than anything else. She hated for her

119

berserker clan to be thought of as anything other than
unique. "Wrinkled dry dead thing crying like a baby
when I chained you up with those vermin you called
mother, father, brother."

A chuckle in his mind; not his. He did not feel her
intrusion, but he knew that she was there, hovering
slightly beyond. He drove on, trying to discern which
direction the laugh had come from.

"Laughing at what I did to you, Natasha? You won't
find it funny when I catch you this time. You think ten
years was a long time in the ground, smelling your family rotting around you? Feeling their flesh grow cold,
wet, fluid? Or did you eat them to stay awake, just for a
little while longer?"

She laughed again, a sound so filled with confidence
and hate than Cole slowed the Jeep, shivering. *Fuck
you, Mister Wolf.*

He came to a junction and turned left.

"Still awake then, vampire?"

I'm no vampire!

"I bet you're sucking the life out of that poor man
already."

She was silent but still present, and Cole narrowed
his eyes as he tried to put direction to the slithery
touch now evident in his mind. He veered left and
right on the road, striving to sense which way was
closer.

Warm, Natasha said.

"I'm going to find you and kill you," Cole said. "I'll
kill him, too."

Why should I care? the girl said, and Cole smiled when he heard the doubt in her voice.

"Get out of my head!" He had to cover what he had heard, hold it to himself for whatever advantage it may yield him.

I'm not in your head, Mister Wolf . . . I'm below it, down here rooting through all these things you want to forget. Would you like me to describe some of them to you now? Dredge up these memories for you to feast on? They're all here, awaiting their fair showing. Here, this woman Sandra Francis with her long red hair and—

"Shut the fuck up!" Cole hissed. He swung the Jeep left into a narrow lane, and the sense of his mind being invaded grew warmer, wetter.

Warmer.

"You *want* me to find you."

There's always fun in the chase.

He pressed his foot down on the gas and flicked the headlamps to full beam, taking corners at a mad speed, careening into a high bank, wheels spitting mud and gravel as they squealed against protruding stones, away again, light dancing and vibrating across the road ahead of him as the Jeep bounced and jolted from side to side.

Warmer still . . .

Cole reached over and grabbed the .45 with his left hand, clicking off the safety and resting it between his legs. It was a cool, comforting weight. He fought with the steering wheel as the vehicle splashed through a deep puddle. A house flashed by on the left, white-washed walls reflecting headlights back at him. Its occupants were probably tucked up cosy in bed, unaware of what had passed them perhaps only a few minutes before. They were dull sheep, sleeping and working, breathing and eating, never questioning the realities they were brought up to hold as truth.

Cole had seen things, done things. He knew that all such realities were lies, invoked because they painted comfortable pictures out of unnatural, unbearable paints. The truth was never easy to accept. It could drive a man mad. His own madness, his own unbearable truths, were buried deep. And he liked it that way. They spoke to him sometimes, but usually only in dreams, and he had become adept at forgetting his dreams.

Sandra with her long red hair?

Cole shook his head, and the point of one of those hidden memories sank back down into safe, impenetrable depths.

Ooh, very warm now Mister Wolf. Be seeing you soon. Don't forget to have fun, because fun is what it's all about. What else is there? Only death, and decay, and ten years of purgatory, you bastard. You'll never win, Cole. Never!

"What game are you playing?" Cole said, but Natasha did not answer, and he suspected that she had fallen silent for now. *Is it just this?* he thought. *Maybe it was a tease and they went the other way. There's no rule to this little bitch, no rhyme or reason.*

There was a hollowness in his chest at the thought of her being out, a void where hope had once existed. So many times over the years he had considered returning to the Plain, excavating the grave, pulling out

Natasha's corpse and finishing what he had started. But he was scared and in denial. Even with everything he knew of the berserkers, he had believed that she would be dead. And that belief, that hope, had kept him away. That, and the certainty that unearthing a corpse that spoke to him would drive him mad.

Around the next corner a tractor blocked the road.

Cole stomped on the brake and clutch, fighting the juddering wheel, the Jeep shuddering as the ABS kicked in, the farmer turning in his tractor, his face big and pale and comically shocked, mouth open and one hand coming up to protect his face against the two tonnes of metal hurtling toward him. Cole shouted and pressed the pedals harder, actually standing from the seat and bracing himself against the steering wheel. The tractor jumped forward as the farmer sped up, a reaction as useless as it was automatic. And the one thought that screamed out in Cole's mind was, *What the hell is he doing out at three in the morning?*

The Jeep hit a pothole and bumped to the left, burying its nose in the hedge. Cole was thrown forward, seatbelt locking across his chest and biting into his neck. It knocked the breath from him and, winded for the second time in an hour, he slumped back in his seat and gasped for air. The Jeep's bumper had nudged the tractor's big rear wheel, but only slightly. The farmer drove on for an extra few feet—as if afraid that the Jeep would leap ahead again, like an animal lunging at its prey—and then pulled over into a gateway.

"You alright?" the man shouted, jumping from the

tractor and waddling up the road. He was wearing a boiler suit and Wellington boots, and in the glare from the Jeep's headlamps he looked like a lumbering puppet. Cole sucked in a breath at last and let out a hooting laugh, realising as he did so that he had been grasping the .45 so tightly between his knees that he could feel bruises forming there already.

"So do I just shoot this twat?" he said, laughing so hard that a string of snot powered from his nose. *I'm losing it*, he thought, *too pumped up, too careless*.

The farmer reached the Jeep and held out his hand as if to open the door. But then he looked inside, and whatever he saw in Cole's face caused him to move back a few cautious paces, eyes downcast. *Dominant male*, Cole thought, snorting again. He gave in to the laughter as he restarted the Jeep—it had stalled after striking the hedge—and by the time he scraped between the tractor and the far hedge he was guffawing almost beyond control. But it felt good, it felt like regaining control, so he let it come some more.

"Nearly there!" he said, laughing again. "Nearly there for you, Natasha! I've been warming my gun so that the bullet's not too cold when it goes into your skull." His head hurt, his leg was stiff with dried blood, and every time he turned the steering wheel it felt as though blades were slicing into his hands. "Soon," he said.

Cole glanced once in his rearview mirror. The farmer was already climbing back onto the tractor, probably trying to get his story straight so he could tell his fat wife later.

Natasha was there then, probing his mind, seeing how close he was and withdrawing again. She left something behind, an echo of herself. To Cole it felt like fear. He smiled.

He held the .45 in his right hand as he steered; dangerous, but he was unwilling to drop the gun now. If that had been Robert's car back there and he'd fumbled the pistol instead of clasping it between his knees, he could have lost his best chance. So no more risks. Not now he was so close.

And why does she want *me to find them?*

"She's sick," Cole said, "and mad. She's been under the ground for ten years." He expected a smart answer from the living dead girl, but she had truly gone.

He looked left and right, searching for any gates to driveways, or narrow lanes, or parking areas. Roberts and his wife must have hired a cottage for the weekend, which would be good for Cole. No one else around to witness what was about to happen. If he was really lucky, the bodies would not be found for some time.

A few minutes later he saw the glare of car headlamps through the hedge to his right and he slowed down, killing his own lights. Moonlight was enough to see by at this speed. There were sparse white clouds in the sky now, like smudged paint on a blank black canvas, the stars splashes. He lowered his window, saw the entrance to the driveway, turned off the engine and coasted to a stop between the gateposts, blocking any route of escape.

The pistol felt good in his right hand.

It was Robert's car. Luck had lead Cole on . . .

Luck and her, *luck and* Natasha, *because she* wanted *me here.*

He wondered where she was, and guessed the boot. Roberts would not have wanted to put something like that, something old, mysterious, dead, on the backseat where anyone could see it.

The car's rear lights were still on, and there seemed to be a commotion in the driver's seat. Cole squinted, glancing aside to allow his night vision to make out the shapes, and then he smiled. Perfect. He felt no thrill at killing, took no pleasure; it was a job well done that pleased him.

This would be over very soon.

Opening the door he heard a woman's voice, raised and muffled, angry and relieved, and as his feet crunched down on the gravel he was glad she was making so much noise. This way, Roberts would not even hear the gunshot that killed him.

The interior light of Robert's car was on, and Cole saw him look in the rearview mirror, his eyes widening, mouth dropping open to shout a warning.

"Shit!" The last thing Cole wanted to do was to hunt these people down. This had to be quick.

He cupped his right hand in his left, braced his legs and started shooting.

CHAPTER SIX

Tom had heard gunfire once before in the last twelve hours, but this was different. Out there on the Plain he had heard the blast and that was all; no bullet swishing by, no echo, no ricochet, no evidence of the shot other than the sound itself. Now it felt as though his whole world was exploding.

It took him a few seconds to associate what was happening around him with the gun blasts coming from behind. As he looked in the rearview mirror the back windshield shattered, misting and showering down in a thousand pieces. The mirror itself smashed, firing glass shards at his face, and a hole the size of his fist appeared in the front windshield. Something hammered on the roof once, twice, as if someone had taken to the car with a sledgehammer. The whole vehicle shook. The passenger seat rattled in its bracings, and a puff of stuffing erupted from its front face. It drifted lazily down onto the mat as the car stereo and heating panel exploded in a shower of plastic, glass and wires.

Jo had slumped down over his lap, hiding from the shooting. He could feel her shaking with fright, mumbling her terror, and he put his hand on her head to show her he was still there. She was wet with the sweat of fear.

The noise was incredible. The various sounds of the car being destroyed around him—*Go back, go back!*—the explosive gunshots, much louder than he could have imagined—*Go back go back, now!*—and his own screaming, so loud and yet so detached from him that for a few seconds he wondered whether it was Jo.

Go back, Daddy, back, back, he's hurting *me!*

Tom tried to lean forward in his seat to offer less of a target, but Jo was heavy in his lap, still jerking and gasping from the shock of what was happening. Her legs protruded from the open door, the most exposed part of her, and he was terrified that one of them would catch a bullet.

It hurts! Natasha screamed, and suddenly Tom realised what she had been saying, and why, and he knew that she was right. He turned the ignition key, slipped the car into reverse and slammed his foot on the gas.

The shooting paused as the car stared to move, and Tom guessed that Mister Wolf was reloading. Good timing. He turned to look back over his shoulder just at the instant when the rear of his car struck the front grill of the Jeep, jerking him back in his seat. Jo pressed against his stomach and chest, and Tom gasped. He saw the man leap away to one side, roll on the gravel and stand again, fumbling in his pocket with one hand and holding the gun with the other. For a second their eyes met. The man frowned, cocked his head to one side, holding Tom's gaze. And then Tom saw the game of distraction Cole had been playing when he brought up the gun and aimed it at his head.

The bullet exploded the seat's headrest as Tom drove forward again. He braked quickly and reversed into the Jeep once more, careful to keep Jo's legs safely clear of the impact. He felt hot metal glancing across the back of his scalp, opening up fresh wounds.

Hurts, hurts!

The car struck again and he kept his foot on the accelerator, wheels spinning in the gravel and sending small stones flying, the stench of the burning clutch filling his nostrils, the Jeep moving back now because the man had somehow, miraculously, left the parking brake off.

The gun exploded again and again, punching holes in the car. Jo shook but Tom did not look down, could not, not now that there was the slightest chance they might escape. He could smell something other than the clutch, something that must have been the sweet tang of a gun growing hot.

"Come on!" Tom screamed, and the Jeep rolled from the driveway and back out into the road.

Jo jerked on his lap and then lay still. Tom looked down and saw a blossom of blood on her back, spreading slowly outward from a ragged hole in her dressing gown. "Jo?"

Footsteps, running on gravel.

He kept his foot on the gas.

Another engine roared and a tractor ploughed into the side of the Jeep, shoving it several feet along the road with a screech of tires and the howl of breaking metal.

"Jo?"

There was room now to reverse between the Jeep and tractor—tangled together as if they had rolled off the production line as one—and the gatepost, and as Tom saw Mister Wolf standing directly in front of the car, leveling his pistol, he spun the wheel and ducked down over Jo. Two bullets thudded into his seat. He felt the warmth of Jo's blood on his cheek where he was pressed against her back. Her legs and the open door snagged the gatepost and then flipped free again. The car hit something, scraped by, and Tom sat up in his seat, blood and tears dropping from his chin and cheeks as he twisted around and reversed quickly up the road.

He was sobbing, blinking fast, trying so hard to keep his eyes clear so that he did not bury them in the hedge. More gunshots followed him but he did not care now, would not care if one of them struck him in the neck. At least then he could hold Jo one more time before he bled to death.

There's still Steven, Natasha said.

"Shut up!" Tom shouted. He aimed the car around a bend and steered its smashed rear into a gateway, knocking the gate from its iron moorings. It fell slowly, as if wanting to remain standing. He saw dawn blurring the night in the east. Jo's blood ran warm on his legs. He twisted the wheel and drove forward, away from the cottage and the Jeep and Mister Wolf, who wanted so much to kill him.

Me, Natasha said, *it's me he wants to hurt, Daddy, not—*

"I said shut up!" Tom screamed, and two wheels churned briefly along the grass verge before he regained control.

Jo was still and silent, and he could see now that the bullet in her back had not killed her. How could it, when there was so little left of the back of her head from those first few shots?

He touched her there, hoping that somehow, as he drove, he could share in his dead wife's final thoughts.

Tom was aware that he was dreaming, but that awareness gave him no control. He had slipped from a chaos of nightmarish images into this almost filmic episode, and though he could feel the sudden outside influence that drove this—it was more like a memory than a dream, yet one that someone else was remembering for him—he could do nothing to steer or influence its course. He sensed that it would be bad. He tried to close his ears, his eyes, but he was asleep, and dreams paid little heed to external senses.

Besides, it was fascinating, like a car crash or a train wreck. He *had* to watch. And it distracted his mind from . . . from . . . something awful that he could no longer quite remember.

"It's good to forget, for a while," said the man in the

boat. He looked straight at Tom and smiled, a pained expression that showed far too many teeth. "But you'll always remember again in the end. Watch now. Remember."

Asleep, his dreams hijacked by Natasha's memories, Tom watched.

The man in the boat was not alone. There were four of them, two adults—a man and a woman—a young boy, and Natasha, through whom Tom was viewing this memory. They were all dressed in similar grey-green clothes, almost militaristic. The adults sat stony-faced, but the boy seemed excited, forever standing and being told to sit again, babbling and being hissed at to remain silent. He was panting like a puppy at play. The adults seemed to speak to him without moving, and Tom heard whispers in his mind.

"Almost there," the man said out loud. His legs were jerking up and down, feet tapping the deck beneath them. His hands clasped at his thighs. He turned to the woman next to him, his wife, and smiled, and kissed the side of her face. "Remember, it's not us doing this," he whispered. She turned away as if she could not face him, and looked across at her son. He did not echo his parents' apparent sadness. The boy was standing again, keening as he jumped up and down on the spot, hands twisting the legs of his plain trousers into tight knots. His eyes were changing colour.

A voice came from elsewhere, dull and distant and

lifeless. *You leave no one*, it said, and a shape stood above them, blurred against the skyline.

Try as he might Tom could see nothing outside the cockpit where the family sat. They were totally enclosed. The only reason he knew this was a boat was because Natasha's memory told him so, and the only way he could be certain of the movement was by the shadows of the radar mast gliding up and down across the cockpit as the boat dipped and peaked the waves. The little boy was running back and forth now, four steps left, four steps right, and the movement must have been blurring him in memory because his arms seemed to be growing in length, his legs thickening. It was as if Natasha's memory in Tom's mind was slipping, and its images were slurring.

"Peter . . . ," the woman said, but she trailed off when the man put his hand on her arm. The boy's eyes shone as if they caught the sun.

One minute, the distant voice said, and the shadow of the speaker rose and fell across the woman's face as the boat traversed another wave. She turned and looked directly at Tom—at Natasha—and smiled a smile he remembered his mother giving him so many years ago. It spoke of unquestioning love, and a motherly instinct to protect.

The man leaned to the side and spoke to the woman. She shook her head, both angry and scared, and he held her closer and spoke again, keeping her still so that she could hear everything he had to say.

Then he let go, pulled away and began to blur.

Tom tried to draw back. Something had changed here, a sudden jump in the reality of things that he should not be seeing. And yet he was prisoner to this dream, a passive viewer of Natasha's memory being played out in his own head, and he was trapped here watching and hearing, tasting and smelling the truth of history. He tried to close his eyes but was already asleep. He would have turned away had he any control. Instead, he saw the family go berserk.

The voice rose into a shout, its words indistinguishable from the snarls and screams coming from the cockpit. The young boy Peter was on his hands and knees now, fingers and toes clawing at the timber decking and leaving deep scores in its surface. The slashed wood shone bright in the sun. He shook his head, and spittle and blood flecked the deck around him. The adults seemed to speed up, their movement jerky, as if this were a movie with every third frame removed.

The view flipped onto its side and began to vibrate as Natasha fell to the deck.

I don't want to see this, Tom thought, and Natasha said, *No, but you need to. And it's only just begun.*

Ten seconds, the vague voice said, and Natasha looked up at the shadow looming above them. Its stance showed fear. Its voice held awe. Its hands were weighed down by a blocky, heavy object that could have only been a gun.

What are you showing me? Tom thought, but there was no reply, because this was pure memory once more. As the boat thudded onto a beach and a high door in its bow fell open onto wet sand, he became a part of it.

The rest of the dream, the memory, the nightmare
came to him in brief glimpses, each of them more confusing than the last, and more terrifying. To begin with
Tom could make little sense of the individual images,
but the memories viewed through Natasha's eyes combined to evoke a sense of impending action, and a dis-
tinct emotion: dread.

Natasha ran onto the beach behind the adults and
her younger brother Peter. The sands were deserted, a
beautiful golden spread marred here and there with
blots of driftwood or seaweed drying in the merciless
sun. At the head of the beach where the dunes began,
maybe fifty yards away, sat a huge house made of glass
and steel, an architect's wet dream sparkling with daylight and holding mystery behind its shaded windows.
There were several cars parked beside the house, none
of them worth less than fifty grand.

Several people stood around the house and hunkered
down on its balconies. They flashed. It was only as Peter
flipped onto his back and writhed like a landed fish that
Tom realised the flashes were gunshots.

A blur here, like film forwarded sixteen-speed, the
images distinguished only by their redness.

They were in the house. It was light, airy, ultra-
modern, all steel and slate and glass. The father was
holding a woman against a wall and emptying her chest
cavity onto his feet. Heart, lungs, shattered ribs
slopped out, their impact smothered by somebody else
screaming. He bit at her lower jaw and tore it away,

and as he turned Tom saw just how much he had changed.

Blur.

Natasha was running along a corridor. It turned left and right, doors flashing by on either side, but it was blood that laid the trail she was following. Another turn and she came across the crawling man, mangled leg dragging behind him like a gutted fish. The man collapsed on the floor and turned, attempted to raise a gun, but one slash of Natasha's claws ripped his hand apart, sending the weapon spinning against the wall in a rain of blood. He screamed, Natasha leaned in, and there was a howl that can only have come from an animal as the memory turned red.

Blur.

Peter was in the kitchen, thrashing at a body on the floor. He leaped onto it, screeched, flaying with his hands and feet, jumped off, landed on the work surface, turned to look at Natasha, opened his mouth wide—his mouth, filled with too many teeth and meat and a scream that was not possible—and jumped onto the body again. His head shook and tugged and the body slid across the tiled floor, leaving bits of itself behind. It was barely recognisible as human, other than its clump of blonde hair matted with brain. Peter jumped off again and came at Natasha, but there was no panic, no fear, only a primal sense of sibling love.

Blur.

Some people—the survivors—had locked themselves into the basement. Natasha's parents were down at the door trying to tear through, but it was steel-lined, and their claws and teeth screamed on the metal leaving only shiny slashes behind. Peter was a few feet away trying to dig through the wall. Natasha loped down the steps to join her family, leaving bloody footprints behind.

Blur.

The door stood open now, and there was shooting, and Natasha's mother was dancing against the wall as a man emptied an Uzi at her. None of the bullets seemed to be hitting her; chunks of plaster blew out, shards of concrete block rattled to the floor, and when the magazine was empty she stopped dancing. And growled.

The man cried out as Natasha's mother ripped into him, and then through him.

Screams came from the basement. Natasha plunged into the darkness to join in the final slaughter.

Tom screamed himself awake. Sunlight blazed in through the shattered windshield, and for a moment he thought he was on that beach, perhaps facing the house of steel and glass and waiting to see what would emerge from it. He screamed again, his memory of the nightmares rich and fresh—he could taste the blood, smell the guns—and then someone whispered to him, calming, soothing.

Don't worry, don't cry, it's all memory.

"It's not mine!" he said, turning in his seat to see Jo lying in the back. When he had finally stopped he managed to push her from his lap out onto the road, then haul her up into the backseat. He had scraped her legs doing so, and there were speckles of black tarmac in the scratches. He had tried to pick them out, crying the entire time.

Jo stared at him through half-closed eyes. The blur of his own tears seemed to make her cry.

There's more, the voice said, *more to see*.

"I don't want to."

You must, Daddy, if you want to know me.

"I don't! Since I found you everything's . . . just . . ." He slumped back in his seat, wretched, hopeless. *Hospital*, he thought, *police*, but somehow both seemed futile.

It's not my fault, Natasha said, her voice breaking in his mind. He felt her in there, her awareness melded with his own, and his tears were for both of them.

Tom climbed from the car and took a look at it for the first time. He had driven for an hour after Mister Wolf's attack, lost in a blind panic, treading the waters of grief as Jo cooled across his lap. How he had not crashed he had no idea, because he could recall little of the journey. He must have passed through other villages, and yet he could remember nothing of observers reacting to the ruined car and the dead woman in his lap. Perhaps because he did not see them meant that they could not see him.

The car was a wreck. It was a wonder that it had driven anywhere, such was the violence that had been wrought upon it. The sides and rear were buckled and dented, all the windows smashed, and more than a dozen bullet holes perforated the chassis. The driver's door and the rear door were speckled with Jo's blood. It was not obvious, there were no great smears or splashes, but Tom knew what he saw. His dead wife's blood. On their car. On the car he had driven for an hour, with Jo dead across his lap.

He fell to his knees and buried his face in his hands, Natasha's bad dreams fading to be replaced by this, his own living nightmare.

I'm hurt, Daddy, Natasha said, and Tom glanced up at the boot of the car. It was crushed and buckled from where he had repeatedly struck the front of the Jeep.

"Good," he whispered, and he meant it. "And I'm not your daddy. That man . . . that *thing* is your father, not me." He tried not to focus on any one image from the dream.

You rescued me, she said, sobbing. *You found me. You birthed me from the earth, and you're as close to a daddy as I have. I'm only a little girl. I'm only—*

"You're that thing from my dream!" He shook his head, as if doing so would rearrange and resolve the images that had invaded his troubled sleep. "What are you? What were you *doing?*"

There's more for you to see before I can explain, Natasha said, voice hitching as her sobs dried up. *But now Mister Wolf will be coming. He hasn't finished. He wants me dead, and you as well because you're helping me. He wants everyone dead. He was human once, but he lost all that, and now he's just a bad man.*

"Human?" Tom said, tipping his head back and staring at the brightening sky. He was not entirely sure what that meant.

We have to move on, the voice said, quiet and considered. *We have to go, because of Steven.*

"Where is he?"

The blunt question must have surprised Natasha because she fell silent for a few seconds. Tom could still feel her in his head, but the sensation stilled like a held breath.

I can't tell you, she said.

"Why?"

I can't. I'm not sure, not really, but the closer we get the more certain I'll be. And it's dangerous there. Very dangerous. If he's still with them, they'll be angry, and strong, and well fed.

"Who are you on about? I don't understand. I don't understand any of this."

They kept us hungry, Natasha said. And then she drew back into herself and left Tom alone, alone with his dead wife and that already familiar sense of abandonment.

Cole had never enjoyed killing. Those few occasions he had killed—his old friend Nathan King recently, and the times before—had been out of necessity. King had died because he knew too much and he had started blabbing, but really it was all down to the berserkers. Cole had promised himself ten years ago that he would have to be as heartless, ruthless and vicious as them to catch the ones that had escaped or, ironically, to prevent them from being noticed. He knew that he could never truly match them, but he had tried. Through the doubt and the self-hate, he had tried.

After killing Sandra Francis six years before, Cole had cried. Curled up in bed the tears came, and he stood immediately, went to the kitchen and cut himself across the back of his left hand. The pain gave the tears a different reason, and the blood brought back memories that had given him some form of justification. If the scientist had talked, helped him, revealed everything she knew about what made Natasha special, perhaps he would have let her live.

Now, standing over the kneeling farmer and pressing the hot barrel of the .45 to the back of the man's skull, Cole would have cheerfully seen the fool's brains splatter his shoes.

"Fucking idiot!" he shouted. "It's early, you should be in bed, not driving around the fucking lanes wrecking cars. Idiot. *Idiot!*"

"I . . . I . . . ," was all the farmer could say. He was shivering, sweating and crying. Instead of inspiring pity this only increased Cole's anger.

"Stop stammering and tell me what you're going to do about it. Tell me!"

The farmer had seen most of what happened. The shooting, Roberts ramming the Jeep into the road, the blood on the woman's legs where she lay across Roberts' lap. Cole knew that he had hit her several times, and that was bad, that was wrong. But right now he was too enraged to feel sorrow or regret. Now, his blood was up.

I'm berserk! he thought, and although the idea was horrific, it was strangely satisfying as well. "I'm almost as mad as them!" he said. Cole's finger tightened on the trigger and he pressed the barrel harder into the farmer's neck. The old man swayed on his knees and then tumbled onto his side, crying and raising his hands to ward off the bullet. He could have been anyone's father, probably had grandchildren, showed them around the farm, let them feed the chickens and play in the hay barn . . .

"I . . . I . . . ," he continued to say.

Cole knelt next to him and pressed the gun up under his chin. "I said, what are you going to do about it?"

The farmer began to shake his head. The pistol barrel snagged his jowls and they bulged with each shake.

"Better start talking," Cole said.

"Who . . . who are you?"

"Army."

"That man . . . that woman . . ."

"That's none of your business. Now listen, old man, this is way beyond your understanding. Got that? This is nothing to do with you, but you've seen me, and you've seen everything, and I have to tell you my finger's about two pounds of pressure away from spreading your brains across the ground. Like that idea? You want me to air your head?"

"No . . . no. . . ." He shook his head again, fat jowls catching on the gun barrel, and Cole's anger started to dissipate. Later, he thought that the old man's obesity had saved him. He had actually looked funny down there, kneeling on the ground and shaking his head, blubbery cheeks going one way, neck wobbling the other. If he had not made Cole smile, unintentional though it was, he may well have never milked his cows again.

"You love the queen?" Cole said. He almost smiled again, but then the thought of Natasha rooting in his mind came back to him, the sense of her intruding there, doing her own secret things down in the underground of his subconscious, and he thought maybe he'd never smile again. "You love your country, old man?"

The farmer nodded, eyes never leaving Cole's. *I wonder what he sees there*, Cole thought. *I wonder if he thinks I'm mad? He has no idea . . .*

"I need a car," Cole said. "That man you saw has taken something from Porton Down, and I have to recover it. And thanks to you, my Jeep's fucked."

"Dear God, am I infected, is that it?" the farmer asked. "Please, not me, not my children."

"You know of the place, then?"

The farmer nodded.

Cole leaned back and took the gun from beneath the farmer's jaws. Perhaps threat was no longer the way. "No, you're not infected," he said. "But that man had something in his car, something deadly, and he doesn't even know he's got it." And if he did, would it make any difference? If he knew what Natasha could be, would it change anything that had happened? Probably not. People like that were selfish. Never saw the big picture. Didn't understand the implications of what they were doing, and why. That was why Cole was here with his gun. His gun was one of the implications. If only he could get close enough to put a bullet into that shriveled monster's head.

"And they've sent you to catch him?"

"Something like that," Cole said. The idea had crossed his mind of telling the relevant authorities about what had happened, but it fled just as quickly. Not now. Not after last time. They had made it quite plain that they didn't give a shit for what they had done with the berserkers. It was down to Cole, and really it always had been.

"Are you a special agent?"

"What, like James Bond?"

The farmer smiled, but it dropped quickly at Cole's cool expression.

"I need a vehicle," Cole said. "As you so kindly wrecked mine, perhaps you'd be able to lend me one?"

The farmer nodded. "My farm's a mile away," he said. "I have a car, you can borrow it but will I get a receipt?"

Cole brandished the gun again casually, and the farmer nodded, his eyes wide and amazed.

"You'll get your car back," Cole lied.

The farmer stood and brushed himself down, and Cole urged him to walk on ahead. He was no threat— the shambling old man probably couldn't even raise his dick, let alone a fist—but Cole wanted him in front simply so that they did not have to talk.

He had some thinking to do. And while he was thinking he had to do something that made his skin crawl, his balls shrivel and his scalp tighten: he had to open his mind.

* * *

Cole taunted Natasha, and very soon she answered back.

Fucker . . . useless . . . think you can get me? Piece of shit . . . worm . . . fuck you, Mister Wolf . . .

The words flew in from a distance, vague and almost unheard. Cole could barely feel Natasha's slick, sick intrusion. They were more like echoes. She must have been a long way away.

"I'm not finished yet," he mumbled, shouting it with his mind, but he did not think she heard.

"What?" the farmer said.

"Not talking to you."

"You talking to HQ, eh?"

"Just keep walking." *Holy shit, he thinks he's in a fucking movie!*

It was dawn now, and the sun was smearing the eastern hills with a palette of oranges and pinks. Cole loved to watch the sunrise, welcoming in the new day and wondering how different it would be. Each day offered renewed possibilities and a refreshed chance at life, and even in his darkest moments a spectacular sunrise would not help but touch him.

I wonder if Nathan's been found yet, he wondered, and a flock of rooks passed across the sunrise. Cole closed his eyes briefly and imagined he were one of them. He envied the animals their simplicity of life. Their main purpose was to survive and procreate; his own purpose was borne out of revenge. A particularly human trait, revenge. It served no aim. It was like a fox coming after the hounds.

He had lost his own meaning in the world.

Cole opened his eyes and brought himself back to the here and now. Back to the unnatural.

His objective was now divided. On the one hand, he could not let Natasha reach the other berserkers. He had gathered evidence over the years that she was different somehow, altered, experimented upon by Porton Down and . . . improved. That was the one word the scientist had used before Cole shot her. *Improved.* He had no idea what they had done to her, but he did know one thing for sure; it would have only been to make her more deadly. And once reunited with the others, she could well become too powerful for him to take on his own.

On the other hand, finding the escapees had, until today, been his prime concern. What he would do then he had not even considered, because the prospects were too terrifying. Call in the army, perhaps. Give them the opportunity on a plate to clean up an old mess.

Or maybe after so long, he would go it alone.

The escapees had been silent for ten years. Cole scanned the news every day, always looking for signs that they had been active, but there was nothing obvious. Murder, death, missing people, all these happened, but not in any great numbers in any one place. Not in Britain, at least. If the monsters had gone aboard . . . well, he would know soon enough. If Natasha looked to be making for the ports or an airport, this would be a whole new game.

Either way, he had some fucking vampires to hunt and kill.

* * *

Even though they cut across fields it was more than a mile. It took almost half an hour for the farmer to lead Cole to his farm, and ten times in the last ten minutes of their walk Cole daydreamed about putting a bullet in the fat man's arse. Roberts and Natasha were getting farther and farther away, and every minute wasted meant that finding them again would be harder. Cole listened for Natasha, inviting her in, and her random words soon faded with distance into mumbles, and then whispers, and after that he was uncertain that he heard anything at all. His subconscious told him that she was still touching him, her words so quiet now that they were shadows rather than voice, and he was sure that she was still there. Raving. Gloating. And luring him on . . .

Luring him on, because that was the only way she would ever find the others.

"That's it!" Cole said as they entered the farmer's yard. A fat woman stood at the doorway to a rundown house, and a tall youth emerged from one of the sheds, both of them staring at the farmer and seeing the fear in his eyes.

"Yes, that's it," the farmer said, pointing to the BMW. "I'll get the keys. Er . . . you want me to get the keys?" He stood there in the cow shit and awaited Cole's permission to leave.

Cole smiled. "Yes, the keys," he said. He slipped the .45 into his jacket, hoping it had not been noticed but seeing in the fat woman's eyes that it had. He looked from her to the farmer to the tall youth standing beside the steel shed. The boy held a shovel in his hands as if it could swipe a bullet from the air. Too many John Woo movies.

"What's wrong, John?" the woman asked. Her voice was firm, the fear well hidden. Cole guessed that however surprised and scared she may be, she would stay in control. The boy, however, was already growing pale as realisation set in.

"I'm taking your car," Cole said to the woman. "It's a matter of national security." *Damn, maybe* he'd *seen too many movies!* Instead of smiling he turned to the boy and stared him down.

"You're not taking my car," the woman said.

"Janet, he's army!" the farmer said, waddling across the yard, hands held out to his wife. Cole realised he had an ally in this man, someone for whom the extraordinary was a break from the mundane day-to-day. Never mind the woman he had seen Cole shoot, never mind the fate of the man who had crashed his way out of the cottage driveway. This was an adventure.

"Has he shown you ID?"

"No. But he has a gun."

"Oh then he *must* work for the army!" The woman stared across the yard at Cole, glanced down at the pocket where he'd slipped the .45, then back up at his face. *What do you want?* her expression said, and Cole glanced across at the black BMW and shrugged. *That's all.*

"Is that a real gun?" the boy said.

"It's real alright!" the farmer said, turning from his wife to the boy. Easier reaction there. Not so much hostility. "I've just seen a gunfight!"

This guy's a gem, Cole thought. The farmer had already forgotten that the other party in the "gunfight" had not possessed a gun.

"Look, Janet," Cole said, stepping forward with his hands held out from his sides, "I really do need your car, and I really am going to have it. I didn't exaggerate in what I said, though I could have put it better. You'll get the car back, and you'll have a letter of thanks and some small reward for your troubles." The woman's expression hardly changed. *Hard bitch*, he thought. "You'll get a new tractor, too!"

"He shot the tractor?" the boy asked.

Cole sighed and shook his head. This was getting more ridiculous by the minute! And then the woman spoke, and ridiculous turned to crazy.

"I don't believe any of what you say. There's a loaded shotgun on the wall three feet from me. You show me ID right now or I go for it."

"Janet—"

"You don't want to do that, Janet," Cole said, drawing the .45 again. "What do you think this is, a movie?"

"No, I don't watch them. This is me protecting my property and my family."

"You go for it and I'll shoot the boy first."

Damn, he didn't have time for shit like this. Random thoughts began to fly at him, his own ideas coming together at high speed, reacting to the trauma of the last few hours. He was not used to being confused, and he was not used to someone getting the better of him. Roberts had been at the nasty end of Cole's pistol and yet he'd escaped, and now here Cole was wasting time arguing with a bumbling idiot farmer, his TV-addled son and the fucking Terminatrix!

He did not have time . . .

Natasha is drawing me on because while I'm still hot after them, Roberts will keep on going . . . I take this BMW and that fat bitch will be on the phone to the police in seconds . . . I could kill them. Slurry pit. Be ages before they were found. . . . And just what is it Natasha has? How is she "improved"?

The woman was glancing back and forth from him to the boy. Cole looked at him, back to her, then to the farmer. "Oh, for fuck's sake!" he said. He put the gun back in his pocket. "You—John—go and get me the car keys and I'll be on my way."

"Don't you move, John!" the woman said. She had edged back into the doorway and reached inside the room, and Cole expected her to bring out the shotgun at any moment. Then he'd have two choices—run or shoot her. That was somewhere he didn't want to get to—*ten seconds ago I was thinking about killing them and throwing them in the slurry pit, wasn't I? Wasn't I?*—but unless something changed very soon, that's just where he would be. Run or shoot.

"Shit." Cole looked around the farmyard, saw a herd of cows looking out from a barn with sad faces. Back to the woman. She was farther into the house now, and maybe her hand had already found the gun. The boy stared at his mother, wide-eyed. John, the fat farmer, turned·in circles, seemingly at a total loss.

And every second Natasha grew farther away.

Cole pulled the gun and shot one of the cows.

The herd panicked, perhaps more at the blast of the gun than because one of their number was thrashing on the floor of the shed, its skull ruptured and pumping blood into the shit-covered yard.

From the house Cole heard the clatter of the dropped shotgun. Janet disappeared inside.

"John, get me the car keys," Cole said, already running across the yard. He guessed he had a few seconds before the woman gathered her senses. The reality of the gunshot would have muddled her mind. The sight of the cow dropping and sprawling in its own bloody shit had been enough to send her running, and Cole knew from experience that people unused to violence took time to react to it. Even if she had gone for the phone, her hands would be shaking too much to use it.

He leaped straight up the steps into the kitchen, almost tripping over the dropped shotgun, carrying on through to the hallway where he found Janet fumbling with the phone. He snatched it from her hand, dropped it and shot the connection box from the wall. The gunshot deafened him, and he hardly heard her scream. She stared at him wide-eyed and petrified, and yet there was still a glint of defiance in her eyes, a look that said, *I'm scared shitless, yes, but give me a minute and you'll regret ever having found this place.*

151

Cole believed her, and he could not help but be impressed. *This is the sort of person I'm fighting to help*, he thought, and the realisation was yet more validation for what he was doing, and what he had already done. He heard the crack of Nathan's neck and the woman scientist pleading for her life a second before he shot her, and he saw justification for those actions in this woman's hearty defiance.

He showed her the gun, waved it once in front of her face and then left the house, picking up the shotgun on the way.

The farmer and his son were standing together by the BMW, staring intently at the doorway. As Cole emerged the farmer muttered something unintelligible, tears coming to his eyes.

"I shot the phone box from the wall," Cole said. "To be honest, I think it would take more than a silver bullet to kill your missus. Now, I'm going. I guess you have mobile phones, or another phone elsewhere in the house, but I'd really appreciate it if you held off using it to call the police. I won't waste time pleading with you, but I'll say this: I could have shot you all. I could . . . have shot . . . you all. That way I'd ensure that I get away, and it would give me a lot more time to catch the man I'm after. And the more chance I have of catching him the better it is. For everyone. Am I getting through? Comprendez?"

The farmer nodded, eyes still wide.

"I should be talking to your wife," Cole muttered. He nudged the farmer aside and pressed the remote locking button. The BMW opened up to him, he climbed in and started the engine. Smooth. Fast. But he'd have to dump it within the hour.

Shame.

"When will we get—"

"The cheque's in the mail," Cole said. Then he slammed the door and screeched away, spraying cow shit from beneath the wheels.

CHAPTER SEVEN

Those echoes of Natasha had been too remote, she had offered no clues, and Cole had no idea which direction to take. Logic dictated northwest, back toward Wales and Roberts' home. But something else nagged at Cole, and the more he thought about it the more elusive it became. He headed north, listening out for Natasha, willing her to come back to him with her taunting faux-child's voice, hating the idea of her in his mind but knowing that it was the only way to track her. The fact that he now believed she *wanted* him to follow changed nothing. She would slip up, or Roberts would make a mistake, and Cole would need only the slightest opportunity to put a bullet in the bitch's head.

He threw the farmers' shotgun into a field beside the road—it was too difficult to hide—and the .45 was back in the holster on his belt. The magazine had been reloaded. The near miss at the cottage had angered him, but he was doing his best to put that anger to good use.

He was trying not to think of the woman he had killed that morning. She had been in the way, that was all.

None of this was his fault.

"She didn't *feel* improved," he said. "She felt *dead*." Natasha and her chains had knocked him out on the moor, and even though he had not seen her in the darkness he had felt her, a damp, slick thing, filled with no signs of life at all. Cold. Wet. She had been below ground for ten years. Cole could still remember putting her there, the cries for mercy that turned into screams of rage as the soil was piled in on top of her. *I'll see you again*, she had said.

I'm a good man, he thought for the thousandth time, and he pictured the farming family he could so easily have left weighted down at the bottom of their slurry pit.

And then it came to him. Not dwelling on what was nagging him brought it home; her voice, when it was loud enough to hear, had come from the northeast. He was not certain how he knew this but the knowledge was welcome, and undoubted. When he had picked up her voice on the way to the farm something inside had clicked, a direction-finder that he was unaware he even had. Turning his head left and right now did nothing, but when he heard her again, he would be sure.

At the next junction he turned right and headed east, reading a map book as he drove, trying to find a road that lead northeast.

Who knew, he might even luck out. Find the right road, come across Roberts burying his wife in some field, kill him and open the boot and stare down at Natasha, gloating right back at her as he placed the .45 against her leathery skull and pulled the trigger.

Just how is she improved?

Yeah, right, it would be that easy.

"Yeah, right."

Fucker . . . , he heard a few minutes later. *Eat my shit, Mister Wolf . . . lost . . . going . . . fucker.*

Yeah, right.

Tom remembered a story his mother had told him when he was in his teens. It had affected him strongly then, and now it seemed to say a lot about the situation he was in, both literally and in a spiritual sense. He found some solace in it; there was precious little else to comfort him. And remembering the story brought him somehow closer to his mother. However old a man may be, he always wants his mum in times of crisis and stress.

She was a nurse for much of her life, and when she was in her twenties she had befriended an elderly patient in the hospital where she worked. He was in his nineties, a veteran of two World Wars, blinded at Dunkirk, and a compulsive gambler. Horses were his preference, and he chose them by name alone. He liked names, he said, because they told him much that his ruined eyes could not. Tom's mother would take him on trips from the hospital during her days off, sitting with him at the bookies' while he placed bets and stared at the ceiling, listening to the races broadcast live over the radio. If he lost he would smile and pat her hand, and if he won he would buy her lunch and tell her about his life. She was more than content to listen, she said, because he was a fascinating old man. Whether he talked about the trench hell of World War I or his time on a farm as a youngster, his stories were always rich and compulsive. Perhaps such storytelling talent had something to do with being blind.

One day, on the drive back to the hospital, she looked in her rearview mirror and saw him smiling up at the ceiling, a look on his face she had never seen before. "What a beautiful light!" he said, and he was still smiling as his head rested back against the seat.

She pulled over and felt the old man's wrist, but she already knew that he was dead. She drove to a police station and told them what had happened, and when she said she was a nurse they suggested she should drive him to the hospital herself. So there she was, in the middle of London, a corpse in the back of her car with betting slips spilling from his pockets and that beatific grin forever on his face. She received more than a few strange looks from pedestrians and other drivers, and by the time she arrived at the hospital she was laughing through her tears.

Tom knelt in the front seat of his ruined car and stared back at Jo's corpse. There was no grin on her face, other than the clown's smile painted there in dried blood. And no one could mistake her as sleeping. Not with the wound in the back of her head, and the amount of blood on her nightclothes.

"I hope you found the beautiful light," Tom said, reaching back to touch his dead wife's hand. "You *were* my light. I'm sorry, Jo. It's all my fault. I'm so sorry."

Natasha, perhaps using her child's honest sense of what is right and wrong, remained silent as Tom wept.

Later, Natasha said, *He's coming for us.*

"So what can I do about it? He's a killer, he's got a gun. I have my dead wife and a child's corpse in a ruined car. It's finished." Tom found no hope in that morning's dawn, and the potential only for pain.

Not for Steven. Daddy, all this was for Steven, wasn't it? How can it be finished when it's only just begun?

"I don't believe you," Tom said. He was sitting in the driver's seat, trying to work out what to do. He could think of nothing.

Natasha retreated to a deep corner of his mind and began to sob. *I'm only doing this for you,* she said.

He wondered how a dead girl could cry. "I don't believe that, either."

The girl was silent, still sobbing, and she withdrew and left him alone.

Tom gasped at the sensation of being abandoned and leaned back in his seat. *Was* she lying? Could Steven really still be alive? He felt in his bones that he could, and if there was even the slightest chance that his son was not dead, he owed it to himself—and to Jo—to try to find him. There was little else left for him now, nothing to go home to, no future . . .

No future. His hopes and dreams of a gentle old age

spent with his wife had been blasted away by that bastard's gun.

Grief birthed anger, and Tom realised that he had
been angry since that first encounter on the Plain. It
had kept him going, boosted adrenaline into his system
and given his aging muscles precious fuel to drive him
on. He had excavated a mass grave and crashed his way
from a frontyard under fire. That was not real, not him
at all, and yet he had mud under his fingernails and the
dead wife to prove it all.

And the thing in the boot. He had that, too.

"Natasha?" he said.

Daddy?

He ignored that. Let her have her own dreams for
now, whoever or whatever she was. "Natasha, how do
you know where Steven may be? You have to tell me
what you know if you want me to trust you. Look at it
with my eyes . . . I'm sitting here talking to fresh air,
and a corpse I just dug up is communicating with me in
my head. You have to understand my doubt. You have to
accept my uncertainty."

I already showed you something about me while you slept,
she said. *That was honest, wasn't it? It's bad to lie. Only
naughty children lie. I'm not naughty. I'm a berserker, and
my family were berserkers, and they kept us hungry so that
we would do those things for them.*

"Who?" But Tom already knew.

Them. The men. The soldiers.

"But why use you? Why not do it themselves?"

There's more to see, Daddy. I can show you if you like.

But not yet, and not here. Mister Wolf is coming, I can feel him, he's getting closer. We have to go. You have to take me away from here. I can show you the way, but you're the only one who can look after me.

"We have to go to the police," Tom said, staring into the hedge beside the car. "Jo is dead. She was murdered. We have to tell the police. Have to. They'll catch him, they'll protect—"

Me? Natasha said, and her voice had changed. Still a little girl's voice, but older and wiser now. Harder. *They'll protect me? One look and I'll be sent for tests, cut apart. And you, what will they do to you when they find me in your car? How will you explain me? And Mister Wolf is one of them anyway, they'll know him, they won't stop him, or maybe he'll kill them, too, and we have to go, because the Wolf is coming and I can't stop him and you won't stop him, not again. Nothing can stop him. He killed my family and he'll kill me in the end, if we don't go now.*

"You're confusing me."

I'm telling the truth, Daddy. I wouldn't lie to you. He's a bad man, and no one can stop him, not the police, not you, no one. Our only chance is to find the berserkers that got away before he does, and then they'll help us.

"Got away? Who got away? Your family were dead in that hole with you."

"There were others who escaped before I was buried."

Another mystery, Tom thought. "But why would they help us after so long?"

Because I'm one of them. The statement was so obvious that Tom could imagine no possible lie behind it.

She was one of them, and they would help her. And him? Her new daddy?

"You're confusing me, and—"

We have to go. He's coming!

"We can't just drive away, not with Jo like this, we have to take her—"

He's getting closer.

Tom shouted an incoherent scream of rage and hopelessness, and he felt Natasha in his head soothing and calming, touching those places that she somehow knew would work.

Shhh, shhh, I love you Daddy, shhh.

"Are you good?" he said, not sure how else to ask. He knew what he meant; he only hoped that Natasha understood as well.

We were good, she said. *All of us. Just different. My daddy . . . my first daddy . . . told me that they stole our innocence and forced us to do what we did. He said to never let it change me.*

"Do you want revenge?"

I just want my family back. She sobbed again, her voice coming from farther away as if she were trying to hide. *I just want to be with people like me. Will you be my daddy? Will you?*

Tom nodded once, and she seemed to hear that. He was glad, because it was not something he thought he could actually say. Not yet.

He had no choice but to abandon the car. It was smashed up and shot to pieces, and to drive it any farther would be to risk being stopped. It was almost eight A.M., and there would be people on the road by now. Tom was surprised that no one had yet passed them on this narrow lane. And besides, it had Jo's blood on the seats. He could smell it, and he could smell her, the subtle lavender perfume she favoured growing stale as her body cooled beneath it.

Somehow, for now, he was keeping at bay the madness that her death must bring.

For the first time since leaving the Plain he opened the boot. It squealed, twisted metal protesting at being forced, and as the lid popped up he knew that it would never close again.

Natasha lay against the back of the rear seats, the heavy chains still wrapped around her body. She looked no different from before. Her smell was one of dampness and age, muck and must, and Tom stepped back a pace or two while fresh air swilled the boot.

I'm cold, she said. *I'm hungry. Will you hold me?*

Tom did not want to move any closer, but the vulnerability in that child's voice pricked at his heart. He could remember Steven when he was a little boy, standing at their bedroom door and saying there was a goat in his bedroom. Each time Tom would take him back and show him that there was no goat, and each time Steven would end up in their bed, snuggled between them in their warmth, already back to sleep by the time Tom and Jo settled down again. It was his voice, and their love for him, and secretly they had both quite liked having their young son in with them. He would twist a little finger into their ears to wake them at six in the morning, but he had a giggle that would banish the early hour and welcome in the sunrise.

Tom moved closer and stared down at the body. It was the first time he had seen her in daylight. "Is that really you?" he said.

It's me, Natasha said. *Look what he did to me. Look what Mister Wolf turned me into.*

She looked like a child carved out of wood, wrapped in old cloth, constrained in chains, buried and left to rot. Veins and ligaments stood out in stark relief against her stretched skin. He could see old yellowed bones. The chains were rusted the colour of dried blood. And there was movement, tiny earthy insects crawling here and there where clumps of soil were stuck to her body or the chains, while others burrowed in hollows that gradual decay had formed in her corpse. A golden centipede made its way across the boot's carpet, afraid of the light.

Tom reached in, grabbed the chains and dragged Natasha to him. He gathered her up, grunting, amazed that he had carried her so far last night, and lifted her against his chest. He looked down into her face, terrified that she would smile. He would drop her and run, because nothing like this could be alive, not alive and moving like when he had first taken her from that pit . . .

I'm hungry Daddy, she said. *I haven't eaten for so long. And being out, being free . . . I'm hungry.*

"You're confusing me." Brief images from his dream flashed by and he staggered beneath Natasha's weight.

Gnashing jaws, severed limbs, Natasha's real father holding the woman against the wall as he tore out her innards, her little brother Peter, shrugging off the bullet wounds and thrashing around on that body on the floor, and her words came to him again: *They kept us hungry.*

Oh no, Daddy! she said, *Never that, never, ever that for you. You saved me!*

"I saved you," he said, and he pulled her close to his chest.

Perhaps the bullet still in her body moved. Natasha screamed, and for a second she seemed to fill his mind with the effort, being as wholly *there* as Tom himself. And then she calmed with a groan and a sigh, and something scratched his chest, and Tom sat down in the grass like a mother nursing a newborn child.

Tom drifted. The presence of Natasha in his mind was stronger than it had ever been before, so large and powerful and potent that it seemed to drive him into a fugue, a state of conscious dreaming that quickly took on a feel and taste he had known only recently. *The house*, Tom thought, *the room, the basement . . .*

The countryside vanished, and Natasha was feeding him memories as he fed her his blood.

This time they told him so much more.

She stormed into the basement, brushing aside the remains of the man her mother had just killed. He slapped against the open door and slid down its metal surface, a stain of blood and flesh that drove Natasha into greater frenzy. His torn face quizzed her intentions and she snapped at it as she ran by.

Inside, her family was already at work.

The basement was huge, much larger than the footprint of the house above, and partitioned with several large glass screens. There were more than just a few survivors down here; there must have been thirty men and women, spread throughout the several glass-walled rooms, and as Natasha and her family stormed in, every one of them seemed to have a gun in their hand.

Her father was a few paces away, his arms and legs flailing as two men and a woman pinned him against a wall. His head thrashed from side to side, blood flew, a man fell away, the flash of gunshots strobed the air, and then her father knelt and leaped, kicking out and digging his toe into the woman's eye as he went. The remaining man followed him with gunfire, and even though several bullets thudded home he kept on running and leaping. Every time he landed it was on a different person, and each time he leaped again he left a mess of rent flesh and broken bones behind. Blood trailed from his bare feet, and torn flesh and clothing were caught on his long talons. Bullets traced the air after him, and his wild screeches matched the sound of shattering glass.

Natasha ran into the melee, slashing out with her hands. She knocked a gun from one woman's hand, and as the woman knelt to retrieve it Natasha grabbed the back of her neck, long nails piercing skin and sinking in, fist squeezing tighter and tighter.

A man ran into her, lashing out with a knife and burying it to the hilt in her shoulder. Natasha screamed, saliva and blood spattering the man's face and neck. He let go of the knife and backed away grinning, then suddenly stopped grinning. Natasha followed, dragging the woman behind her, fingertips almost meeting inside the woman's neck. The woman squealed and thrashed, reaching back and batting ineffectually at Natasha's arm and hand. The man glanced down at the woman, then back at Natasha.

Have her! Natasha shouted, but it came out as an animal roar, nothing intelligible in that violent outburst. And there that brief period of coherence ended. Natasha screeched, power thudding through her child's body and firing every nerve end, rage pumping her blood and spasming in her muscles, pain singing from every bone that sought to distort and be something it could not. Her jaws opened wider, her arms grew longer, fingers were pincers, nails were claws, and her teeth throbbed in her gums at the thought of fresh flesh ready to part beneath them. She took a bite out of the woman's face and then threw her at the man. As he caught the body and stumbled back, Natasha's little brother fell on him from above and ripped out his throat.

There were still some people left alive, a core of defenders that had retreated to a far corner of the basement thinking that their guns would protect them there. Natasha and her family ducked down behind tables and furniture, slinking through the rooms, smash-

YES! ☐

Sign me up for the Leisure Horror Book Club and send my TWO FREE BOOKS! If I choose to stay in the club, I will pay only $8.50* each month, a savings of $5.48!

YES! ☐

Sign me up for the Leisure Thriller Book Club and send my TWO FREE BOOKS! If I choose to stay in the club, I will pay only $8.50* each month, a savings of $5.48!

NAME: _____

ADDRESS: _____

_____

TELEPHONE: _____

E-MAIL: _____

☐ **I WANT TO PAY BY CREDIT CARD.**

☐ VISA   ☐ MasterCard   ☐ DISCOVER

ACCOUNT #: _____

EXPIRATION DATE: _____

SIGNATURE: _____

Send this card along with $2.00 shipping & handling for each club you wish to join, to:

Horror/Thriller Book Clubs
20 Academy Street
Norwalk, CT 06850-4032

Or fax (must include credit card information!) to: 610.995.9274.
You can also sign up online at www.dorchesterpub.com.

*Plus $2.00 for shipping. Offer open to residents of the U.S. and Canada only.
Canadian residents please call 1.800.481.9191 for pricing information.
If under 18, a parent or guardian must sign. Terms, prices and conditions subject to change. Subscription subject
to acceptance. Dorchester Publishing reserves the right to reject any order or cancel any subscription.

JOIN NOW!

ing through glass partitions where they had not already been destroyed by gunfire. Where they found someone living—a man hiding in a cupboard, stinking of piss and fear; a woman taking huge snorts of white powder from a shattered glass vial—they slaughtered them, relishing the splitting of their bodies, spreading insides across the tiled floor. Where they found a dead body they slashed at it on their way past, or perhaps paused to swallow a ruptured eyeball or take a mouthful of exposed breast. It took only a minute to come together, Natasha and her brother, their father and mother, all of them coated in blood, their own, and others', mad, raging, berserk. Her brother spat gobbets of meat from his mouth and slashed at metal furniture, his nails squealing across its surface. He was still young, still learning to direct this rage.

They did not speak, because in this state such communication was all but impossible. Tom, part of Natasha through her memory and yet still an independent observer, realised that everything for the berserkers was instinct. Like a pride of lions on the hunt, or a flock of birds weaving back and forth across the sky, they knew what to do and when. Natasha's father growled and broke left, her mother moved to the right, and Natasha and her little brother waited for a few seconds, preparing to leap over the bank of metal cabinets they hunkered behind.

The humans gathered in the corner of the room were shouting and screaming and crying, letting off bursts of gunfire at shadows thrown by flickering lights.

Natasha could smell their fear, and it was good. She could also sense the meat of them, their pumping hearts, their pulsing blood, the flesh of their thighs and the tender taste of their throats. She glanced sideways at her brother and tried to smile, but her tooth-filled mouth would not allow her. He tried to smile back.

Their parents roared at exactly the same moment, launching their attack, diving into the humans unfortunate enough to be on the outside of the group. Guns exploded, bullets whined and whistled around the basement, thudding into walls and ricocheting from furniture.

Natasha and her brother leaped onto the metal cabinets and looked down at the violence below.

There were maybe ten people left alive. Their father was to the left, standing on his hind legs disembowelling a man while a woman fired at him again and again. His body danced and jigged, feet kicking him from the wall, jumping from the floor, dodging bullets as his face and hands remained working on the man. He turned suddenly on the shooter, snatched her gun and buried it barrel-first into her face. One of his claws caught the trigger and the back of the woman's head erupted into the air.

To the right their mother was a blur of thrashing limbs and snapping teeth. A man fell before her, screaming as she pulled herself up his body and opened it every inch of the way.

Someone shouted, someone else pointed, and bullets screamed at Natasha. The memory blurred as she danced left and right, jumped and powered down from the ceiling, bounced from the floor. The whistle of bullets passed close by, and their paths sometimes left hot streaks across her skin. And sometimes, they struck her. Peter whined behind her as a bullet found home. He fell to the floor beside her, growled, and they leapt together. Both of them found meat.

The lights went out as one last desperate burst of gunfire found a switching panel. The stench of an electrical fire added to the odour of opened bodies. But the humans were all dead or dying and already the rage was subsiding. For the berserkers, there were wounds to heal and expended energy to replace.

Natasha and her family settled down to feed.

Do you see? Natasha asked. *Do you see now what they made us do?* Her voice was weak and tired, barely there at all. Tom could feel her inside his head but there was not the sense of invasion there had been before. He almost had to search to hear her voice.

"I saw," he said. "But I don't understand."

I'm tired, she said. *So tired. I haven't fed for so long, Daddy. I need to go away for a while.*

"Wait!" Tom said, "we have to decide where to go, what to do."

Yes, we have to leave, she said, *to leave, he's coming, Mister Wolf is coming . . . but I'm really only a little girl.* She faded away at last. Tom could not be certain what he heard in those final few words: vulnerability, or hopelessness.

He sat there in the morning sun, the unearthed girl in his lap, cows staring over the gate at him with disinterest. A sparrow hawk hovered high overhead, stalking something a couple of fields away. Bees buzzed the hedge, and a tiny wren darted in and out of the undergrowth, picking insects from leaves, wagging its tail to gain balance each time it landed. Tom wished that he could find his balance so easily.

He loved the countryside, and right now it was shielding what had happened from the eyes of the world. His battered car, his dead wife . . . he could see her feet and lower legs through the open back door. *Jo,* he thought, but suddenly the idea of that body being his wife was alien and distant. She was somewhere else now.

Tom stood, carried Natasha and her chains to the car and set her down on the bonnet. It was only as he let go that he realised how easily he had moved. He paused, standing still, trying his best to discern exactly what had changed. Eyes closed, he heard so much more. Hands over his ears, he saw more. His head no longer hurt, and the aches and pains in his limbs had faded. He thought back to the memories Natasha had shared with him . . . but it was more than sharing. He had seen what had happened in that house. She had not told him about it, nor explained it, she had *shown* him. In the same way that she came into his mind to talk to him, so she had invited him into her mind to know more of her.

And what did I find? he thought. *That she's a monster? Some sort of wild animal, immune to bullets and knives, im-*

possible to kill, a killer herself? But he shook his head and looked down at the strange body on the car bonnet. She was more than an animal, and more than simply a killer. She was more than human, not less. She was, as she had told him, a berserker.

Do you see what they made us do? She had whispered before slipping away into a deep sleep. *They kept us hungry.*

Tom had to leave. He felt refreshed and strong and ready to move on, and though the grief over Jo sat heavy on his shoulders, there was still a numbness that held back the tears. He looked through the shattered windshield at his dead wife on the backseat, and it was not her. *That is not Jo!* There lay the body he had touched and loved for over thirty years, and yet she was not there. *She's dead,* he thought, *dead and gone forever and I'll never see her again, never smell her or taste her or talk with her again for all eternity.* But though the rage and grief were there, something kept their full effect at bay, a numbness that promised worse to come.

Perhaps it was the unreality of what was happening. The impossibility. Natasha had thrown him into a dream world, a place where dead girls spoke in his mind and a man with guns came after him. A place where an unearthed corpse wanted him to be her daddy. Maybe it was that; the unreal, surreal place his world had become.

Or perhaps he really had gone mad.

"We have to go," he said, and out of that unreal daze a panic began to descend. He was parked just off a country lane with the body of his wife in the car and a ten-year-old corpse wrapped in chains on the bonnet. He could not afford to drive the car any farther. Natasha and her chains were too heavy to carry very far. His wallet contained about fifty pounds in notes. Looking around he could see no signs of habitation nearby; no farms, no isolated houses that may offer him transport or a place to hide. He scratched absently at his chest and his fingers came away smeared red. He had been cut there, perhaps by flying glass when Mister Wolf blasted at his car with his gun. Tom rubbed the blood across his fingers until it dried, sticky and crisp, and he wondered why he felt so strong.

Desperation, he thought. *Fear. Panic. All simmering just below the surface of whatever's keeping me going.* "Crash and burn," he said, and that was what he would end up doing. But while he still had energy to stand and the will to move on, he was more than willing to let instinct and events take over. Just like Natasha and her family in the basement of that house, dodging or shrugging off bullets, raging at the wounds, letting instinct lead them on.

In the distance, Tom heard the roar of a car's engine. It sounded like the growl of a wolf approaching its prey.

CHAPTER EIGHT

Cole listened out for Natasha. He had been driving for half an hour, and although he had not heard her again, still he was sure that he was going in the right direction. It *felt* right. And for now he had nothing else to hang onto but that.

He tore through the country lanes, barely shifting down a gear to negotiate blind bends or humpback bridges. He had already had one collision today; he hoped that was his share of accidents for a while. And besides, the faster he went, the more chance he had of catching the old man and the girl. *She lured me on*, he kept thinking, *she wants me to follow*.

People were traveling to work now, and here and there he passed other cars going in the opposite direction. Their drivers greeted him with a uniform expression; shock and disgust. *Slow down!* they all said with their glares, and he grinned back and pushed down on the gas as he passed them by. He was doing all this for them, these sheep, these innocents who thought that nine to five, Coronation Street and a meal out on Saturday was all there was to life. None of them had a clue about what was really happening in their world. None of them knew the risks he took, the life he had given up to pursue the berserkers and try to keep the innocents safe from harm. And if he took time to stop and tell them they would call him mad.

Let them. It had been years since he had let his own peculiar madness be an upset.

And then there they were, the old guy standing beside the parked car, staring straight at Cole with eyes as wide as a rabbit's in a headlamp's glare.

"Holy shit!" Cole stepped on the brakes and swerved the car across the road, sliding it sideways to prevent careening into the hedge. *I can't be this lucky!* he thought, but there was Roberts, moving back and forth with indecision, the fear of an innocent who had seen terrible things etched on his face.

Cole was out of the BMW and running at Roberts almost before the wheels had stopped spinning. He paused a few steps away and aimed the .45 at his face.

"She's not here!" Roberts said.

"What?"

"I hid her. I know you want her, she told me, so I hid her where you'd never find her."

Cole paused, trying to work out whether or not Roberts was telling the truth, or if it even mattered. Roberts had seen Natasha and knew what she could do, so he needed to be removed from the picture. "Where?" he asked.

"If I tell you, you'll kill me."

"I'm going to kill you anyway."

Roberts moved back one pace and leaned against his wrecked car, glancing down into the backseat. Cole followed his gaze and saw the dead woman's legs through the open door. "You think I care?" the old guy said. "You killed my wife, you bastard." There was little emotion in his voice, no real trace of anger or rage or anything else that could be dangerous. Numb.

"I'm sorry," Cole said, keeping his voice equally neutral.

"So kill me," Roberts said.

"Where's the girl?"

"I told you, I hid her."

Where? Cole thought. *Just where? He could have stopped anywhere between the cottage and here, hid her in a barn or shed, beneath a hedge, out in a field, anywhere . . . but wherever she was, she would be found again.* He could kill Roberts now, but his job would be far from over.

"Tell me where."

"No. You've hurt her once before, I won't let you—"

"*Hurt* her! Do you even know what she is, you stupid fuck?"

"A little girl you buried alive."

Cole shook his head, snorted. "Look, I don't have time for this. Tell me where she is and you'll join your wife quickly, no pain, you won't even hear it coming. Don't tell me, and I'll shoot you again and again until you do. Believe me, I could use a whole magazine and you'd still be conscious."

"You won't do that," Roberts said.

Cole braced himself, lowered his aim until the sight rested on Roberts's left collarbone, then swore because he was right. Cole could kill him with few qualms, but torture was not his thing.

"Okay, I won't do that, but let me appeal to you. Please. You have no idea what she is, or what she can do, and you have to tell me where she is."

"So that you can kill her?"

"Yes, exactly! I should have killed her ten years ago instead of doing what I did. That was stupid of me. I should have known she would have risen again at some point."

"I don't know what the hell you're on about, but I won't let you hurt her again. She's an innocent."

"Innocent! What has she been telling you?" Cole said, genuinely amazed. "Has she told you what a wonderful little girl she was, how sweet her family were? Has she really?"

"She told me that she and her family were turned into killers." Roberts seemed to be gaining confidence, and that pissed off Cole because *he* was the one with the fucking gun!

"They've *always* been killers," he said. "They're berserkers. They're not human, not like you and me. They're a different breed, a whole race apart. Yes, we— the army—used them, but they went willingly enough, let me tell you. They used to spend their long lives hiding from us because of the persecution their kind suffered centuries ago. They'd slink through shadows and take someone here, there, now and then. They *eat* us! They *eat* people! But we caught them and gave them the chance to do it for real, to revel in what they are. Because they're very, very hard to kill, and they never make a mistake."

Roberts looked at him for a while, a cool appraisal that left Cole unnerved and wondering whether he had underestimated this man. "And after that, you think I'll change my mind?" he said.

"I can't believe your mind's made up the other way anyway," Cole said. "Look at all that's happened since you found Natasha." He glanced down at the feet protruding from the rear door of the car, but Roberts' gaze did not waver.

"You killed her," he said. "Not Natasha. You. With that." He nodded at the gun.

Even as Cole glanced at the gun in his hand, he knew his mistake. *Sly bastard!* he had enough time to think, and then Roberts was upon him, punching and swearing and kicking, and there was *no way* he could have moved that quickly. One second he was safely under the sight of Cole's .45, the next Cole was stumbling backward under a frenzied assault, tripping over his own heel and landing heavily in the road, and Roberts fell on him and plucked the gun from his hand, turning it around, pressing it into Cole's right eye so hard that he thought his eyeball would pop. *Oh no this is it this is it.*

"Feel nice?" Roberts said. "Feel good?" But even then Cole could see the confusion in the man's eyes.

"Please . . . ," Cole said.

Roberts nodded. "I'm sure that's what she said, too."

He pulled the trigger.

Click.

Nothing. He was holding the gun as though it were dirty, resting it in his hand rather than grasping it tight.

Click.

Again, nothing.

Holy shit, what am I doing?

The man on the ground looked up at Tom, his left eye wide, breath held, his expression one of terror and outrage. Tom stared down at him—*what in the name of fuck am I doing?*—and almost smiled, the situation was so unreal.

Mister Wolf started to twist and writhe, and Cole knew it would only be seconds before he was toppled off, and then Mister Wolf would wrestle the gun back and reverse the situation, and he knew how to use the gun, the safeties, whatever had gone wrong with Tom's attempt to shoot someone in the face.

I almost shot him in the eye!

Tom leaned back, twisted around and swung, bringing the gun in low and hard against the side of the man's head. In the movies Mister Wolf would have been out cold with barely a mark on him, but in reality the skin of his temple split and he cried out, swearing and wriggling harder beneath Tom's weight, swinging his fists, then changing his tactic and grasping at Tom's clothing in an attempt to pull him off. Tom hit him again, this time putting all his strength into the swing. It made a sickening *thunk* as it hit the man's skull, and this time he did not shout as loud. His hands fell from Tom's sides, his head rolled back and forth, and beneath his flickering eyelids Tom could see his eyes turning back in his head.

Oh God, I may have killed him anyway! The gun's barrel was matted with a bloody clot of hair. Mister Wolf's temple was a mess. He twitched, and his right heel scraped at the road once, twice.

Tom stood and backed away. He held the gun in both hands, aimed at the prone man even though he was still unsure why it had not fired before. He took a good hold of the stock this time, and as he squeezed he felt the grip slide in tight. Safety.

Now, if he so wished, he could kill.

Tom sobbed out loud. Tears came, and as much as he tried he could not hold them back. He had no idea what had happened just then. He fell to his knees in the road, gun barrel resting on the tarmac.

I moved so fast. One second here, staring into the barrel of a gun. Next second there, pressing it into his eye and pulling the trigger twice, ready to see his head explode and his brains spew out all over the road. And in my mind at the time, feeding the rage . . . Jo? No, not Jo. Not my dead wife. Someone else . . .

Natasha.

Something had taken him when Mister Wolf

pointed the gun at him, some unknown madness that had given him speed and strength. That had not been Tom, not at all. The anger had been his, but not the willingness—the *eagerness*—to kill. Tom thought he could never do that, no matter what. Not even to the man that had killed his wife.

He had moved so quickly. And with that came a recollection of the dream-memory Natasha had shared with him; the speed with which she and her family had moved through that huge basement, and the power of their bodies as they dodged bullets and shrugged off knife wounds in their state of crazed hunger.

Tom stood slowly, looked around, shook his head to bring himself back. Right now he had the upper hand, and he could not afford to lose his position of advantage by cracking up. Later, perhaps. But not now.

"Natasha?"

There was no answer from the mummified girl. Still asleep after her feed. And Tom rubbed the wound on his chest again, still putting it down to flying glass when he had really always known the truth from the second her teeth touched his skin.

The BMW was still running, parked across the road so that no other vehicle could pass by. It would only be a matter of time before someone else came along. If Tom could make the most of the next few minutes— think logically, not crack up, not let what was happening get to him and drive him over the edge—then he and Natasha would be away from Mister Wolf for good. There was a car just waiting for him, though it was likely stolen. He would not be able to keep it for long, but perhaps after the next hour or two, if he drove carefully and quickly, he would be far enough away to find safety.

At least, for now. Tom was under no illusion that there would be a reckoning, a time when he would have to go to the police and tell them everything that had happened. Between now and then, however, he had to do whatever he could to move on.

He jumped the gate and went behind the hedge to where he had left Natasha. A snail had crawled onto her face in the few minutes she had been in the grass, and Tom flicked it off and stepped on it in disgust. The subtle crunch of its shell beneath his shoe felt good. He picked her up, chains and all, and was she slightly heavier than before? He could not really tell; the fight and its emotional recoil had drained him.

"Natasha?" he said again, but if she heard him she chose to remain silent. He stood there for a few moments, looking down into what was left of her face, trying to discern any form of expression there. But her living death was expressionless; everything she felt or thought was shown only on the inside.

He placed the girl on the backseat of the BMW and covered her with Mister Wolf's jacket. Back at his ruined car he carefully bent Jo's knees, hating the cool feel of her skin and the way her legs already seemed to be growing stiff.

"Jo," he said, feeling everything, able to say nothing. "Jo." He closed the door.

He ran back to the BMW and opened the boot. It was filthy inside, strewn with old sacks and dried grass and leaves, but he found what he was hoping for in one corner: a toolbox. He undid the straps holding it in and emptied it in the boot. Then he shook his head, cursed himself and hurried over to the prone man.

Got to get everything right! he thought. *Got to get the order of things right. There's always order in things—the right order, and the wrong—and if I get this wrong now then I'll be caught, and there's no way my story will be believed. I've got a bloodied gun, my dead wife, a child's corpse and this pistol-whipped killer lying in a country lane. What story could the police concoct from this? And what about the army, or whoever it was this bastard worked for? Got to get this right. Jo, in the car. Mister Wolf beside the car. Then Natasha's chains. Then Mister Wolf again.*

Then the gun.

Dragging the man across the road was harder than he had expected. Whatever strength had come to him had drizzled away again, and he grunted and huffed as he pulled Mister Wolf by the legs. The man mumbled something as they approached the ruined car, and Tom stood over him again with the gun pointing at his face. But the mumbling stopped, the breathing became harsh and uneven, and Tom lifted him into a sitting position against the car.

That done, he returned to the BMW and started rooting through the spilled tools. All the time he kept an ear open for any approaching vehicles, wondering just what he could do if someone came along now.

There was surely some believable story he could come up with given time, but right now he was not in the mood for creating stories. Right now, he simply wanted to leave.

He found a pair of bolt croppers. They were old and rusty, but still the blades had been kept sharp and oiled, and the action was smooth. He leaned into the car, uncovered Natasha and got to work on the chains. He wanted to cut them as little as possible, because he had need of them. It took four broken links before he was able to unwrap the chains totally from Natasha, taking care not to pull off parts of her body as he extracted a few sections that were buried deep with her rotten clothing. Finally the last length came away. "You're free," he said, and from somewhere far away he heard a sigh.

Mister Wolf was still leaning against the ruined car, unconscious,. His chin rested on his chest, dribble darkened his shirt, and blood dripped from the wound at his temple. Tom thought he saw him breathing, but he did not want to move close enough to see for sure.

It was time to find out whether his plan would really work.

The chain was long enough to wrap twice around the man's head and the steering column of Tom's wrecked car. Tom joined the chain at the base of Mister Wolf's neck with two of the broken links, using the bolt croppers to squeeze the snipped ends together. He supposed that the man would be able to work the chain around and perhaps prise the snapped links apart, but he would not be able to see what he was doing, and it would take a long time.

Someone would have found him by then.

Lastly, the gun. Tom cleaned it as well as he could with his shirt, found the button that ejected the magazine, then placed the unloaded weapon on the ground beside Mister Wolf. He pocketed the magazine, then stood back to survey his work, frowning. He knelt again, grabbed the gun, lifted the man's hand and curled his finger into the trigger guard, pressing it onto the trigger.

Shit, he had no idea what he was doing! In the movies this would work, but this was not a bloody movie. He was not quite sure whether it was real life, either, but whatever it was he had to get going. Whatever he had done here would be found soon enough, and while Mister Wolf answered questions with the police, he and Natasha would be gone.

"Gone for Steven," Tom said, standing, glancing into the car at his dead wife, remembering the birth of their son. Jo had been screaming, and Tom had been crying so much that he could barely see. "Gone for Steven, Jo." Damn. She had died without even knowing there might still be a chance.

Something touched his crotch.

"Move and you lose them."

Tom looked down. Mister Wolf had raised his head, lifted the gun, and now he was pressing it into Tom's scrotum.

"No bullets," Tom said, revealing the tip of the magazine in his pocket. But something prevented him from moving; he had never touched a gun before, and he had no idea how they really worked.

"Always keep one in the hole," Mister Wolf said.

Tom bit his lip. Learning all the time.

"I'm going to shoot you now."

"What's your name?" Tom asked.

"Huh?"

"Your name? What's your name?" Tom looked down. The man was frowning, right eye swollen half-shut and thick with blood, face pale, and his head was swaying from side to side as if it hurt to hold it up.

"Cole."

"I'm Tom."

"You're dead."

"I'm *Tom!*" He had no idea what he was doing. Stalling for time? Trying to start a conversation with this killer pressing a gun into his balls?

"Huh?" Cole looked woozy, and his head dipped down to his chest, then up again. The gun never moved a millimetre. "Shut the fuck up, Tom," he said. His voice sounded stronger. His left eye focused on Tom's face and stayed focused. "Where is she?"

"I told you, I hid her back—"

"I'm tied up with her chains, shithead."

Damn! Tom pursed his lips and looked along the road. *Please come now, please come now, someone, anyone, please please I don't want to die like this, with my balls blown off for the birds to come and take away. . . .*

And then Natasha woke up.

185

Tom squeezed his eyes shut as he felt her worm inside his mind, her presence fresh and seemingly renewed. She rooted around, finding things. She felt vibrant and . . . alive!

Only one bullet to dodge, Daddy? she said. *Well then, he's in pain, dizzy, and I'll be able to give you one chance.*

"What . . . ?" Tom said, but Cole suddenly cried out in pain and pushed the gun harder into Tom's balls. *Here it comes,* he thought.

Cole squeezed the trigger. For the first time in his life he was actually looking forward to killing someone. His head hurt like hell, his temple felt weak and mushy, and the headache meant he could barely even open his one good eye. The piece of shit deserved to die.

He squeezed harder.

"What?" Tom said.

Natasha came. She erupted from Cole's subconscious, throwing open the doorways of his deeper mind, gushing up into the foggy streets of his awareness, shouting and screaming and raging like the insane berserker she was. There was no sense or meaning to her outburst, though he read the hatred it contained. He could not make out any single words, but her mockery and derision was obvious in the scream, driving into and filling his waking mind with such loathing that he could only shrink back under its assault. She gave him the violence she had always possessed. He tried to curl into a ball. He dropped the gun and grabbed his head in both hands, ignoring the pain from his temple, feeling the sticky blood there and wishing the wound would vent Natasha from his mind.

"Get out," he whispered, because he had little strength for anything more.

Get out get out get out! she screeched, whining like a little girl who knew far too much.

"Leave me," he said.

Leave me leave me . . . Mister Wolf, fuck you, you can suck my ass, fuck you Mister Wolf, you'll lose, you've already lost!

"No," Cole said. And with a monumental effort, fighting through the agonies of his body and the torture in his mind, he opened his eyes, saw the gun lying next to him and reached for it.

A wavering, fuzzy shape grew smaller in his vision as Roberts fled.

Cole screamed, aimed the gun and fired.

Cole fell away from Tom, dropped the gun and curled into a ball.

Daddy, it's time to run, Natasha said, her voice calm and considered. *One chance, Daddy. He's got one round, and you've got one chance.*

Tom panicked, dropped the bolt croppers, stepped over the groaning man and headed for the BMW. His balls ached, he felt sick, the painful glow radiating up from his stomach almost bending him double.

Quickly! Natasha said.

"I'm moving."

"Leave me," Cole said from behind him, and Tom

glanced over his shoulder, wondering what she was doing to this killer's mind. Something horrible, if his expression was anything to go by. Something that gave him pain. Tom was glad.

"No," Cole said. He raised himself on one elbow and grabbed the gun.

Run, Daddy, dodge, fall, he's going to—

The shot blasted out, startling Natasha deeper into Tom's mind, and he sensed her own profound shock as something punched him in the back and sent him sprawling across the tarmac.

Shot, he thought, *I've been shot.* There was no pain, no real sensation other than being winded, and he hoped that this was as it had been for Jo, this shocked numbness before death.

Death . . .

"I'm dying," he said.

Daddy! Natasha gasped, and he could hear her tears. *Wait . . . it's not that bad. Stand up. Stand up now!* Her voice changed on those last three words, losing their childish lilt and taking on something of age, experience, something that spoke of power and adaptability. And fury. She was enraged.

Tom groaned, pushed himself up onto his hands and knees, stood. From the BMW he heard the squeak of leather as something moved inside.

Natasha screamed in his mind, a long, loud, incoherent exhalation of pure rage. Cole had heard this before, years ago when the berserkers were at their fiercest, mad and hungry and craving the feel of living flesh between their teeth. Then they had been contained at Porton Down, and their psychic abilities had never been so strong. Now, Natasha had changed.

He tried to crawl away but the chains held him tight. Neither could he escape his own mind.

Cole screamed, but he could not hear himself.

He scrambled around on the ground and found the bolt croppers Tom had dropped. Instinct grabbed him and he snipped and cut, hardly aware of what he was doing, pulling hard at the chains until they parted and he fell to the ground. He crawled then, across the road and into a ditch. The terrible effects of Natasha's scream lingered.

It seemed like hours before the roar started to fade. But by then Cole was lost to the world, unconscious, prowling the dark places of his mind for somewhere to hide from this monster that pretended to be a little girl.

When darkness found him and took him away, he was glad.

Tom pulled himself upright against the car, still waiting for the pain to kick in. At least he could stand.

Come here, Natasha said.

He looked into the rear seat and saw the bundle that was Natasha. It seemed to have moved. Her arms had separated slightly from her body, and the face had turned toward him. There was still no expression there—no sign of anything other than the death mask he had seen before—but her attitude had changed.

Whereas before she was a mummified corpse, now she was something that seemed to crave its erstwhile animation. He stared at her face, tried to remember just how he had placed the body on the seat, and then the signs of movement were obvious.

Here, she said again, a young girl's voice, yet the command impossible to ignore.

Tom leaned into the car, and that was when the pain came. He groaned, froze, hoping that lack of movement would quell the fire that was growing in his lower back. But it did not. Stoked by his spasming muscles the agony roared louder, and Tom thought, *I won't remember this pain, it's nothing, it's a signal, the damage is done and there's nothing worse going on now, it's a signal that's all, a signal, and oh fuck it hurts!*

Quickly! Natasha said, and though his eyes were closed Tom sensed slight movement again. *Lie down beside me.*

Tom slumped across the car's backseat. He felt Natasha's corpse against his chest and tried to pull back, but he had no strength, and he lay there with Natasha pressed between himself and the seat.

Closer, Natasha whispered. *Closer, Daddy.* Even through the pain he heard a quiver to her voice.

His eyes squeezed shut—not so much because of the pain now, but because he no longer wanted to see what was happening, what was moving, why he could hear the squeak of leather—and he felt a stab of pain in his chest. And then there was slight movement there, as if he were being tickled by a feather, and darkness came to calm his pain.

"Someone will come," he whispered.

Don't care, the girl's voice said in his mind, following him as he sank, turning into an echo and then fading away altogether.

From the darkness came the sound of the sea, and then its salty smell mixed with the odour of blood, and then he saw the boat. The darkness never went altogether—it was there at the edges, threatening to bleed back in at any instant—but Tom viewed this memory out of Natasha's mind, and try though he might he could not pull away.

The four of them—Natasha, her brother and their parents—were in the same boat that had brought them to the house. It was powering across the waves, thumping and jarring as it leapt from crest to crest. They sat in the sunken well at its centre, unable to see anything but sky and the occasional splash of spray against the deep blue afternoon. The sun shone bright and aloof overhead.

The deck around their feet was awash with blood. Some of it was their own. They all bore injuries that should have killed them, and yet they seemed more alive than ever. The strange adaptations that had been evident in the house—the elongated limbs, distended jaws, lengthened nails—seemed to have receded, but the bullet holes and stab wounds were still visible. Some of these weeped blood, but others already seemed to have stopped bleeding and scabbed over, especially her brother's. There was a dark spot on his face and two on his neck where bullets had struck home, and now they were little more than heavy bruises. No signs of holes in the skin. No fresh blood. He smiled at Natasha. His pain was palpable, yet in the smile there was an adult knowledge as well, the calm certainty that everything would be alright. Even at this tender age, Peter knew that these wounds would not be the death of him.

Some of the blood was theirs. But most of it came from what they had brought with them.

Huddled between where the berserker family members sat, cowering on the floor, three naked people wallowed in the mess. There were two men and a woman. One of the men pressed both hands to his throat, trying to stem the tide of blood pumping from a ruptured artery, while the other man and the woman watched wide-eyed, afraid and yet unwilling to help.

Natasha's little brother—he must have been maybe seven years old—left his seat. He splashed through the blood on hands and knees, and the three captives cowered back, the man without the ruptured throat keening like a pig in pain. Peter paused, growled at the whining man and laughed when he started to cry. Natasha's mother and father watched with parental fondness, smiling past the pain of their own healing wounds. Peter suddenly darted to the bleeding man, pulled his hands away and took a long, deep draught of the dark red blood. Still on hands and knees he returned to his seat, glancing at the naked woman as he passed by. She remained silent, eyes downcast. Perhaps if she did not see them, they would not see her.

The writhing man grabbed at his wound again, pressing hard, starting to moan now as he felt death's approach.

"You're so greedy," Natasha's mother said. Her throat was raw from the scream of the hunt and the ravaging of flesh, her voice a knife on bone.

"Yummy," the boy said, licking his lips and rubbing his stomach. Natasha laughed. Her father smiled at her and his son, then looked down at where the naked woman cowered. She was doing her best to avoid their gaze, legs and arms drawn in to make herself as small as possible. There were terrible bite marks down one side of her body, the skin ragged and torn.

"What's wrong?" he growled. She ignored him. He kicked out, his heel catching her head and flicking it back. "What's wrong?"

She looked up at last, defiant. "Fuck you," she said, and they all laughed, and their laughs were deep and harsh.

Natasha looked down at her own bloodied body and drew her hands over the wounds. Each touch brought pain, but each pain brought comfort, because she would mend. None of them had been using silver bullets or blades. It had been quite a battle, and a good feed, but now she was tired and looking forward to getting back home. At least, *she* thought of it as home. Her mother and father frequently spoke to her in her mind, telling her of another place entirely, and sometimes she dreamed of the darkness and the silence and the places where her kind may one day live in peace, as they had before. They had told her of home, but there was a huge implied history to their discussions, a deep and rich past, through she had never probed further. She sensed that they were keeping her ignorant of many truths of berserker history for her own good. *The Man seeks to know everything*, they often warned, telling her to guard her thoughts. *He would know, and he would kill us all, because he's not like the others. He's different. He sees the bad without the good, and he sees the differences between us whilst ignoring all the similarities. The Man hates us because we're not like him. Sometimes, honey, that's all a man needs to hate.*

"We don't really need to take anything back, do we?" her father croaked.

"There's plenty for us when we want it at home," Natasha said. "But still, there's something exciting in taking it from the hunt."

"Surely you're not still hungry?" her mother asked. She was a thin woman, slight, and her skin displayed evidence of at least four healing bullet wounds.

"I'm always hungry," her father said, glancing above Natasha's head at something out of sight. He smiled, and even though his teeth were back to normal by now, it still looked like a growl. "I'm a berserker. Eating people is what we do."

Natasha turned to see what he had been looking at, who he had been talking to. Standing above her on the boat's main deck, eyes bearing their own peculiar human hunger, a soldier watched the continuing bloodshed. The soldier whom her parents referred to as The Man.

To Natasha, he was like a scary monster from a children's book, and she called him Mister Wolf.

Tom snapped awake, panicking. He had no idea where he was. He looked around the car, expecting sea water to flood in at any moment, wondering why he could no longer feel the boat leaping from wave to wave. He could smell blood but there was no one else in sight, no one but the shriveled thing suckered to his chest.

"No!" He pushed away, wincing as the pain roared in his lower back. *Cole. I saw Cole through Natasha's eyes. Watching them, and enjoying it.* "Leave me alone!" he said.

Natasha rolled back against the leather seat. Wet blood glittered around her mouth. She did not move, but Tom sat up anyway, pressing his hand to his chest and feeling the warm trickle of blood running onto his palm and down his wrist.

No Daddy, she said, *it's not like that, not always. And never for you. I'm trying to help you. Can't you feel, can't you sense the pain drifting away?*

Tom pushed back against the front seats, staring at Natasha's mouth as he heard her voice in his head. No, those lips were not moving. No, her limbs had not shifted position. She was propped against the backseat and there she remained. And yet his blood surrounded her shrivelled mouth, and the pain in his back from the bullet wound was a fist of fire twisting in his insides, its fingers flexing and reaching and tearing . . . but it was bearable. Awful, making him want to scream, but bearable.

195

Can you feel it? Fading away? Listen to me and it will get even better.

"How?" he asked. "Why? Am I in shock?"

Not shock, Natasha said.

Tom almost laughed. Almost. "I've never been shot before. I *am* shocked, let me tell you."

Not shock, she said again. *I'm feeling better, so you are too.*

Tom glanced down at his chest, the lip of torn skin there that still dribbled blood into his opened shirt. "Have you been drinking my blood?"

Only a little. Her voice was quiet and tentative, the voice of a child found doing wrong.

"You told me you weren't a vampire."

We're not! she said, more determined now. *They thought that at first. Especially him, Mister Wolf. Teased us with garlic and crosses and . . .* She laughed, a dry rustle that matched her physical appearance. *My mummy and daddy went along with it because it amused them. They did their best to sleep in the day and wake at night, even though it upset my brother and me, and Mister Wolf and the others thought they knew what they were doing. Funny. It was funny. Even the day they found out we were fooling them, it was funny.* She trailed off, as if that day were the last time she had found cause to truly laugh.

"I've been shot," Tom said. "I've been *shot!*" He leaned forward over Natasha's body and rested his forehead on the backseat, turning slightly so that he could look along the road at Mister Wolf. He was still lying half-in a ditch beside the road, an arm and leg splayed out onto the tarmac, the rest of him almost hidden from view. He was not moving. Tom wondered what Natasha had done to him, and how, but he thought he had a good idea; he had felt her dark psychic fingers exploring his own mind, and he had no doubt they possessed strengths other than those he had already experienced.

We really do have to go now, Natasha said. *He'll be awake soon, and he'll have more bullets.*

"But I've been shot, I'm bleeding. I can't drive like this."

Listen to me, Daddy. If you listen to me you can do it.

"I think the bullet's still inside." He checked his stomach and abdomen, feeling gingerly for an exit wound, but he found none. Only the pounding pain in his lower back, and the feeling of something being very wrong inside. *Is that just the bullet grinding around,* he thought, *or has it moved stuff in there?*

We have a connection, Natasha said, and Tom suddenly thought of her dried mouth clasped to his chest, his blood leaking into her desiccated body. The image was thrust into his mind, not conjured, held there for his inspection and turned by memories other than his. He sensed the blood flowing from beneath his skin, and felt it enter Natasha's mouth. He could sense the draining from his veins, and taste his own blood upon another's tongue. And wherever he looked, whichever way he turned, he felt calmed and soothed by the exchange. It was as if bad blood were being bled from him, taking pain along with it, and yet it was good blood when imbibed. Strength came to him, and something unknown seemed to stir in Natasha's mind.

There, Natasha said. *See?*

"But I don't understand," he said, reaching back and feeling the ragged mess of his back. Blood still coursed between his fingers, and when he shifted a fresh flow warmed his skin.

You don't need to, she said. *It's enough for now to accept it and let it help. We have to go.*

"I don't think—"

You can drive.

"I'm not sure—"

Daddy . . .

Tom looked down at Natasha's body, her face, eye sockets holding the shriveled eyes like old raisins. And even though he saw no movement, he felt her smile.

Thank you, she said.

From outside the BMW, above the rumble of the engine, Tom heard a groan. He looked across the road at Cole's arm and leg, saw the fingers twitching and the foot dragged across the ground. "He's waking."

Natasha was silent but her smile remained in his head, the gratitude apparent. *I can't let it end like this*, he thought. *Not here, and not now.* He moved slightly, waiting for pain to tear up his insides, but it was little worse than a bad toothache. A toothache the size of his entire lower body, true, but it was a rich, vibrant pain, not debilitating. He shifted some more, stepping carefully from the rear seat, standing, turning, closing the door and resting in the driver's seat. *I've just been shot in the back and now I'm going to drive*, he thought, and the idea was so alien that it made no sense whatsoever, gave him nothing to grab onto. Here was Tom, entire life spent behind a desk, most daring exploits usually involving having four pints instead of two on Friday evening pub visits, who now sat covered in his own blood, a ten-year-old body talking to him from the backseat, an ex-army killer lying twenty feet away, and his dead wife in a car farther along the road.

There's still Steven, Natasha said then, and she knew exactly what to say to turn his mind back to the present.

Tom nodded, thought fleetingly of his young son playing soldiers in their back garden, and slammed the driver's door.

Cole sat up in the ditch. He shook his head, putting his hands to his temples as if to contain his dizziness. Then he looked straight at Tom, and his expression was unreadable.

"You killed Jo," Tom muttered. He reversed the BMW, went forward, back and forward again until it was facing along the road at his own battered car. His wife was in there, dead and cooling, Cole's bullets still wrapped up in her organs and flesh.

Steven, Natasha said again.

Tom nodded, gunned the engine and slipped it into first gear.

Cole stood on shaky legs. He still held the pistol in one hand, and the other delved into his jeans pocket and came out with a slim silver shape. A fresh magazine.

Tom thought of Steven laughing as he blew out the

candles on his tenth birthday cake, and Jo ruffling his hair and smiling at Tom, her eyes as alight as those candles with the knowledge of the blessed life the three of them had together.

Steven, the girl said yet again, and behind the voice in his mind was a sudden sense of promise and hope.

As Tom changed into second gear and pressed down on the accelerator, he swerved the car across the road. The offside edge caught Cole across the thighs and sent him spinning over the ditch and into the hedge. Tom looked in the rearview mirror and saw the killer disappear in a shower of leaves and limbs.

The pain nestled at the base of Tom's back and Natasha stroked his mind, calming, soothing, telling him all the things he wanted to hear.

CHAPTER NINE

Cole had not thought about his ex-wife for months. They had divorced soon after the berserker programme had been closed down, when Cole had buried Natasha and her family, and the others had escaped, and he had not seen her since. Sometimes he had to look at a photograph to remember what she looked like. He missed her sometimes, but it was always the idea of what she represented that he mourned the most: normality. A real life, with wife, kids maybe, and an existence other than the one he had led for the last ten years. His life was an obsession, and there was no room in an obsessive's life for anyone else. He had shut her out without even knowing it, and by the time he realised what was happening, she was gone.

He thought of her now, as Roberts aimed the stolen BWM straight at him, and it was because he could think of no one else who would give even a microscopic shit that he was dead.

Instinct probably saved his life. Unable to tear his eyes from Roberts's face—eyes wide, skin smeared with blood, hate painted red—Cole started to fall back, letting gravity lure him down toward the ditch he had only just climbed from. The car closed in, Cole pushed with his feet, and by the time the car's wing clipped his thighs he was already moving back into the hedge. The car gave him rough assistance.

His shout matched the berserker bitch's screech of glee in his head.

Cole's feet left the ground, and he tried to spin in the air to protect himself from the worst of the impact. All he succeeded in doing was presenting his face to the hedge instead of the back of his head, and he managed to bring up his hands as the spiky growth welcomed him in. The impact was relatively soft, but sharp. Branches pricked at his hands, cheeks, neck and chest, while his lower body landed awkwardly in the ditch, a protruding rock thumping his stomach and winding him. Dried leaves fluttered down around him, and something squealed and hurried away deeper into the undergrowth.

He waited until gravity had settled him down before slowly taking his hands away from his eyes. *Lost them again*, he thought, staring down into a pile of leaves and rabbit droppings. He remained still, sucking in a breath when he could, waiting for the pain of broken bones to kick in. The noise of the car striking him had been a dull thud instead of a crack, and he knew that pain was a fickle thing, sometimes shouting in with a roar, other times laying in wait until its target had begun to think themselves lucky. He had suffered enough pain—and dealt it, too—to know that he had a few more seconds yet until his fate became clear.

If he had broken a leg or arm, the chase was over. If he was merely bruised and winded . . . even then, Roberts would have a long headstart. Cole was not sure he could get away with stealing another car again so soon, especially looking as roughed up and bloodied as he did. Of course, he did not have to be so polite next time.

"Bitch!" he said, hoping to provoke some response. He imagined the berserker child chained to the headless bodies of her brother and parents, closed his eyes again and laughed at the image, projecting it as hard as he could lest she still hid in the underground of his mind. No secrets hatches opened, no darkened alleys spewed forth her rage, and Cole could only assume that she had left him alone for now.

What if I don't hear her again? he thought. He could try to follow, but without any clues he had no idea where they were heading. London? The coast? Farther north? Berserkers were excellent at hiding—the escaped family had shown that over the last decade—and without any leads at all, Cole would never find Natasha.

But he had shot Roberts, he was sure. Misty as his vision had been, head shrieking with Natasha's intrusion, he had seen the man stumble to the car after the gunshot, kept his eyes open long enough to see the first bloom of blood on the back of Roberts' jacket. And with a silver bullet from a .45 nestling in his back, he wouldn't get very far.

Cole's wife came to mind again. Tall, beautiful, never understanding, and he wondered where she was now.

Opening his eyes again he slowly pushed himself upright. The pain was merely terrible, nothing worse. He spat and watched his bubbly saliva and blood hanging on a small branch in the hedge. No bones ground together. There seemed to be nothing burst inside. He laughed. His head throbbed as if struck by a nuclear hangover, his face and neck bled from a dozen lacerations, but he had managed to survive being run over by the man whose wife he had killed earlier that morning.

He supposed he could consider himself lucky.

Brushing leaves and mud from his clothes, Cole looked around for the magazine. He had kept a grip on the .45, and it only took him a few seconds to locate the mag and click it home, loading one in the pipe. He felt happier like that, at least. If only he'd been able to put one of these silver bullets into that shriveled fucking bitch.

"Damn!" he shouted, finding another wound in the meantime. One of his teeth had somehow shattered, and parts of it were embedded in his upper lip and gum. He opened his mouth and let blood and speckles of tooth dribble out, leaning forward so that most of it missed his clothes. *Don't want to ruin my look*, he thought, snorting, trying not to laugh again because it hurt too much. He probed the broken tooth with his tongue, finding sharp points and cutting himself again.

"Fuck!" he spat, and a flock of starlings took flight from the field across the road. The cows stood there, still looking his way, calmed now after the gunshot. "Seen enough?" he asked. They stared, chewing their cud like nervous football managers. Damn, he was such a mess.

But not as much of a mess as Roberts. Dead wife, his life fucked, shot in the back, he surely couldn't go much further. However much the little bitch was urging him on, dick-stroking him in his mind, soothing and cajoling . . . he'd be bleeding. He'd be hurting. Someone like that couldn't go forever on adrenaline and fear alone. He was a normal guy, and he would grind to a halt. Cole had to make sure he was in the vicinity when that happened.

Climbing from the ditch, resting one hand on his thigh to push himself up, Cole realised that he had pissed himself.

That bitch!

A car came around the corner from the direction the BMW had taken. It was an old Mazda MX5, growling through a holed exhaust. Cole bet the owner thought that sounded cool.

He'd pissed himself. Probably when she'd screeched at him, invaded his mind, driven him down into his own darkness. It was her fault.

"You bitch!"

As the softtop approached, Cole raised the gun. The car slowed, the driver wide-eyed and terrified, and in her face Cole saw the mockery of the berserk girl, the twinkle in her eyes every time she had called him Mister Wolf, the condescension in the gaze of someone so young.

He pulled the trigger.

He had meant to put a round through the canvas roof, but blood dripped in his eye as he fired. The car skidded to the right, just clipping the rear bumper of Roberts' abandoned car before nudging the field gate and coming to a halt. It rolled back slightly then sat there, engine still running.

There was no movement from inside.

"Shit," Cole whispered, the sibilance pricking his tongue on his ruined tooth. "Shit, shit, shit."

When he reached the driver's door and opened it and watched the woman's body tumble out onto the road, he tried to tell himself he would have had to kill her anyway. No way he could leave her here with a smashed-up car and a body inside. She'd run, and find someone, and the police would have been onto him in hours, if not minutes. She was a brunette and looked as though she had been very attractive, just the sort of woman he sometimes tried to fuck when loneliness got the better of him. The bullet had popped neatly through the corner of the windshield and taken off part of her skull. Blood and brains dripped from the underside of the canvas roof and across the dashboard. Her skirt had ridden up to reveal skimpy black panties and pale, muscled thighs. She was a casualty, and it was people like her he was trying to protect.

Doing his best to reason away his second murder of

the day, Cole dragged the woman to Robert's old car and piled her in with the other corpse.

He did not even bother flicking the skull splinter from the centre of the MX5's steering wheel before driving away.

Tom was numb. His body felt distant, and sitting in the driver's seat his head felt lower than his stomach. He could move his hands on the steering wheel and gear stick, his feet on the gas and brake and clutch, and he constantly twitched in the seat, subconsciously trying to find the pain that should be there. He had a feeling that the bullet was lodged somewhere close to his spine, but at least he was not paralysed.

He felt *unattached*.

And mentally his numbness had spread, a protection against what had happened that was as obvious as it was comforting. As he drove he dwelled on what the last twenty-four hours had brought to, and taken from, his life, and yet his mind only skimmed the surface. The digging, the body, the running, the shooting, the dying . . . all these flashed through his mind with the immediacy of fresh experience, and yet with the dimness of a faded dreams. He could smell the stink of the grave, but digging up those corpses seemed like someone else's memory. He could smell Jo and hear her yawn and see her brushing her hair, but she was someone from the past, an inconsequential part of his here and now.

He could feel Natasha inside, worming her way through his mind, exploring, calming, and he welcomed her in. Because she was protecting him. She was a drug that he needed so much, one that took away the pain and heartache and replaced it with one word, and one aim: Steven.

He drove slowly and sensibly, not wishing to attract attention. He could feel the tremendous damage his body had sustained—she could hide the pain and the immediate consequences, but not the knowledge—and some part of him worried about what the future would hold. Yet somehow he knew that he was safe, at least for now. Safe until they reached wherever it was they were going.

Steven, Natasha said from the backseat.

"Will he know me?"

I'm sure.

"Will I know him?"

Natasha paused, and Tom sensed something that may have been surprise. *What daddy doesn't know his son?*

Tom blinked slowly, eyelids heavy. They were on a dual carriageway now, heading north, and he stayed in the slow lane, watching lorries and cars and motorbikes pass them by. "I only knew him ten years ago," he said.

Natasha fell silent, and Tom guessed that she had gone somewhere else.

He thought of what he had watched her doing when she lent him her memories. Why the army had deemed it necessary to send in the berserkers, he could not fathom. There had been lots of people and lots of guns, yes, but surely one single bomb could have wiped out that drug den as easily as four berserkers? Perhaps it was political. Perhaps it had been a test. But then Tom thought of the faces he had seen through Natasha's eyes, and he realised the truth: it was all about fear. Whoever those unfortunate people had been in business with would find them at the house, or what was left of them, and their hearts would be stricken with the terror of their discovery.

Fear. It was a powerful weapon. He wondered just how much it had backfired on the staff of Porton Down, and why. And much as he felt a trace of that fear as well, he hoped that Natasha would soon show him what had happened there.

The girl was still away. His mind was his own—still hazy, distant from the pain that should be ravaging him, but his own—and Tom concentrated on driving. He had no idea where they were going. But he thought that when they finally arrived there, Natasha would let him know.

Cole waited for Natasha's scream to come in again. His mind felt clear for now, but he knew that there were depths, unplumbed hollows beneath the streets where his darkness ran deep. Anything could be hiding down there. As he drove he strolled the byways of his mind, peering into darker alleys, always afraid to shift manhole covers or venture into tunnels in case he found her waiting for him. He had always feared that he would. And in a way she *was* always with him, a nightmare that he had never quite been able to put down.

The steering wheel was slippery with blood. The CD

oozed Tori Amos; Cole had not bothered to turn it off. The car stank from one of those odour eaters that smelled worse than wet dog or cigarettes, and it was burning the inside of his nose and giving him a headache. He found the little plastic turtle stuck to the underside of the dash, ripped it off and threw it from the car. He kept the window down, cleared the air, and now he could only smell blood. That was fine.

His trousers were still wet from where he had pissed himself; he could smell that too. His hand and calf still dribbled blood from where he had cut them climbing the fence. His legs hurt from the BMW impact, his left much worse than the right, and he feared that soon the bruising may prevent him from driving. His head thumped and throbbed, pulsing with nightmare echoes from the roar Natasha had driven into him, so loud and powerful that it had forced him down into his own dark subconscious.

At least she had not been waiting there for him.

Cole ignored the aches and pains and drove on, not knowing where he was going, simply aiming in the direction Roberts had taken. And much as he hated the prospect, he knew that once again he needed Natasha to slink into his mind if he were ever to find her again.

"Where are we going?"

Tom glanced in the rearview mirror, raising himself so that he could see down into the backseat. Natasha was still where he had left her, a shriveled dead girl, but somewhere inside that carcass was the blood she had suckled from him. He wondered where it was and what good it had done her. She did not respond.

"I feel weak," Tom said. "It's almost lunchtime. I need to eat. I haven't eaten since . . ." *Since before I dug you up*, he wanted to say, but somehow it seemed impolite.

Natasha was still away.

The road had turned into a motorway. He kept his speed down, wondering about stolen cars and number plates and police cameras, but there was nothing he could do about that right now. He had a bullet in his back and a body in the rear seat; stealing another car was hardly an option. Besides, he would not know how to do it. He was just an office worker.

Tom hummed a tune that he did not know for a while, but then he recognised it as a song he had written before Steven's death. Something about race, and bigotry, and acceptance. He could not remember the words, but he found himself tapping out the drum beat on the steering wheel, and remembering how guitar strings had felt beneath his fingertips. It felt good. For a few minutes, it took him away.

"There's an exit coming up," he said. "Natasha? Where do we go from here? How long do I drive? What happens now?" That last question was as much for him as the berserker girl he had taken out of the ground. *What happens now?*

He felt her return. She was wild, like a tornado falling from out of nowhere, touching down and setting the air reeling, the land vibrating, the whole world shaking with something that was either joy or rage.

211

Perhaps both, Tom thought, because even then she was looking after him and there was no fear. *Perhaps both, because for her I think perhaps they may be one and the same.*

In the backseat, with a crackle like a fistful of stick being twisted together, Natasha sat up. And Tom heard her true voice for the first time.

"I've found them," she said.

CHAPTER TEN

Cole tried to shove down the guilt, but it kept rising again to remind him it was there. He drove it into darkness but it dragged him with it, and that darkness was painfully familiar. It stuck to him like blood on cloth, and however much he tried to distract himself it was always waiting there for him.

I'm a good man, he thought, and the sun glinted from a splash of blood on the dashboard.

Deep in the underground of his unconscious he thought he heard a wail. He turned up the car stereo, wound down both windows, pressing his foot to the gas so that he had to concentrate more on taking sharp bends and small humps in the road. Yet still he heard the echoes, and they were not fading away. Everything you ever see or hear or taste remains in your mind, so it's said, only waiting to be retrieved. And he knew that all four people he had killed in his life—three of them in the past two days—were still inside him. He would meet them again. They would rise up and speak to him, and it was purely his strength or weakness, his doubt or conviction, that would see him through.

I'm a good man!

He only hoped that he found Natasha by the time that mental showdown came.

"Who have you found?"

Tom had stopped looking into the mirror. He had seen Natasha sitting up once, and that was enough. *She held my arm when I dug her up,* he thought, but up until now that had been a memory he'd kept shut out, weighed down, away from everything that was happening. Because there were only so many edges he could walk, and that was one from which he would surely topple.

Them, Natasha said in his mind. She had spoken just now, Tom was sure. The voice had been that of a child, but one that has seen too much; croaky with age, weak with decay, yet filled with excitement. *Sophia, Lane and their children, the ones who escaped. The other berserkers! The ones Mister Wolf wanted dead, so he killed my family instead.*

"They have Steven?" Tom's heart was suddenly light in his chest, skipping instead of beating. The car drifted into the centre lane, and a lorry driver leaned on his horn until Tom twitched the wheel and brought them back.

Probably, she said. *They probably have him.*

"You told me they *did!*"

I said there was a chance.

Tom frowned and looked in the mirror again, the girl's face frozen and inscrutable. She remained sitting upright. Her hair was wrapped into a solid muddied knot at the base of her neck. He should wash it for her. And really, through the haze of everything that had happened, he was not exactly sure what she had said about Steven. All he knew was that there was a chance, and right now that was enough.

"Where will they meet us? What will happen? How many of them are there?"

I'll tell you where to go and when to stop, Natasha said. *And Daddy, don't be afraid. I'm here with you. You helped me, now I'll look after you.*

"You can't move!" Tom said, wincing as his raised voice seemed to allow in the pain from his back. "You can't do anything. How can you protect me?"

I'm a berserker, like them, Natasha said, and then she was silent, the question obviously answered.

Tom drove on. The pain in his back—*I've been shot, shot by a fucking gun, and the bullet's still in there sucking in infection, and I might be* dying!—throbbing in time with his heartbeat, yet never bad enough to make him woozy or faint. Something Natasha had done was seeing to that. She had fed from him—whatever she claimed to the contrary, he knew that was what had happened— drinking his blood, taking strength from it, and giving him something back in return. There was no other explanation for how good he felt, considering all that had happened to him. She was taking care of him.

Stop thinking, she whispered in his head, *stop worrying, drive on.*

"Am I going mad?" he said, and Natasha withdrew to allow him his own mind.

He drove on. Midday came and went, and Tom slipped into some sort of daze, feeling the miles drifting by but having little recollection of the moments in between. He was tired, hungry and thirsty. He supposed veering into an almost hypnotic state was a defence mechanism.

The motorway swerved and swayed northward. He kept his speed to about sixty, and most cars and lorries swept by as they edged up toward eighty. A few people looked his way, but he did not return their stares. He was aware of pale faces pressed to windows, and only when their vehicles moved on did he glance over at them, catching brief glimpses of faces which all looked the same. Whether they saw Natasha or not he did not know, and he was not sure what they would make of her if they did. A dummy, perhaps. Or maybe they would see a scarecrow, or a pile of cloths, or a strange plant being transported south to north. None of them stopped, none of them swerved away from him in surprise, the drivers losing the steering wheel as they reached for their phones to call the police. They simply moved on, and he would never see them again.

He drove on, mind focused ahead, the events of the past day and night as hazy as a dream.

The landscape was wide and flat. Fields were being harvested, some of them already worked and left with stubble where their crops had grown. One or two had already been ploughed under, and Tom thought of the life that would rise from the turned earth. Clumps of trees were dressed in orange and yellow, sprouting from a carpet of colour where many dead leaves had already been shaken loose. The sun bore down on one wooded hilltop and it shone gold and ochre across the land-scape, like a beacon to anyone seeking the true splen-dour of nature. Such beauty in death. Such colour in decay. Everything in nature had a reason, and Tom spent a while musing on why dying leaves should look so attractive. Dead animals' colours were dictated by rot; sour colours, non-colours. Natasha, back there in the rear seat . . . there was no colour to her, just grey-ness, browns, nothing striking at all. The colour of death for plants was much more pleasing. Coming up with no answer as to why this was, Tom was pleased. Nature *should* be enigmatic. It was not up to humankind to pretend to know nature, and it was not right that someone like him should know such secrets on a day like today.

He thought of his office, his desk, his room filled with dusty musical instruments at home. But that all seemed years and worlds away.

Occasionally, Natasha would stroke through his mind, only touching him briefly, and he saw the new strength in her. It pleased him, and frightened him. *Will you be my daddy?* she had asked, and he had never con-sidered the consequences of his reply.

The traffic slowed, then stopped, and then began

moving again at a crawl. A few minutes later they passed a lorry in the ditch, its driver sitting on the back steps of an ambulance chatting with paramedics while they gave him the once-over. He looked at the BMW as Tom passed by, and his gaze shifted from Tom to the backseat, his eyes flickering away, back again, away. A policeman standing in front of the ambulance looked as well, his eyes fixed on Tom until Tom looked away. *They'll be looking for the car,* he thought, and as he accelerated he looked up at a traffic sign spanning the motorway. Place names and road numbers made no sense, but he saw the small black specks of cameras above the signs, pointing both ways. Farther on there was a camera atop a tall pole, aimed directly down at the slow lane. And as distance lessened between the BMW and the camera Tom was sure the camera moved, tracking his progress, following him like eyes in a painting.

"They'll be looking for us," he said. Natasha did not answer, and he wondered where she was. Back with Cole, checking whether he was dead or injured? Or ahead with the berserkers she was taking him toward? He could not tell, and he would not ask.

Miles rolled by, Tom's strange daze continued, noticing everything around him but casting recent events into something of a dream. Sometimes he remembered his dreams, mostly not, and this one seemed to be fading as every minute and mile passed. The memories were still there, but the feelings and emotions were not. The last day of his life was turning into a movie. He thought of Jo, dead in their car, and it was as if she were an actress he had once known. He should have cried at that—he tried to force a tear—but a new model Mini cut him up and made him swerve, and his cursing dried up any sobs that might have come.

When Natasha next spoke in his mind, almost an hour after Tom had last heard from her, her voice made him jump and let go of the wheel. He grabbed it again quickly. The sudden movement had stirred the pain in his back and Natasha came in, calming fingers in his head, easing the pain away. How she did it he did not know; he was simply thankful.

I've been talking with them, she said. *They're coming for us, all of them. They'll tell us where to meet, and then they'll take me home.*

"Steven?"

Yes, they have Steven.

Tom began to cry. The tears were sudden, hot, streaming from his eyes and blurring his vision. He shook. "I need to stop," he said, "just for a while. I need the toilet, and food and drink."

Of course, Daddy, Natasha said. Her voice broke and she paused, as if expecting him to say more about his son.

But Tom did not ask. Right now, weak and in pain, he was not sure he really wanted to know.

He composed himself enough to drive the three miles to the next service station. He pulled off and parked as close to the main building as he could, partly to remain inconspicuous, but mainly because he had no idea how far he could walk. He sat for a while, gasping past sobs, forcing the tears to stop because they would attract attention. If the police caught him now, there would be no future. Natasha would be taken away and buried again. He would be arrested and charged with God knew what. And Steven . . . he would remain wherever he was now, doing whatever he was doing.

That was what Tom did not want to know. Not yet. After the memories Natasha had shared to show him her story, he had begun to fear that his son would perhaps be better off dead.

"I need to leave you for a while," he said. "I'll cover you with my jacket. You don't look . . ."

Don't worry, you can tell me, Natasha soothed.

"Well, someone would have to come close to see what you are."

Do what you need to do, but please come back soon. We're so close, and they can help me.

"Who are they? How many of them are there?"

Four, she said. *That's all that survived. Lane and Sophia, and their children Dan and Sarah. And you'll meet them soon enough.*

Tom sighed and rested his hands on his thighs, ready to get up. It was going to hurt. No matter what Natasha was doing to him, this was going to hurt. And then he realised one vital factor he had totally missed, and cursed his stupidity.

He had been shot. His jacket, shirt and the back of his trousers were caked in blood. His collar too, from the head wound that still throbbed. He was still covered in muck from excavating the mass grave yesterday.

He was a fool who would not get ten feet before someone noticed him.

"Oh Natasha . . ."

I can help, she said.

"How?" Even now he sometimes forgot her psychic
fingers in his mind, probing his thoughts, hearing him
as he heard her.

I can make them look away.

"They'll still notice, I don't understand—"

But I can only do it if you take me with you.

Tom sat silently at that, shifting the mirror and staring back at the girl. Her wrinkled face returned the
stare; no smile, no movement. Perhaps sitting up had
drained her strength.

He looked around the car; foot-wells, glove compartment, turning cautiously in his seat to glance at the
backseat. There was nothing he could use to cover her.
He would need his jacket for himself—it was bloodied
and holed, but not as bad as his shirt—and he could see
nothing else. And then he remembered the boot.
When he had searched it for tools he had seen an old
blanket, spread across the floor in a vain attempt to
keep it pristine.

"Not pristine any more," he said, smiling. There was
blood everywhere, front and back, and grave dirt was
ground into the leather seats.

All he had to do was leave the car, walk around to
the boot, open it, retrieve the blanket from beneath
the tools and anything else that might weigh it down,
return to the rear door, lean in, wrap Natasha's corpse

and carry it into the service station. And then he would have to rely on her to help, in whatever way he could. *I can make them look away*, she had said, and the sense of her in his mind made him believe that.

Piece of cake.

Taking a few deep breaths, Tom looked around. There was a small car parked next to him, its owners absent. A few people milled outside, smoking or drinking or talking into their mobile phones. No one seemed to be looking at him in particular, and more importantly he could see no sign of any police nearby. He touched the door handle and looked in the mirror at Natasha. The door opened with a portentous *click*.

As soon as Tom exited the car several people looked at him: a man walking his dog on a small grassed hill beside the main building; a lorry driver using a cash machine; a mother and her young daughter just exiting the main doors. He was the centre of attention, and they could not help but see the guilt on his face. A burst of dizziness hit him and he leaned back against the car, closing the door and looking up at the sky as if admiring the day. He held onto the handle, sure he was going to pitch left or right at any moment. He could feel something warm running down his leg, and he hoped it was blood.

Daddy! Natasha called. *Stay awake! Stay standing! Don't fall down!* There was genuine concern in her voice, and he realised that had been all but lacking up to now. He shook his head, confused.

"I'm doing my best," he whispered, then bit his lip.

222

Covered in blood and dried mud was bad enough; talking to himself would be sure to mark him as a loony.

When he felt steady enough he lowered his head and opened his eyes. He needed to focus on something, centre his vision to still the crazy gymnastics his balance seemed to be enjoying at the moment. He stared at a huge menu for the burger bar. When the cheeseburger stopped wavering from side to side like a zeppelin in a hurricane he took another deep breath, closed his eyes again, counted to ten.

Nobody was watching him now. Perhaps they had seen the state he was in and decided to move on. Or more likely, he was simply not their business. Strangers are like forgotten photographs to other strangers: the negative is there, but the image is never printed.

Tom shifted sideways with his back against the car. It would look weird to anyone watching, but not as weird as a bloody bullet hole in his back.

And just what the fuck is she doing to me? he thought. *Or am I still in shock? Bleeding my life away without even feeling it?* He had no answers, and if Natasha heard, she remained silent.

That fuzziness remained, a veil over the past that seemed to dilute its importance. "Jo," Tom whispered experimentally, but he did not cry.

He reached the boot and popped it with the electronic key. Now there was no alternative but to lean in and expose his back. "Help me now if you can," he said, but Natasha was silent once again. He moved the spilled tools aside, shifted an old pair of shit-caked

Wellington boots, then gathered up the blanket covering the floor of the boot. It had been chequered once, but successive spillages of livestock food and countless assaults by muddied footwear had turned it into a uniform grey. Filthy. *Just as likely to attract attention with this,* he thought, but then Natasha was back, her young voice filled with excitement like a kid on her way to the zoo.

I've been talking with Sophia. They're not far away now. They'll tell us where to meet, and they know somewhere safe. Isn't that fine?

"And Steven?"

A pause, so slight that Tom thought he had imagined it. *He's at home,* she said.

"And where is home?"

It's a place . . . , Natasha said, trailing off. If she'd had eyes, Tom imagined she would be staring into the distance. *My mother used to tell me about it while I was falling asleep. Below the streets of a city she never named are the tunnels, and below them the caves, and way, way below them is home. Humans have never been there, only berserkers. It's huge, alight with fires that have burned forever. The food is the richest, growing from the purest ground. Water collects in pools, the cleanest there is, and there are fish like nowhere else in the world. Some of the dwellings carved from the rock go back to a time before humans walked on two legs. There are other tunnels leading to other places, but it's home that berserkers always return to. The cradle of our existence. It's . . . somewhere I can barely imagine, let alone explain.*

"I suppose we'll both see soon enough." He curled the blanket into a ball and slammed the boot shut, hissing as pain punched him in the back. Something ground around in there, like a rat clawing and gnawing through his flesh in search of another organ to rupture, and Tom had to lean forward and rest against the car, eyes closed once again. "Oh, Natasha, I'm going to go, I'm going to collapse and that'll be it, no home, no Steven—"

Don't you fucking dare!

His eyes snapped open. Fear swiped him around the face, and it was as effective as a real slap. The dizziness retreated. The pain decided to stay put, and he could feel it waiting in the shadows for its next opportunity to mess him up.

He had never heard her speak like that. That had not been a little girl's voice. Those had been the words of someone used to being in control.

What is she doing to me? he wondered yet again, and he thought briefly of what Cole had said.

Mister Wolf might be here soon, the girl said in his mind, shouting, drawing him away from his own thoughts. *And we won't get away from him again, not with you shot like that. You're bleeding, Daddy.* Her voice dropped again, changing from a shout back to a childish whine. *So much blood! Get in the car and hold me before we go, and I'll make sure we both have the strength for this.*

"What are you doing to me?" he asked.

Helping you. Making you strong. Keeping you alive.

"I don't even know what you are."

I'm a berserker, just like I've told you and shown you. Sit with me for a minute and I'll dream you some more, show you the truth.

He opened the back door and sat down in the car.

Pick me up, hold me like you did before.

Tom manoeuvred Natasha into his lap and cradled her like a baby. He felt a needle-prick at his chest, and this time she moved in his arms, a grotesque shuffle that raised his hackles and sent a tingle down his spine.

We'll both be well soon, she said, and then he felt her withdraw from his mind as she began to feed.

With his free hand he spread the dirty blanket over the strange girl. Then he leaned his head back, relishing the warm waves of comfort that spread through his body and took away the pain.

Soon they took the light as well.

"I've shown you what we are", Natasha said, "and now I'll show you what they did to us."

And this was her real, true voice, and she sounded just like a little girl.

Cole had lost them. He was sure of this, just as he was sure that the MX5 was dying. It coughed and gasped, and something sounded as if it had come loose in the engine. Of all the dumb fucking luck . . . But then he *had* murdered the car's owner, so he supposed there was some cosmic justice at work here.

He was on the motorway heading north, simply because he could move faster that way and it felt as though he was getting somewhere.

The car spluttered again and jerked, and at sixty that was not good. He'd have to pull off soon, or risk having to stop on the hard shoulder. If that happened and the police decided to stop and see if there was any problem, he'd have trouble explaining the blood and brains and bone all over the car's interior. He could try, he supposed. But it would not be easy.

I'm chasing a monster I buried alive ten years ago, officer, because some stupid twat dug her up without having the slightest fucking idea what he was doing. And now he's doing his best to take her to more of her kind, where she'll be looked after and tended and brought back to the land of the living, and I'm afraid of that because there's something about her, something they did to her at Porton Down. And though I don't know what it is, I am certain that, along with the Black Death, AIDS and a dashing of the Ebola virus on your morning cornflakes, you wouldn't class it as Good News. Oh, the car? Yes, well, I accidentally blew the driver's head off when I really only meant to put one in the car body. Pretty brunette. Just the kind of woman I'm trying to protect.

No, that would never work.

Cole took the next exit from the motorway, the car died on the roundabout and he managed to roll downhill into a small petrol station. There was a garage behind it, one car inside with its oily guts strewn across the ground. As the MX5 curved to a halt the mechanic strolled over, lighting up a cigarette on the way.

"Shit!" Cole climbed from the low car, cursing at the increasing pain in his bruised thighs. "Don't worry, mate," he said, nonchalant as he could be. He could feel a splinter of bone stuck into his rear from where he had sat on it. *How bloody casual can I be like this?* he thought. The .45 was a comforting weight in his belt.

The mechanic looked him up and down. His eyes grew wide, he took a long drag on his cigarette, then nodded. "Yep. S.E.P." He turned and walked away.

"What?"

The mechanic spoke over his shoulder, still walking. "Somebody Else's Problem. Douglas Adams. Phone's in the shop."

Cole stared after the man in amazement. "Maybe my luck's changing," he muttered, but then he pictured the woman he had killed, her pale thighs and black panties and ruined head, and he knew that Lady Luck would never smile at him again.

He limped to the shop, digging his mobile phone from his pocket. Hopefully they'd have toilets inside, and from there he could make the call he had been contemplating for the past hour, one which he had always promised himself he would never make. The call that would guarantee that he would be tried for at least four murders.

He had already tapped the number in, ready to dial.

"I'm too committed," he said as he entered the shop and spied the sign for the bathroom. The girl behind the till stared at him, never stopping chewing her gum.

Cole thought of himself as a good person, God-fearing and good. A splinter from an innocent woman's skull could prick his ass, but that did little to change his mind.

In the bathroom he checked that all the cubicles were empty, stood where he could see the door and pressed DIAL.

The phone was answered after four rings. It took some discussion and several minutes on hold for him to be passed through, but in the end the familiar voice came on, and Cole felt his instant dislike rising to the fore.

"Major Higgins," Cole said. "So you're still licking Her Majesty's ass?"

They were in the enclosed rear of some sort of vehicle, being transported to Porton Down. It was moving fast and the roads were bumpy, and if it weren't for the safety belts they would have been thrown around the interior of the cab.

There were no windows, and only one weak light. Strong mesh formed six separate cages, three on each side, with a walkway down the centre. The sliding doors to these cells were open today. Natasha sat across from Peter, and their parents sat in the stalls next to them, none of them speaking. Her father seemed to be asleep, but she could see the glint of his eyes beneath his lowered eyelids. Still pumped up from the exertions of the day, his animal instincts kept him awake. Her mother sat with her head resting back against the side of the truck, mindless of the bumps and knocks, staring at the short strip-light in the ceiling. Her face was pocked with two old bullet wounds, put there only hours before. By the time they reached Porton Down the wounds would be totally gone. The effort of healing was tiring her, and Natasha saw her eyelids droop.

Her brother sat wide awake before her, still alight from the hunt. His recent wounds were mere shadows, echoes of pain, and he twitched slightly now and then to shrug off another memory. He had healed quicker than all of them, as he was the youngest. In humans a child will heal faster than an adult, and so it was with them.

They were contained. Though the doors to the cells were unlocked and the light was on, the truck's rear door was bolted and deadlocked from outside. There was an electronic lock as well; Natasha could see the empty housing where its internal control had been removed. Mister Wolf had taken pleasure in telling them that the truck was heavily reinforced for their own safety. It was fully wired up and could be injected with a massive electrical charge. For their protection. Finally, there was a container of nerve gas fitted into a delivery container between the ceiling layers. Again, for their protection. He had smiled whilst telling them this, though there was no comfort behind the expression. *Fuck up*, it said, *and I'll gas you myself. Make one move to get out, and I'll light you up like Christmas.* Her father had nodded at Mister Wolf, walked around the truck, tapped at walls and kicked tires, and then smiled at the soldier as if he had already discovered a flaw in the vehicle's security.

Natasha was tired but could not close her eyes. She had been cooped up like this with her family many times before, and every time they had remained awake. It was not the fear of confinement, nor the obvious fact that they were prisoners that prevented them from sleeping. It was the knowledge that, one day, they would become expendable. Only one of the humans had ever shown any sign of truly understanding what they were and what they could do, and Mister Wolf made no secret of his desire to be rid of them. His mistake was assuming that the berserkers were unnatural, a slur on creation. If he could only see into their past. . . .

Peter's eyes flickered left and right, scanning the corners of their cells, ever-vigilant for a hope of escape. He would not find it, Natasha knew, not here and not now. And she guessed that he knew that, too. Her father, eyes almost closed and yet fully awake, waited for a more obvious chance at flight. And her mother felt every vibration of the road through her skull, each twist and turn of the truck. A couple of hours after setting out from the naval port she opened her eyes and announced that they would soon be home.

Home. Natasha could not remember the real home—the place her parents spoke of often, but only silently in her mind—because she had been a babe in arms when they were caught. Their enclosure at Porton Down was all she knew, other than the places they were sent to on occasion to feed and destroy. Her brother had been born in captivity. Perhaps that explained why he, more than any of them, was constantly on edge and ready to fall over. The slightest upset would set him raging; the smallest scolding drove him berserk. No problem for his family, but for the humans it made for a challenging time. It was a wonder they had not already tried to destroy him, but they knew the strength in a family.

The truck slowed, the road flattened and became smoother, and they all sensed that the vehicle was now in an enclosed space. It took a few minutes after it had stopped for the doors to be opened, and Mister Wolf glared in at the berserkers.

"Home sweet home," he said. "You know the drill. One at a time, the boy first, then the girl." He wore a heavy pistol on his belt, and Natasha could smell the silver bullets from where she sat. The huge garage had several observation posts built into its thick walls, and there would be a sniper in each one, high velocity rifles loaded with silver trained on the berserkers as soon as they left the truck.

"It's in the truck we could take our chance," her father had whispered to her mother one day. Neither of them knew that Natasha had been listening; they thought she was asleep, mouth bloody, stomach full. "In there, it's only that bastard Cole who has us covered. We'd only have seconds, but it could work. Freedom."

"And the nerve gas?" her mother had said. "And the shock? Could we survive that?"

"Perhaps not all of us—"

"I'll do nothing to risk our children. They're all we have. If keeping them alive means we have to stay here, then that's what we do."

"You think they'll ever let us go? You think they'll

ever decide we have rights as well? We're animals to them! Assets!"

"I don't care," her mother had said, and as she turned away she had seen Natasha watching and listening from where she lay. She smiled, and Natasha smiled back, but inside Natasha had hated the look of defeat and acceptance in her mother's eyes.

Natasha remembered, and Tom saw. He knew this was only memory and yet it was pure experience as well: smell and taste, touch and sound. He could see everything that Natasha had seen, feel what she had felt.

He was a dark figure in the car, head tilted back and to the side, dribbling from one corner of his mouth. In his lap sat the blanket-covered body of an undead girl. At his chest her dried lips worked around the small wound, drawing blood. On his back the blood had dried and the wound had scabbed, flesh already knitting where only a couple of hours before a silver bullet had blasted its way through.

His blood held a taint, but only a taint. And tainted blood was better than none at all.

Natasha drank, flexing her fingers, muscles contracting and flesh filling out.

Tom slept and saw the past.

Anyone who glanced into the car and saw something strange immediately went on their way, and within two steps they were left with only a feeling of disquiet. Two paces further and they were concerned only with what they were going to have for lunch.

* * *

"What are we having for lunch?" Peter said.

"You're not still hungry!" Natasha said, aghast. He really was an eating machine. She'd heard the saying that a puppy will eat until it's sick; he was the same. His stomach was still swollen with the berserk feast they had enjoyed the day before, and now he was craving again.

"There's plenty there," Mister Wolf said. He was accompanying them along the corridor to their quarters as usual, one hand resting on the butt of his pistol. Natasha knew that he knew it would be useless; if they went for him, he'd be dead before he saw them move. But it seemed to give him a sense of comfort, and perhaps power as well. They were the animals and he was holding the gun. He was in charge.

"We've done your dirty work for you again," her father said. "Now we'd like to eat."

"I thought you'd eaten enough to last you a week," Mister Wolf said, glaring at Natasha's father with a stare that said, *I'm so scared of you I don't know where to turn.*

Her father knew this, but rarely played on it. If you got the better of someone like Cole, he would make it his mission to find a way to pay you back. Exposing his weaknesses only made him need to feel stronger. There was nothing he could really do to them, not without reason—he had his orders from way above—but he could make their lives uncomfortable if he so desired. And if his superiors ever questioned his actions, he would put it down to "training." He used that word a lot. Training. As if they were dogs.

"I'll have food brought to you," Mister Wolf said. "All of you." Everything he said had an undercurrent of threat. He hated them. He was a small, weak, insecure man, and Natasha feared him more than anyone or anything she knew.

There came a blank spot in Natasha's memory—a forgotten period, or something she did not want Tom to see—and then there they were, the berserkers, all together in the place at Porton Down where they had been kept for years, together like patients in an asylum or animals in a zoo. They were gathered in their courtyard, a large landscaped area with a pool and fountain, shrub planting, seating areas, a patio and barbeque, and a heavy steel grille spanning from wall to wall, supported on thick stone columns. The whole grid hummed gently. The sun shone through, but its power and beauty was lessened by the mesh, tainted by incarceration. The place smelled of lavender and the potential for death.

Natasha's parents sat quietly playing chess. Her brother larked with Dan and Sarah, two other young berserker children, a rough and tumble version of tag where the one who was "it" had to chase the others on all fours. The other berserker adults—Lane and his wife Sophia—were lying out in the sun, shielding their eyes and whispering.

This was when the change began. Because Lane and Sophia were whispering of escape, and their plan did not include all of Natasha's family. She remembered, and Tom saw, and with this knowledge came a feeling of dread at what was to come next.

Tom woke up. His neck ached from where he had been leaning back. Natasha was huddled in his arms, a cold dry shape that seemed to have taken on fresh weight since he had fallen asleep. He was filled with trepidation. The world was loaded with threat and primed with violence, and for a few seconds he did not want to move lest he kickstarted whatever was to come. He looked around without moving his head and saw people passing by outside, glancing into the car, meeting his eyes and looking away quickly, walking to their car or toward the restaurant as if they were used to seeing blood-soaked men huddled in rear seats with childrens' bodies.

Five more minutes, Natasha said, and she sounded desperate and demanding, her voice striving for normality but dripping with something more animal and vital. Tom looked down and saw bubbles of blood between her mouth and his chest. He was feeding her; more accurately, she was feeding from him. He closed his eyes to see how he felt about this, and was surprised to discover no feelings at all. He was ambivalent to what Natasha was doing.

Yet still that sense of dread, hanging around him like an acid bubble about to burst.

It's inside, she said, *it's in my memory, and I'll show you what I can remember . . . five more minutes, Daddy, and I'll feel better and you'll know what they did. What he did. And then you'll know why we have to move on.*

She drifted away, and so did Tom, falling back into a sleep that invited the movie of her memory to return to him. It skipped and jumped as if cut and spliced from recollections that made no sense, and Tom fell into frame, scared and daunted, yet eager to know.

Natasha walked in from the courtyard, glancing through the door into their dining room. Three people were chained to the wall in there, and though she only caught a glimpse, it looked as though one of them had died. That was bad. Probably Lane had done that, angry that he had not been allowed out on the latest jaunt. He got like that sometimes—petulant, spoilt, like a child that has had its favourite toy taken away. He would never take it out on another berserker, and he could not risk doing anything to the soldiers on the base, so it was their food that suffered. He had probably supped blood until he was drunk from it, then continued until he was almost asleep, suckling from habit rather than necessity until the man died. Natasha was sorry. The food had been there for over a year now, and she had grown quite attached to him.

She walked on. The fate of their victims was the least of her worries right now. She had told her parents that she was going to her room to read, but in reality she had simply wanted to leave the courtyard because of the thickening atmosphere out there. Something was happening. It got like this sometimes—angry and loaded—and Natasha usually put it down to the electrical grid above their heads. But other times she shrank away from such tall tales, telling herself to grow up and try to understand what was going on. There were group dynamics at work here that her child's mind found difficult to fathom, but at least she realised that something was occurring. Her brother, oblivious, played tag with Dan and Sarah, still too young to know. *All children are born animals*, her mother once had told her, *human and berserker. But with its first breath a berserker child is different, and every breath henceforth increases those differences.*

Natasha walked through the communal living area—blank walls, functional furniture, a TV and overflowing bookcase—and headed back to the bedrooms.

Someone was following her.

She darted into her parents' room and hid behind the door. A few seconds later Dan walked by, singing softly to himself and clicking his fingers, something he did when he was nervous. He paused outside Natasha's closed bedroom door, listened briefly and then walked on, singing changing to humming. He had obviously grown bored of playing tag.

He's doing something, Natasha thought, but she had no idea what.

Her memory jumped, blinked, skipped reels—and she was in Dan's room trying to stick something into his mouth so that he did not bite off his tongue. He was thrashing on the bed, moaning and screaming, foaming at the mouth, eyes turned up in his head, and though she had already seen the syringe and blood drops on his bed she did not know what they meant. She was shouting for help because Dan looked as if he were dying, and she had never seen a berserker die. Humans yes, plenty of times, often by her own hand. But never a berserker. Her cries merged with his screams, and her parents soon came running.

Not Lane and Sophia, though. They stayed away.

Her father took over trying to hold down Dan's tongue. He stuck his fingers into the boy's mouth, wincing when Dan clamped down and bit hard, and Natasha thought that the taste of another berserker's blood would have calmed him down. But he kept thrashing and screaming past her father's hand, and soon the loud siren that announced the opening of an external door went off.

Dan pushed Natasha's father away and sat up.

His screaming and thrashing had brought on the change, and foam was still bubbling at his mouth. His eyes glinted red, hands twisting into claws, and as he stood Natasha saw that blood was dripping from his sleeves and trouser legs.

"Dan," her father said. She heard something in his voice then that spoke volumes, and later, when everything was ending, she thought that even then he knew what was to come. Perhaps he had known for some time.

Dan growled, shivering as the fury burst through his veins and lit up his child's body like a radiator. He sweated blood. He shook his head, pink saliva speckling the walls of his room.

"Dan, whatever you're going to do, don't. Nothing will work against them, you know that, they—"

"Weak!" he said, spitting blood. The word was barely

discernable past his mouthful of teeth, and whatever he said next came out only as grunts and snarls.

Natasha's father glanced at her and motioned her back against the wall.

From outside there came a scream, bloody and wet, and then the sudden explosion of machine guns.

Natasha's memory jumped again, and then slipped into a series of rapid images that reminded Tom of a trailer for a movie . . . a horror movie, where they showed all the best, bloody bits in order to lure in the viewers—Natasha ran along the corridor, her father holding her hand, Dan loping ahead of them. As he emerged into the living area a stream of bullets threw him against the wall, their silver coatings already melting into his bloodstream to poison and kill. But Dan howled, spun on the floor and stood again, leaping across the width of the room to land astride the soldier doing the shooting. He ripped off the man's head and threw it at the glass wall between the living area and courtyard. It left a bloody question mark on the window before bouncing beneath a settee.

Her mother ran in from outside, hunkered down low, her brother clasped to her chest. He was already raging and dribbling, but her mother cooed to him, trying to calm him down and prevent the change. "I want no part of this!" she said, and her father said, "I don't think we'll be given any choice. Where are they?" Her mother turned to look back into the courtyard and a bullet struck her face, exploding one eye and spilling hissing blood and brains across the boy clasped to her chest. "No!" her father screamed, and Natasha smelled the silver, the stench of burning blood and poisoned flesh, and she knew straight away that her mother would not be rising again. *The syringe*, she thought, wondering what Dan had injected and hating him for not sharing it.

She and her father ran toward the glass wall—her father carrying her raging brother beneath one arm—and then turned back when they saw what was happening outside. The courtyard had become a battle ground. Soldiers poured through the door from the control centre—some they recognised, a couple they did not—fanning out, firing, throwing grenades. Mister Wolf was probably with them, but Natasha could not see him. Out there too, Lane, Sophia and their children flashed across the courtyard, powering through bushes, over paved areas, blurring around bullets, ripping out throats and spewing blood, bouncing from walls, taking occasional hits only to rise again, stronger and more enraged than before. Natasha saw the smudges of terrified faces. A torso trailing guts splashed into the pond. The fountain turned red. A grenade exploded by the window and starred the glass, and her father grabbed her hand and pulled her away, back toward their rooms. "Mummy!" Natasha said, but she knew that her mummy was dead.

They hid in her room, lying down beside the bed. Her father had slammed the door again and again, smashed a hole in the wall and fused the security lock. It pushed four heavy bolts into the door from the wall, trapping them inside, making certain that they were set apart from Lane and Sophia and the escape these two had obviously planned. They would be trapped here now until the soldiers came to let them out. He cried and raged and swore as he never had before in front of his children. His tears were for his dead wife and his son and daughter, born innocent and yet guilty of so much at others' bidding. "Daddy, let's go and get them!" Peter gurgled, his face distorting and growing red from the change. But her father held him and kissed his forehead, shaking his head, saying, "It's not our fight," and more gunfire and explosions swallowed whatever else he said.

Lane smashed against the door, screeching, his nails tearing through masonry and snagging on the metal bolts, pulling and pushing and twisting, but even his berserker strength could not bend the thick steel. He screamed through the wall at them, nonsense in his words. "Natasha!" he said, and other things, and "Natasha!" again. "He wants me, Daddy?" Natasha said, and her father shook his head and closed his eyes in despair. The bashing and screaming continued until gunshots and explosions replaced them. There was more fighting and more death, and then it became quiet for some time, the only sounds the sobbing of her father and her little brother on the verge of rage. Natasha was petrified. But her fear and her father's despair kept her from the change.

Mister Wolf, faced splashed with drying blood, pressed the pistol into the back of Natasha's father's head and pulled the trigger. Natasha squeezed her eyes shut, trying her best to un-see what she had seen, cast out the image of her father's face bulging out as the silver bullet melted his brain and poured its poison through his body, and even though her brother was screaming she could still hear Mister Wolf's voice, low and loaded, "I've been waiting to get rid of this scum for so long."

They were dragged through the courtyard by their legs, tied with steel-wired rope, and however much pleading or shouting Natasha and Peter did the soldiers would not let go. She could see why: the bodies of their fallen comrades littered the ground, bleeding and torn and all of them dead. *No Lane, no Sophia or their children*, she thought, and the idea came for the first time that perhaps they had got away. Perhaps after all this there had been a chance after all. A chance that started in a syringe, something to calm the burn of silver and negate its poison. "Where are they?" she asked, and Mister Wolf turned to her—a little girl, that's all she was—and struck her across the face with his pistol. She cried because her daddy was not there to protect her, nor her mummy to calm the hurt. "Shut up, bitch," Mister Wolf said. *They got away*, she thought, and even though they had left her and her family to die, for a while she was glad.

The Plain, her brother's cold execution, the hole, the digging and burying, she remembered all of that, and Tom could barely comprehend the cruelty. In his sleep—where his dreams were Natasha's memories, steered and controlled and yet going only one way—he cried out, trying to shout at Cole for the terrible things he had done. "One more bullet!" he said, and it was Natasha's voice begging the soldier to kill her rather then bury her alive with her dead family. But Mister Wolf looked and saw only what he had been told to see: monsters. No little girl, no dead family, only monsters like those that had murdered his friends and comrades. And bury her he did.

You see? Natasha said. *You see what they did to us, Daddy?*

Tom came around quickly, rising out of the dream and back to desperate reality. Though the feeling of dread had gone—blossomed into the violence and terror of Porton Down—the dream had left him with a sense that all could never be right with the world again. He had seen terrible hidden things that he had never suspected existed. He was privy to awful secrets. And his wife . . .

Daddy, we have to go, Natasha said. She moved in his arms.

Tom gasped and tried to push her away, but the front seats prevented her from going any further. She moved on his lap, her limbs and body twisting slowly, as if performing an endless stretch. Her face had come away from his chest, her mouth bloody, dried lips pulled back from her teeth like those of a hissing dog.

"Are you coming back to life?" he said.

I was never quite dead.

"What are you doing to me?"

Only good. Helping you.

"Helping me so that I can help you?"

Of course, she said, and her honesty made him hate himself. *And helping you because you don't deserve what has happened. None of us do. We berserkers were wronged by Mister Wolf, and now he has done wrong to you as well.*

"You want revenge?" Tom asked, thinking of Jo lying on the back seat of their ruined car . . . the image distant, like a faded black and white impression of crystal clear reality.

I want to be safe, she said. Tom tried not to look down at her face, but he could not help himself. He thought of the little girl she had been in the dream, confused and frightened and forced to watch her mother gunned down, her father and brother executed in front of her. He cried. They were dry tears, sobs heaving at his shoulders and reminding him of the pain lying dormant in his back, waiting to be reawakened. She was helping him. She was making him better. Whether by doing so she was making him into something else entirely, it would not do to consider right now.

"Let's go," he said. "In then out again. Food, drink, toilet, and then we'll go to meet them. Lane and Sophia. We'll go to them and they can take you home." *And I'll find Steven*, he thought, *and will he look like those things that were chained up at Porton Down? Those people, living food, chained to the wall for the berserkers to have at whenever they felt hungry?* "Will he?" Tom asked out loud, but Natasha did not answer.

He looked down at the girl in his arms—the corpse that had started to move—and opened the car door.

CHAPTER ELEVEN

Tom's life had been dominated by the loss of his only child. Since then he had spent a long time thinking about what this meant, and how he had changed, and how Steven's death had affected everything. He had come to realise that there are times that pin your life to the background scope of the universe. These vital moments—not necessarily defining moments, but instants that dictate the course of your life—can be few and far between, or many and varied. They can be significant happenings, or apparently inconsequential events. They set the course of your future and paint the route of your past, and your present pivots around them.

When Tom climbed from the car with Natasha in his arms there came one such moment. A policeman passed by just as Tom nudged the car door shut with his hip. He was tall and thin and tired-looking, but his eyes changed as they passed over Tom and Natasha. Became more alert. Became aware.

A second later the policeman looked away, frowning, and rubbed at his temples as he passed through the sliding doors into the service station, as if trying to massage a memory back into his tired mind.

She's in them as well! Tom thought.

A mother passed by towing two children by their arms. All three looked at Tom and what he carried, and all three looked away again, the children ceasing their struggles and complaints.

In their minds, just like she's in mine.

Yes, Natasha said, *except you know me.*

Tom walked on, crossing the car park and skirting between cars. In a couple of vehicles he saw people glancing at him and then away again, slight frowns creasing their brows. A man tightened his grip on a steering wheel, knuckles as white as his face. A woman picked up a book and opened it, scanning its upside down pages. He approached a group of teenagers wearing baggy jeans and baseball caps, laughing and joking and cursing their way up their pack's pecking order. He paused, Natasha's weight shifted in his arms, and he doubted her. She silenced his doubt when the teenagers fell quiet, all six of them looking down as if comparing their trainer brands.

Tom walked by, passed through the sliding doors into the service station, made for the toilets. More people ignored him, and he felt a thrill at what was happening. He felt invisible. He was invulnerable, even though the bullet in his back was grinding against a bone, injecting his spine with a pain that even Natasha could not swallow whole. Service stations had always struck Tom as impersonal places where nobody really cared; now, he was as far away from the centre of attention as he had even been.

Once in the bathroom he went to the farthest cubicle, locked the door and sat on the toilet seat. His legs and arms began to shake and he had to set Natasha down, resting her back against the closed door. The blanket fell from her face and he closed his eyes, not wishing to see the mummified features that seemed to have changed. *Were her eyes really that open before?* he thought. *Was her mouth really that wide?* Natasha was not with him right then, and he hoped she could not hear his thoughts. He would have hated for her to hear the disgust he could not keep from his mind.

"I need to clean up," he said. His voice called her in from wherever she had been and the body in the blanket shifted slightly, settling. Tom looked away.

He grabbed wads of toilet roll and went about cleaning the blood from his back.

"You were controlling those people," he said.

No, just giving them other pictures in their heads.

"Some of them looked confused."

It depends on what pictures I give them.

"What pictures do you give me?" he asked, trying to remember what Jo sounded and smelled like, unable to do either.

Soon you can mourn, Natasha said. *Soon.*

"You're controlling me—"

No, Daddy! Just giving you different pictures.

Tom unrolled some more toilet paper and dabbed

again at his wound. Most of the blood had dried into a hard crisp across his back and buttocks, and he would need more than dry tissue to remove it. But he was more concerned at the wound itself. It should have killed him. He knew that Natasha was doing something to ease the pain, giving while she took, but the fact that he could find nothing of the hole other than a scabbed mess of ridged skin and blood brought him back to Natasha's memory of the attack on the house. In the boat on the return journey, she had looked at her family and seen their wounds already healing. That was a berserker thing, and now it was happening to him.

Tom cleaned up as best he could, used the toilet, then left the bathroom. Natasha cast herself about again and eyes were averted, comments died on lips, attention flowing away from Tom and Natasha as if pushed away by a magnetic field. In the shop he picked up some food and drink and a couple of T-shirts. He paid the girl behind the till, trying his best to catch her eye, but she looked anywhere but at Tom. He hefted the weight in his arms but the girl did not look. She put his change on the counter instead of dropping it in his hand, turned away from him and ran her fingertips down a rack of cigarette packets, as if the truth to life itself were printed alongside the government health warnings.

"I'm going now!" Tom shouted. Music continued to play through speakers hidden away in the ceiling, people still chattered and ate and stretched road stiffness from their limbs, fruit machines pinged and flashed and lured people in . . . but none of it touched Tom and Natasha. They were ghosts, and by the time they left Tom guessed they would be little more than a niggle in the mind of even the most observant traveler.

Back at the BMW he lowered Natasha into the front passenger seat and strapped her in without thinking. Easing into the driver's seat, fingers stroking the key in the ignition, he looked sideways at the girl. She remained still, and all he could see of her was a matted clump of hair protruding above the tatty blanket.

"You're a little girl," he said. "You're not a corpse anymore."

"Thank you, Daddy," Natasha said, her crackling voice muffled beneath the blanket.

He turned the key and started the car, and as he pulled back onto the motorway, Natasha was a presence beside him as never before.

Cole had never understood the true meaning of frustration until now. The last ten years had been a period of dashed hopes and rekindled fears, and each time he had felt close to tracking down the escaped berserkers something had come along to scupper his plans. He realised now that he had never really been close at all; it was always his mind telling him that he was, giving subconscious meaning to the life he was leading and the things he had done to get there. The memory of people dying by his hand was not an easy one to live with, and it was only the importance of what he was doing that kept him going. He had been angry, yes, and impatient, and disappointed that most leads seemed to lead nowhere. But true frustration had not been a part of his life, not like he felt it now. This was heart-pumping, sweat-inducing, ball-shrinking angst, a burning desire to get moving tempered by the certainty that to stay here was his best hope. Every second he hung around the garage—still ignored by the mechanic, still someone else's problem—Tom and Natasha drew farther away. He opened his mind to the berserker bitch but there was nothing, no sign that she was there, no indication that she was even listening for him anymore. With every breath and heartbeat he lost them some more.

Cole burned his fingers lighting a cigarette, stupidly pleased at the distraction. Pacing the forecourt of the garage was pointless, so he went around to the back, looking for a suitable landing site for a helicopter. It was quiet around there, deserted, a field strewn with old car parts and oily engines like machine's tombstones. Too dangerous for a helicopter.

He walked back to the roadside, looked both ways, swore loudly. Nobody answered so he swore again, giving the finger to a frowning passenger in a passing car. The swearing did not make him feel any better so he continued, varying the words, desperate to purge the feeling of doom that had percolated through his body and which now swung from his bones like shadow monkeys.

He'd made the call almost an hour ago. Shouldn't Higgins be here by now? Didn't he have a fleet of helicopters standing by for just such an eventuality? Or had ten years softened the major? Maybe now he was just a desk jockey killing time until retirement. Cole hated the idea of that, but he thought it likely. Even ten years ago, the major had been unwilling to go to Cole's lengths to track down the berserkers. *They're perfect,* the old fool had said. *There's no way on earth they'd let us catch them, so why even try?*

"Because they're fucking killers!" Cole whispered to the afternoon air, and the accusation echoed back at him from nowhere.

But he had killed for good reasons, hadn't he? He'd murdered through necessity, and always quickly. He had never let anyone suffer. No torture. No sadistic shit. Just a quick bullet to the head, death before they knew it was coming. He thought of Natasha lying beneath his gun, closed his eyes, hoped so much that he would see that opportunity before the day was through. And as if it would help find her, he silently promised to kill her quickly.

"Where the fuck is he!" he shouted. A man filling his car with fuel glanced over and Cole stared him down. The man hurried to the shop to pay, head lowered, and Cole looked at his car. The driver's door was open and the keys were in the ignition.

Back to the shop: the man was staring fixedly at the woman behind the till. She too was avoiding looking at Cole, which made him certain that they were talking about him.

It was a Ford Mondeo, turbo diesel, fast and filled with fuel.

The man glanced at Cole then away again, pretending to peruse the display of wine and spirits behind the counter. Selling alcohol in a petrol station—Cole had never understood that. May as well sell guns in a bank.

He looked along the road in both directions, heart thumping with the potential of the chase to come. No sign of Higgins. He'd described to the major the car Tom was driving, said he'd wait here to be picked up, and the idea that maybe Higgins would pass him by only came to him then, a possibility that he tried to disregard but which was now growing and growing in his mind, taking over, taking only seconds to establish itself and convince him of its veracity. Higgins was going after them himself, and the killings that Cole had perpetrated would be for nothing if he wasn't there to see all this end.

"Fuck!" He flicked his cigarette away and strode for the Mondeo just as the man emerged from the shop. "You better just stay there!" Cole said, pointing, staring, and the man dropped the bag of sweets he had been carrying.

"N-n-no . . ." he said, eyes going wide.

"Just a car," Cole said. "You'll get another. I need it. Don't fucking move." He reached around and grabbed the pistol tucked into his belt, but let it go again. No need to cause such a scene now. He noticed the mechanic peering around the corner of the building, cigarette dipped from the corner of his mouth. "Somebody else's problem," Cole said to both men. "That's me. Leave it that way."

"N-no!" the car owner said, and he took two steps forward.

Cole pulled the gun. Everything froze. Even the sound of traffic seemed to lessen, as if involved in this moment.

"Puh . . . please," the man begged.

Cole ignored him, lowered himself into the car, slammed the door, placed the pistol between his thighs, started the engine and pulled away. Music blasted on, some weird whiny jangly shit, and Cole turned it up so that he could not hear the man shouting at him. He saw him, though, running after the car as Cole drove it from the forecourt and onto the road, performing a perfect U-turn and aiming back at the motorway.

Higgins had left him! That fucking jobs-worth gorilla. At least Cole knew he had been believed; Higgins would already have been told about the excavated grave on the Plain, and it would take only minutes to check with police about the stolen car and the showdown at the holiday cottage. So whether Cole was involved or not, he knew that Higgins would have called in every favour owed to him to get a force together looking for Tom and Natasha. He may have been reluctant a decade ago, but the Major would never pass up a chance like this. Especially so close to retirement.

Cole steered onto the motorway and put his foot down, lifting the car up to one hundred with ease. Traffic was relatively light, and he hogged the outside lane and flashed drivers aside when he drew up behind them. His aggressive driving attracted some angry gestures, but Cole ignored them. If only these idiots knew what he was doing and why. Secure in their own blinkered worlds they had no comprehension of what really existed around the dark corner of their existence. They had no idea of the horrors he had seen, which he now hunted to kill. So he let them throw him the finger, flash their lights and honk their horns, comfortable in the knowledge that he was doing all this for them. His legs ached, he bled from various wounds, he was a killer, and it was all for them.

"What the hell *is* this shit?" Cole ejected the CD. It was bright yellow and decorated with a picture of weird, colourful, fluffy characters. As he dropped it he heard a sound that caused his heart to stutter in surprise.

A baby crying.

CHAPTER TWELVE

Natasha was away again, perhaps talking with Lane and Sophia. Tom was terrified. What he had seen of these berserkers in Natasha's memories was enough to scare anyone, but his mind kept drifting back to what he had seen of their prey. The men and women in the drug house basement, torn and killed and eaten. The two men and one woman they had brought back with them to the boat, naked and shivering and bleeding, little more than fodder. None of them had been with the berserkers later in the truck.

And the people chained to the wall in the berserkers' living quarters at Porton Down. They had looked like corpses, thin from so much feeding, bags of bones that clung on tenaciously to whatever life they had.

Steven would be like that, Tom was certain. There was nothing else for him to be, and the prospect of seeing him in that state seemed worse than believing he was dead. The death of his son was something he had come to live with, if not fully accept. Now, there was a chance that the past ten years would be tipped on their back, and that a whole new history would have to be written for Tom's life.

And with Jo gone—

They're telling me where to go, Natasha said. She had not spoken out loud since leaving the service station. Maybe it was too much effort, or perhaps it pained her. *Keep driving north. They'll be waiting for us and they'll tell us where to find them.*

"Don't you know where they are?"

Natasha was silent for a while, yet still there, and her doubt made Tom uncomfortable.

Well, she said at last, *they're not telling me. I don't think they trust me very much. They know what happened to us, but they don't understand how I'm still alive. I told them about Mister Wolf and what he did, but . . . I don't think they believe me.*

"Do they mention Steven?"

Again that pause, just slightly too long. *No.*

"They must know that Cole's after us. Why would they risk—?"

Because I'm one of them.

Natasha withdrew from his mind and Tom drove on. He kept his eyes on the road and concentrated on staying within the white lines. His back was a throbbing pain now, and it itched all across its base. It was the sort of itch that accompanied healing. Since Natasha's last feeding he had felt better, calmed perhaps, stress suckled away. But however much he tried to convince himself that the healing was charged by his own body, he knew that was not the case. Natasha took, and she gave as well. Just what she gave he could not dwell upon right then. It made him better, it helped him drive, and every moment took him closer to Steven.

And Steven was the only good that could come out of this mess. His son. Tom would take him away and make him well again, guide him through the process of finding home, love him just as much as he had loved his memory for the last decade. They would be a family again.

"My family," Tom whispered, awed. The idea was amazing.

The baby would not stop crying.

For a few seconds after first hearing it Cole had almost stopped the car. He would exit the motorway, return to the petrol station, give the kid back to its father and then leave again. Except it would not happen like that and he knew it. There would be complications. Nothing could ever be that simple. *Oh, here you are, I stole your car and kidnapped your baby but please take the kid back now . . . er, but I still need your car, and you'll recall I have a pistol in the waistband of my jeans?* The police would have been called, the father would be frantic, the mechanic would no longer consider it someone else's problem, and apart from the time he would waste Cole had no wish to become embroiled in some messy forecourt brawl.

And there's the woman I shot, he thought, *her blood all*

over the MX5. They'd have noticed that by now as well. He tried not to think of how frantic the father of the baby would be. *I'm doing this for you and your kid,* he thought. But no good intentions or moral justification would stop the brat from screaming.

"Shut up!" Cole shouted. It worked for a minute and then the crying started again. He frowned, bit his lip and concentrated on driving.

That was when the dead brunette with the pale thighs and black underwear came into his mind.

Cole shouted and let go of the steering wheel, and bad tracking swerved the car over toward the hard shoulder. He grabbed the wheel and brought it back under control, panting, trying to calm his racing heart and wishing he could close himself off to what he had just felt. Because she had been there. That dead woman, brains blasted out by a shot he had not intended for her, had appeared in his mind unbidden, uninvited, and he knew it was more than his imagination because he could smell her, taste her. It was more than just a memory. She had risen briefly from the underground— shifting aside a manhole cover and rising from the darkness, a ghost he had never intended creating—and he had dwelled on her parted legs and skimpy black underwear, hating himself but unable to shake the image.

The baby cried.

"Leave me alone!" Cole said, not exactly sure to whom he was speaking. The smell of the woman was still there, a mixture of Obsession and the decay already creeping into her cooling flesh. Her body must have been found by now, but her mind, her soul, surprised by an unexpected death, had become lost in the darkness of his subconscious. He was sure it would rise again.

She shouldn't be dead, he thought. *I shouldn't have loosed off that shot.*

The baby gurgled in agreement, then started crying again. Cole twisted the rearview mirror so that he could glance at the kid. She was bundled up in pink, and her face had coloured to match her coat. Tears streamed down her face.

"I'll stop soon," he said, "don't worry, there, shhh, shhh." He had no idea how to handle children other than what he had seen on TV. And now he was a kidnapper as well as a murderer. *It's all for them,* he thought, *all for the sheep.*

The woman rose in his mind once more, drifting up out of the dark and revealing herself fully to his scrutiny, and her name was Lucy-Anne. She was there with him, a true presence instead of a simple memory. He gasped, and as he took in the next breath he could taste her, a saltiness to her cooling skin. She moved in his mind and revealed her pale thighs once more, good legs, sexy underwear that she had never expected to display to a bunch of crime scenes officers today. She pulled those panties aside, and much as Cole tried to draw away from what was happening, he could not. He could smell and taste her, and his guilt did nothing to change what he was smelling and tasting. He could see everything but her face.

The baby cried on. Cole drove. Lucy-Anne's ghost

tortured him and he found himself crying, great shuddering sobs that blurred his vision. The car drifted over two lanes and vehicles swerved to avoid him, their brakes smoking angrily. He wiped his eyes and regained control of the car, but Lucy-Anne was still there. She was back in the driver's seat of the MX5, her head blown apart and her legs splayed wide, inviting him in to finish raping her body. He had raped her life with a bullet from the .45, and now there was little left for her to protect. He knew her anger and rage. He ran the streets of his mind to escape her, but she was always faster, always there.

"I'm sorry," he whispered, "I'm so sorry."

The baby cried, and so did Cole. He had never been haunted before.

Tom drove on, observing the speed limit. He breathed shallow, expecting any deep breaths to burst his wound and set the blood flowing again. He felt so delicate.

Natasha was away. She had been gone for ten minutes, and he hoped she was talking with the other berserkers, finding out where they would be. Tom did not think he could go on for much longer. He drove toward the light of Steven's life, leaving behind the darkness of Jo's death. That darkness would fall again, and when it came it would be hard and heavy and difficult to accept. But for now Jo was somewhere away from here, a loving memory that he was reserving for later when things were better. Natasha had done something to help him with this; that made him uncomfortable, yet he accepted it. For now.

The present pulled him on and he went with the flow.

Beside him, like a bag of shells being shaken, Natasha giggled.

Lucy-Anne giggled. It was a grotesque sound and Cole tried to ignore it, but it was insistent, reverberating through all the dark places of his mind and echoing into the streets of his psyche. He could not escape himself, and that was where Lucy-Anne was. Inside. In him. *With* him, because of what he had done to her. Her giggle seemed misplaced but he was not in a state of mind to really dwell on that.

The baby was still screaming, and Cole knew he had to stop. He could not go on like this; guilt would not let him, and neither would the pulsing headache the kid's screaming was giving him. The question was, what could he do? He could not just pull over and leave the baby by the side of the motorway, and to exit would lose him precious time. He was still only assuming that Roberts had driven north with Natasha, and now that Major Higgins seemed to have abandoned him, he could think of no real way to trace them. Higgins would likely have the police at his disposal; road cameras, patrol cars, aerial surveillance. Cole could rely on nothing more than Natasha's occasional mockery to locate her.

He needed her to come to him again, let him know how far and fast they had moved. As ever the idea of inviting her into his mind was ghastly, yet he could think of no other way. Besides, she would have good company in there.

The ghost of Lucy-Anne presented itself again and Cole cringed, trying to see past the image floating across his mind like a shadow over the sun. He saw through her but could not ignore her presence. She was there again, and now he could see her face as well, her ruined head spilling blood and brains over her clothes, her thighs, her legs propped wide in the same way he had seen her spilled from the driver's seat of the MX5. She was inviting him in and he could not pull away, could not avert his eyes as she pulled her underwear aside, and he knew why she was doing this. He had thought fleetingly that this was the sort of woman he liked to fuck, and perhaps she had died right then, at the exact moment of his thinking that. She had grabbed onto that thought and was using it now to tear him apart.

"Shut up!" he screamed at the crying baby.

Lucy-Anne giggled again, a ragged sound as if she were gargling razors. She slipped away and retreated underground, leaving only the smells and tastes behind.

Cole breathed deeply, opening the window to try and purge the taste of a dead woman's pussy from his mouth.

"No!" She was not doing this. He was doing it to himself.

The baby still cried.

The sun glinted from the pistol on the seat beside him, a precise piece of engineering, unhindered by human doubt and faults of the mind.

She came at him yet again, approaching from behind and wrapping her limbs around his mind in a grotesque parody of animalistic lovemaking. She ground her dead self against his imagination and raped it, giggling all along, forcing tears from Cole's eyes at the rancid black guilt he felt. Without thinking he reached for the gun and fumbled it, cursing as it slipped between the seats and thudded to the floor in the back of the car.

And just what had he intended doing with it?

He shook his head and grabbed a tight hold of the steering wheel, so tight that his knuckles whitened and fingernails pressed into his palms, drawing blood. It dripped onto his trouser legs, the warm drops hitting his wounded thighs. They were stiffening even more from where Roberts had run him over. More blood dripped.

He thought of Natasha.

And then she was in his mind, had been there all along, her face wrapped up with that of Lucy-Anne's, her wicked intentions clear even as she performed a grotesque dance with the false mannequin of a dead woman's ghost.

"Get the fuck out of my head!" Cole shouted, hating the little berserker bitch even more than he ever had before. She had fooled him into seeing a ghost, and there was only one reason why she would have possibly done that: entertainment. "Get out you little bitch!"

Temper, temper, Mister Wolf, Natasha said. *You'll upset the baby.* The smell and taste of the dead woman vanished suddenly, replaced by the stench of nothing. Cole had never smelled emptiness, and he suddenly wished for the stink of the dead woman again. However manufactured, and whatever terrible guilt it conjured, at least it was better than this. *But this is your life*, Natasha said. *Nothing. Empty. And soon, utterly pointless.*

"Not pointless when I catch you and kill you," he said.

Well, you're getting much warmer, she said. *Keep coming . . . keep coming Mister Wolf. Everyone's dying to meet you again.* She left, emptying his mind, and he gasped at the sudden sense of being set adrift. Her leaving dragged away all remnants of the faux ghost, and for that he was glad. But rather than relief he was filled with sadness, a realisation that his life *was* empty, had been, and would be forever.

"It's you doing this to me, Natasha," he said, and the baby suddenly stopped crying as if in agreement.

Cole looked in the rearview mirror, stared into the baby's eyes and saw the wonder of potential alight in there. In his own eyes, the fresh glint of determination. "For you," he said, talking to this new human now, not the filthy bitch berserker. "For you I'm doing all this. And you know that, don't you?" The baby stared, seeing only Cole's eyes in the mirror, and it's lower lip pulled down as it prepared to cry again. "Don't cry," Cole said. "Not yet. Not until I've finished. Then you can cry for me, or cry for all of us. There'll be nothing in between."

Shaking, filled with a renewed purpose, Cole drove on.

"What were you laughing at?" Tom asked.

Natasha remained silent and still beside him. He had heard nothing since that gruff giggle, and it had taken a few minutes to find his nerve again after that. It had sounded so adult, and so unlike Natasha.

His question unanswered, he drove on. It felt as though he had been driving forever. Yesterday he had woken to begin his drive out onto the moors, last night he had traveled though the night with the body of a girl in his boot, and today he had been fleeing the bullets of the madman who had buried her, come back now to finish the job. His back ached, not just from the gunshot wound but also from simple road-tiredness. He could not go on forever, and Natasha had promised him that this journey would be over soon.

After that . . . he was not sure.

He passed a police car parked on the hard shoulder. He glanced down at his speedometer—eighty, ten miles per hour over the limit—and watched in the mirrors for the flashing blue light as the car came in pursuit. But it remained parked where it was, fading quickly behind him. Everyone on the road seemed to be going as fast or faster than him. Perhaps the police were waiting for someone special.

"They'd have a field day with me," he said, smiling without humour.

Not far now, Natasha said. *They're on their way, all of them. They'll meet us in two hours.*

"Where?"

A pause, now familiar, one that displayed uncertainty. *I don't know yet.*

"Tell me about yourself," Tom said, and the statement surprised him as much as Natasha. Yet those few simple words seemed to open doors. After everything he had been through with this strange girl, everything she had done to him and shown him, his own statement of curiosity marked a vital change in their day. The imminent threat of Cole was still there, but now there was also the comfort of company.

Well . . . She paused, and Tom could sense her confusion. He heard her shifting in her seat slightly, perhaps uncomfortable. He did not look. He was still uneasy at the fact of her body coming back to life. *I've shown you so much already*, she said. He felt her draw back in his mind, a diminishing presence that gave him room. No probing fingers now, no questing thoughts. She was releasing her touch, remaining there only to talk to him. It was as if that simple question had inspired a newfound respect for the man who had rescued her.

"You've shown me, but why can't you tell me? You asked me if I would be your daddy. I saw what happened to your real father, but I know nothing about him. And really I know nothing about you. Other than thinking you should be dead."

I'm a berserker, being buried—

"I know that, but I don't understand what it means. Tell me, Natasha. I'm tired. Talk to me. Keep me awake until we get to Lane and Sophia. I reckon everything will change again when that happens, and we might not get a chance to talk again like this."

Like this, he had said. Alone. Intimate. But he

267

guessed that by the end of that day, the two of them would likely never talk to each other again, ever. And he knew that she knew, too.

My father was a good man. Berserkers are old, they live a long time, and Daddy was almost a hundred when Mister Wolf killed him.

I cried when Daddy died, but I wasn't given time to mourn for him properly. I'm just a little girl . . . and that's so unfair. When I was buried I cried myself dry. I don't think I'll ever cry again, even when I'm whole. I don't think I can.

Berserkers and humans, I know you wonder about that, I've seen it in your mind. Berserkers are humans, just different. They're made differently, but Mummy always said that doesn't mean they can't live together. And for thousands of years they did. They still do, in fact, because there are thousands of us all over the world. Or so Mummy told me. I don't really know for myself, because Porton Down is all I can remember. When you dug me up and took me away, that was the first taste of freedom I've ever had.

But sometimes I think Mummy lied. Sometimes I think there's just us, and we're freaks, and maybe we were never truly born at all. I'm alone, but that idea makes me lonelier still.

So we lived together, people and berserkers, though they were ignorant of us for a long time. Then my parents were caught, along with Lane and Sophia. I asked them a lot how that happened, and where, and why, but most of the answers were kept from me. The only reason for that is home, the place where berserkers used to live that was beyond the eyes of normal people. A place underground, with almost everything we needed to survive. If I knew all about it and where it was, that would put me in danger, and put home in danger. It was a safe place then and it's still safe now. I think that's where Lane and Sophia went with their children. And I hope that's where they're going to take us. It's so close I can almost taste it.

Things feel different now, Daddy. Now that Mister Wolf has come back, things feel very different. I hope they can go back to how they were years ago, before I was born . . . but I'm not sure they can. We're known now, you see. People know of us. And as Mummy told me, it was always being unknown that made it easy for us to survive.

The berserkers took people, sometimes. You know that. I understand what that may mean to you, but it's the way we lived, the way nature made us. You take pigs and cows and sheep, we took people. At least we murder for food within our own species. Lane and the others must have been doing that these last ten years, but maybe not much, and maybe not near home. We'll see, they'll tell us. And then there's . . .

Natasha trailed off, falling into that uncomfortable silence that Tom was growing to understand. She had things to say that she did not wish him to hear.

"And then there's Steven," he said, finishing for her. "Food for them. Fresh food. Kept in their home like so much fodder."

Don't sound bitter, Daddy.

"He's my son!" Tom said, and a spear of pain bit into his back. *Is that you?* he thought. *Is that you punishing me, Natasha?* "And I'm not your daddy. You saw him shot. I saw that in your memory, and however much you try to shut it out it's still there, fresh and clear." The pain stayed away, but Tom felt as if he were balancing on the edge of a lake of agony. Only Natasha's hand held onto him, and were she to let go he would drown.

You said you'd be my new daddy, she said, her voice hitching, dry sobs taking the place of breaths. Tom remembered how the young Steven made him feel like the worst father in the world with one tear, and Natasha had the same gift. Maybe all children do. Too small to protect themselves, they manipulate the emotions of adults to do so.

"I will," Tom said. "I am. You're like a new baby, aren't you? Birthed up from the ground, growing, learning? And what was the first thing you saw?"

You.

"Me." She stroked his mind and the pain in his back went away, shoved down with the true memories of the past day. It would be back, along with Jo, and when that time came the pain and grief may well kill him. But if he had Steven in his arms by then, perhaps he would be able to fight through them both.

It took Cole another half an hour to realise the enormity of what he was doing. He'd stolen a car, yes, but *he'd stolen someone's baby as well!* The little girl had dropped off to sleep, lulled by the motion of the car, and for that he was glad. But he kept the rearview mirror twisted down, and he continued checking that she was alright. The crying had ceased, Natasha had left him alone and dragged the imaginary ghost away with her, and Cole was on his own. It gave him time to think.

He passed a police car parked on the side of the motorway, glanced in his side mirror, certain that it would come after him. He watched, drove, watched, glanced at the sleeping girl . . . and when he looked back one last time the police car had lurched onto the motorway, lights flashing and smoke clouding up the air behind it from screeching tires.

"Oh shit, here we go," he muttered. He had not considered what he would do if it came down to this—not really—but he had the gun and it was still back on the seat beside him, witing for Natasha. He could not let anything get in the way of that.

The police car was gaining rapidly. Cole considered trying to get away, but that would never happen. The longer the chase went on, the more reinforcements they would call. More cars, a helicopter, road blocks, and he would be a rat in a trap, unable to escape however determined he was, however big his gun. Best to confront them as quickly as possible, hand over the kid and . . . what? Kill two policemen? Shoot them in cold blood so that he could get away and, perhaps, finish what had started ten years ago?

"All for you," he said to the baby's reflection. The image of the dead woman flashed before him again and he gasped, but this time it was only his own memory dredging up the filth Natasha had put before him. He pushed it from his mind and indicated to pull over onto the hard shoulder.

Maybe it'll go by, he thought, *maybe they're after some-one else, on another call. Maybe I'll be that lucky.* But the patrol car slowed behind him and, lights still flashing, pulled over and parked twenty feet behind his car.

"Not long to go now," he muttered. "Not long and it'll all be over. The bitch will be dead and hopefully Lane and Sophia, too. Not long until the end of the day. End of the day." He had to think quickly. He could see the two policemen as shadows in their car, one of them talking on the radio, checking registration num-ber and—

And they'd know he had a gun.

"Why wait?" he said. He looked once more in the mirror at the sleeping baby, then threw open his door, grabbing the pistol as he went.

He walked quickly toward the patrol car, carrying the gun at his side and not yet aiming it. Last thing he wanted was some vigilante motorist deciding to nudge him into the ditch at eighty miles per hour, and bran-dishing a gun at a police car in broad daylight beside the motorway would be just the ticket.

The policemen kept their windows up. He didn't care. On the passenger side he shot out the front tire, took a few more steps, shot out the rear tire, and only then did he tap the barrel against the glass. The policeman's face was inches from the gun and he looked terrified, pale and sweating, his shirt sticking to his chest and shoulders.

"Open!" Cole shouted. He knew they could hear him. "Open up now!" He turned the gun so that it was aiming straight through the glass. The policeman's eyes opened wide, as if trying to look far enough into the barrel to see the round that would kill him. "Three seconds!" Cole shouted, and the door clicked open.

Cole stepped back and motioned the man out. The policeman climbed from the car and kept his back against it, never once taking his eyes from the pistol.

"Driver, out this side," Cole said.

"Where's the baby?" the driver asked. He climbed across the front seats and stood slowly next to his partner. He looked less shaken and more in control, and Cole knew that this was where his trouble could come from.

"In the car asleep," he said. "I didn't know she was in there when I took the car. Now listen, both of you. This has the potential to go very wrong, but I don't want it to. There's a simple rule for both of you to remember over the next couple of minutes, and if you do, everything will go down fine: I have a gun, and you don't." The driver glanced down at the weapon briefly. The passenger's eyes never left it. "You!" Cole said. The passenger looked up, eyes still wide. "I want you to take off your radio, and your mate's, and stamp on them."

"But—"

"Do as he says," the driver said. "He knows we've already called it in." The passenger did so, crunching the radio attachments into the tarmac. He stood back against the car again, still hardly able to keep his eyes from the pistol aimed at his guts.

"This needs to go very smooth," Cole said. "Very, very smooth."

"You don't look too good," the driver said. "You're bashed about, your eye's swollen shut, and you were limping."

"It's been a bad day."

"It needn't continue. If you just hand over—"

"I'm not in the fucking mood for this!" Cole said. He raised the gun, stepped forward and pressed the barrel of the .45 against the passenger's forehead, hard enough to leave an impression in the skin. The man pissed himself. It was more than Cole could have hoped for. "Feels warm to start with, doesn't it?" he said. "Warm and unpleasant. You'll smell it soon. And there's nothing like the feel of cold piss around your bollocks."

"No need for that, son," the driver said. "This doesn't need to get ugly."

"No, it doesn't," Cole said. For one crazy moment his finger squeezed on the trigger. He imagined Roberts standing there before him instead of this unknown copper. He so wanted to put a bullet through the meddling fuck's brain, blast out all the bullshit he'd lived through these past twenty-four hours; Natasha invading his mind, the mockery, the two women he had killed, and the ghost of Lucy-Anne that Natasha had haunted him with.

Then he eased back, lowered the gun, sighed. "You, go to the car and get the kid. Back door on this side, away from the road. You do anything other than open the door and take out the baby, I'll shoot your boss."

The passenger, eyes wide, pistol barrel impression a

white full moon on his forehead, walked stiffly toward the Mondeo.

"You know there's an armed response unit on its way right now, don't you?" the driver said.

"Of course. That's why I want to get away quickly. And next time I stop they may even be able to help."

"What do you mean?"

Cole shook his head and smiled at the thought of relaying everything that was happening. "You have no idea."

"Well, I can't let you leave."

"You will."

"I can't."

Cole stared at the man and could not help being impressed. "You're brave," he said. "But you're not stupid."

The policeman glanced away, and Cole knew that he had won.

The other policeman carried the baby back to the patrol car, both of them stinking of piss.

"I never meant to take the kid," Cole said. "Tell her father that. Tell him to take better care of her. And tell him . . . I'm looking after her. And him. And you two as well, if only you knew it. Now step aside." He motioned them away from the police car with the gun, leaned in and put several rounds into the dashboard radio, the steering column and the gearbox. The gunshots woke the baby and she started crying again.

"See how you like that," Cole said. "It's okay for the first three seconds, then it really starts to piss you off." He turned to walk back to the Mondeo.

"Son?"

Cole paused. The driver had advanced a couple of steps in front of his crippled patrol car.

"Son, drop it," he said. "Wait here with us. You can keep hold of the gun, but don't go driving off again. You do that, and you know how all this will end. You don't want to be just another item on the news, do you?"

Cole considered for a moment, thinking of the various strands now drawing together somewhere up ahead. Roberts and the waking berserker girl; Lane and Sophia and their kids, probably even now coming out from their hidey-hole to meet them; Major Higgins and whatever military presence he had been able to muster; the police armed response units streaking this way even now; and him, Cole, a murderer with nothing left to live for other than the obsession that had taken his life.

"No," he said. "No, I have no idea how all this will end." He walked to the Mondeo, took a few seconds to restock the pistol's magazine, then drove away.

CHAPTER THIRTEEN

Natasha had said he was getting warmer. Cole was trusting everything he was doing now on the word of the lying little berserker bitch, and he hated every aspect of that. It was almost four o'clock, and soon the sun would be setting. He didn't think he could go another night without sleep.

His head still hurt from where Roberts had knocked him out. Since then he had crashed a car, been attacked by Roberts and been run over, and his body was not thanking him at all. He supposed he should have accepted the pain as a small price to pay for the bad things he had done that day, but it inconvenienced him, made it more difficult to drive, so he cursed every ache. His thighs, especially the left, were swelling and stiffening, and the longer he sat still in the car the less easy it would be to move when the time came.

"Where are you, you little bitch?" he said, hoping that she would answer. Nothing.

He drove quickly. There was no point in trying to avoid being pulled over; the police were after him anyway, and the faster he drove the longer it would take for the armed response unit to catch up. Once they were on him it would be over, no way to avoid them, no way to outrun them, and as he'd already shot up a police car they would be taking no chances.

Damn you, Higgins! If the major had kept his word and taken Cole along, perhaps they'd already be on Roberts and the girl. Maybe the major already was. If he had a helicopter and contact with the police, the final battle may already be taking place. *But I don't think so,* Cole thought. And not for the first time he wondered just how much information Natasha could pluck out of his head.

It took ten minutes for the armed response unit to pick him up.

He passed a motorway exit, drove quickly under the overpass and drew level with the entrance ramp when he saw the car streaking down from above. Though unmarked, its speed gave it away, and when Cole looked over he saw two faces pressed against the side windows. They were evidently as surprised as him.

Both men turned quickly away, and that confirmed Cole's fears.

He had only seconds to act. He pressed down on the gas and moved forward, drawing level with the police car as it came down the ramp toward the inside lane. They obviously planned to pull ahead of him and then slow down, perhaps nudge him from the road if he failed to pull over. Cole could not allow that. He had one chance to move on, only one, and that was to disable the armed unit here and now. If he got embroiled in an extended chase there would be others, called in from the surrounding countryside to head him off at the next junction. Cole was a good driver, but he was also realistic; he knew that there was little chance of escaping a police chase.

And if they managed to stop him, he'd likely be shot.

He had seen this done in movies, and it always looked easy. But he was not kidding himself. Making sure his seatbelt was clicked in properly he drifted across the motorway into the outside lane, looked left without turning his head, saw the police car move onto the motorway and pick up speed. And then he turned sharply to the left and broadsided them.

The impact was shattering. The steering wheel jumped from his hands and turned to the right, jerking him back across the road. He passed between a lorry and a minibus filled with pensioners, staring at him with grey disapproval. Horns blared, brakes screamed, and Cole only just managed to bring the car under control before it barreled into the central reservation. It skimmed the metal barrier, throwing out sparks and splinters of metal from its front panel. His door buckled inward and punched his leg, and he screamed out loud as the already wounded limb was subjected to more abuse. He looked left and saw that the police car was still there, its side dented and scraped but otherwise unharmed.

The men were looking across at him again, and this time they did not avert their gaze. Cole smiled and turned hard left again.

They were ready this time, and their driver slammed on his brakes. The police car threw up a cloud of smoke as Cole drifted in front of it, and even before he realised what had happened they accelerated and rammed him from behind. He jerked back in his seat, head bouncing from the headrest, and accelerated away, shifting back into the middle lane as the police car pulled up beside him.

Left again, hard, and he caught them by surprise. Perhaps the police driver thought he'd be too shaken to drive straight into them again. Or maybe he had too much faith in his patrol car's speed. Either way, Cole connected before they could move past him. He kept a tight hold of the wheel this time and twisted it to the left, arms straight, elbows locked, foot pressed to the floor. The sound of tearing metal screamed above the protesting roar of the engine. Wheels juddered as they were torn the wrong way, and the stench of burning rubber filled the car. Glass smashed, cool air whistled in.

The police car ground over the rumble strip between the inside lane and the hard shoulder and kept going. Cole strained left, forcing them farther, and a second before their nearside wheels hit the gravel strip beside the road he swung the Mondeo back out onto the motorway. How he did not collide with any cars he did not know, but he looked in the mirror in time to see the police vehicle throw up a shower of stones as it started to spin. It completed two complete revolutions before a tire blew and it flipped onto its side.

Cole looked away, concentrating on the road ahead, hoping the men would be able to walk away from the wreck.

Less than a minute later he heard a heavy *wukka wukka* from outside. He leaned forward and looked up in time to see two Chinook helicopters pass over the motorway from east to west, fast and low and filled with intent.

"There you are," he said. He drove on, heart racing, pain from his legs keeping him alert, silently calling to Natasha.

And eventually she answered.

We need to turn west.

"Is this nearly it? Is it almost over? I can't be your daddy forever, not like this. You don't need me forever."

I need you now. And even if it does only last days, what you've done for me will be a lifetime. Just because we may not be together, that doesn't mean you won't still be my daddy. Just like you and Steven. You never stopped believing, did you? You never stopped being there for him?

"I still don't know if Steven is alive or dead."

Natasha paused again, that telling silence. *We need to turn west.*

Tom glanced across at her body beneath the old blanket. She seemed to have shifted slightly, as if making herself comfortable, though it could have been the movement of the car shuffling her corpse down in the seat. He had seen her moving, he had listened to her speaking, yet still he found it difficult to believe. "Is Steven as alive as you?" he asked.

I don't know, Natasha replied.

Tom turned off at the next exit. The road curved up and away from the motorway and joined an A-road, aiming west toward where the sun was melting into the horizon. He thought of them driving that far—reaching for the sun—and though the idea was foolish, it felt right. They were heading toward impossibilities. Natasha was leading him out of the world, and he was following willingly. Because however much she said *she* needed *him*, Tom knew it was Natasha doing the leading. It always had been. If he turned the car around now and headed back south, he guessed he would be dead from his bullet wound by sunset.

The road curved through the countryside, passing between low hills and bare fields. Trees and hedgerows caught the sun and burned slowly in its dusky glare, their leaves licking at the air with each breeze. Tom loved autumn. It was a time of death and decay, but also a time of survival. Plants shed their flowers and retreated beneath ground for the winter. Squirrels stored nuts in secret caches to see them through the harsh weather. And though dead leaves spiraled down to rot, their cousins would bloom again in a few short months. Autumn was beauty in death, the future in decay. Tom wondered what Natasha thought of it, this autumn that was her spring.

"Will you become alive?" he asked.

I already am alive.

"You know what I mean. Will you move. Will you . . . grow? Change? Fill out?"

You've seen me move and you've heard me speak. It hurts when I do both, but it feels good as well. It reminds me what being alive means.

"What *does* it mean?" Tom asked, and as the question left his lips its import struck him like another bullet. *What does it mean?* It was a question that he had asked many times before, both out loud, and more often silently. He would often lay awake at night, watching shadows expand across the bedroom ceiling as the moon phased across the sky. The shadows were slow; they had plenty of time. The question would pose itself again at the strangest of moments, and he was never quite ready for it, never prepared to suffer its weight. It would send him into a daydream of confusion, or a spiral of depression. Not because he could not find the answer—he guessed that nobody ever could, not really—but because he believed any chance he had of even guessing was long since past. He was growing old without really knowing what life meant for him. He despaired at that, and the despair only served to cloud his thinking more.

Now, though . . . for the first time in decades, he believed that the possibility of truly considering the question would soon be open to him. Here he was surrounded by life, death and whatever lay in between. Over the past two days he had been living and witnessing extremes— Jo's death, Steven's life, and his own battle to forge on whilst understanding neither. And here beside him the antithesis of logic: a living dead girl. A human, but a berserker. A child, but one with such old wisdom. An innocent who had done so much bad.

It means so much, Natasha said.

"I'm not sure . . ."

Being sure of that is what completes your life.

"But you're so young. Just a girl. How can *you* be sure?"

I've had a lot of time to think about it.

Tom closed his eyes, but he could not imagine ten years beneath the ground.

It's not far now, Natasha said. *Lane tells me there's an industrial estate a couple of miles farther on. It's small, secluded. We'll wait for them. They'll be there soon.*

"And then what?" Tom asked.

Then they'll take me home.

"And me?"

You'll be fine, Natasha said. *I'll make sure. I'll look after you.* And there it was, the admission, the proof that it was Natasha who was in control. She went away, withdrawing from his mind and leaving him alone.

Tom drove on, even less sure of the meaning of his life than ever.

You've nearly lost us, the little bitch was saying. *You're too far away. Always been too far. Too stupid to find Sophia and Lane, too stupid to kill me, and now you're going to lose, and you'll be worth even less than you think. You'll be worth a spit from my mouth, a shit from my arse. You'll be worth nothing, Mister Wolf, and nothing is what you'll get.*

Cole did not answer. That she was talking to him, luring him on, was good enough for him. He was used to her ranting and raging—he'd heard it ten years before, and even though it was now all in his mind, he was already used to it again—and he was happy for her to continue, lose control, even though his prime instinct was to cringe away from the unnatural monster. He felt her down in the dark places, stalking his mind as if looking for somewhere new to surface. Perhaps she would drag up another pseudo-ghost to try to scare him. The echoes of Lucy-Anne's dying voice still haunted him, false though they were. He pictured her pale thighs and black panties, shook his head to clear the image, heard Natasha giggling in the caverns of his mind. *Bitch!* he thought, and he felt her brief spurt of anger.

He smiled. And she was luring him on. He questioned why, but did not let that stop him. Nothing would stop him. Cole nursed the .45 in his lap, silver rounds nestling in the magazine.

"These are for you," he said. "Every single one of them for you."

Couldn't do it before, won't do it this time.

"I will," he said, "without a doubt, without a twinge of guilt, and without an ounce of regret at never knowing how the boffins at Porton Down changed you."

Natasha was silent, her presence huge; speechless.

"So, I know something you didn't think I knew," he said, smiling.

I'll tell you more, she said. *I'll tell you all of it, if you want to know. Do you want to know, Mister Wolf?*

"Fuck you!" he said, and *Yes*, he thought, *yes, I want to know*.

I'd tell you what they did, if only you could catch me, Natasha said, laughing as she pulled away.

How Cole wished he could fire a bullet after her retreating mind.

The others, Lane and Sophia and their children . . . he was trying not to think about what had happened before. It got in the way too much. It obscured his purpose, threw up a roadblock between him and the bitch he was after, and he did his best to keep that past down in the underground with all the other ghosts. Yet he could not shake the memories of their escape from Porton Down, and the things he had found afterwards. The syringes. The strange drugs. The antidote to the silver that Sandra Francis had made for them.

His only way to skirt past the roadblock was to believe that their antidote had worn out.

Five miles from the motorway Natasha told Tom to turn again. A minor road curved down into a shallow valley, ending at the entrance to the industrial estate Lane had told her about. It was five thirty when they arrived there, and they drove into the main car park against the flow of traffic. Most people were leaving for home, and a few scattered lights remained on in several buildings. The sun had settled in the west and spread an orange glow across the hilltops. Sunlight caught stray clouds and lit them like Chinese lanterns. The car park quickly emptied until there was only the BMW and two other cars. One industrial unit still had its roller door open, and a man and woman were working on a large piece of furniture inside. Their radio gave dusk a classical theme.

Tom opened the window and turned off the engine. He breathed in deeply, enjoying the fresh air, relishing the coolness that seemed to light up his body as the sun illuminated the clouds. Beside him Natasha sat still, silent, away. He wondered where she was. Talking with them, probably, the other berserkers. Planning, scheming, working out the best way home. He pulled down the blanket and looked at her face. There was nothing to see.

He heard a car engine somewhere, but it faded and stopped without him seeing its lights. He tensed in his seat for a few seconds, wondering whether Sophia and Lane were here already. All he knew of them was what he had seen in Natasha's memories, and he had not liked anything he saw. They had abandoned Natasha and her family; why would they come to rescue her now? *Because I'm a berserker,* she had said, but she also told him that they were simply another species of human. And humans were always prone to betrayal and deceit. Perhaps they would not come at all. Maybe they would give the police an anonymous call, lead them here, and sit back in their home—wherever that may be—knowing that the last trace of their past at Porton Down had been destroyed.

"Natasha?" Tom said, but the girl was still away. Her frozen face offered no clues. He reached for her, fingers outstretched, but he could not bring himself to touch that leathery skin. There was some of him in her now, he knew, and the small wound in his chest prickled at the thought.

His back itched. Itched when it should have burned, annoyed when it should have killed. Yes, there was some of him in her, but there was some of her in him as well. Perhaps much more than he knew.

He closed his eyes and sought out his rage, fearing what he would find.

Natasha came back just as Tom heard the sound of something approaching.

"No!" Natasha said, her voice the grind of swallowed grit.

"What?" Tom asked. The sound grew louder, a regular, fast beat.

I never believed Cole would give us to someone else, she said in Tom's mind. *I always thought he'd want us for himself. Daddy . . . I'm sorry.*

"What are you on about? I don't understand. Are they here, are Lane and Sophia and the others here?" Tom looked around the industrial estate car park. The man and woman in the open business unit had downed tools and were standing at the door, shielding their eyes against the fading sunset, looking south down the valley. The woman lifted her hand to point and the noise suddenly grew louder.

Tom recognised that sound. Helicopters. And he suddenly understood Natasha's anguish. Mister Wolf had yet to catch up with them, but he had spread the word.

"Now what?" Tom asked. Pain speared into his back, Natasha began to cry, and their whole world exploded into action.

CHAPTER FOURTEEN

From Tom's right came two gunshots in rapid succession. He looked that way, startled, expecting to see Cole running at them from behind the undergrowth marking the boundary of the car park. What he saw instead made him gasp out loud, and he closed his eyes and called for Natasha, afraid that he was back in one of her dream memories. If that were the case and he opened his eyes again, who knew what terrors would be awaiting him?

They're already here! Natasha gasped, and in his mind Tom sensed an uneasy shadow of betrayal. He opened his eyes to see Lane and Sophia running toward him across the car park. They were dressed in black, moving fast, and both carried weapons. Lane had a pistol in one hand and a long bulky tube over one shoulder; Sophia held a rifle in both hands. Both of them were looking at Tom, and he could not hold their gaze. The setting sun seemed to catch their eyes and turn them red.

"You're Tom," Sophia said when she reached the car,

a statement rather than a question. "You were followed by the police. We just killed them, but they led others here." She stood beside the BMW, her breath barely raised after running across the car park, and pointed the rifle at his face. "I don't trust anyone. Understand? No one. You have no special privileges, and I'll shoot you the second I think I need to." She was having to raise her voice above the roar of the approaching helicopters, and Tom glanced up to see the shadows of two huge aircraft approaching. And as Sophia knelt next to the car, he saw what Lane had been carrying.

The male berserker was kneeling with the tube balanced on his shoulder, one hand holding the wide barrel, the other closed around the grip and trigger. Dust and rubbish swirled up around him, hissing against the body of the BMW. He did not even close his eyes.

"Stay in there!" Sophia shouted as she ducked down beside the car. For a few seconds there was a rattle merged within the roar of the helicopter rotors, and chunks of concrete erupted around Lane. Bullets ricocheted toward the buildings and Tom saw the man and woman duck back inside their unit.

Lane jerked as if punched. He slumped forward and then sat upright again, stilling himself, ignoring the second burst of machine gun fire as it blasted into the ground between him and the BMW. The tube on his shoulder coughed and spat its deadly load.

Tom fell across the front seats and gathered Natasha beneath him. He could still sense her confusion as a massive explosion brought daylight back again. The car shook as if shunted by a juggernaut. Its windows smashed inward, a blast of warm air sizzled the hairs on the back of Tom's neck, and something thunked against the car's roof. For a second he thought they were being machine-gunned, but then he realised that pieces of the helicopter were raining down.

He sat up and leaned around in his seat, looking back.

Two hundred yards away, a giant burning mass dropped from the sky. It struck the ground in an orchard beyond the car park, crushing trees, sending ripe apples tumbling to the ground, burnt black and dry. One rotor continued to spin, fanning the flames. The other had speared off into the dusk. There was another explosion, even larger than the first, and the shell of the aircraft bulged outward and scattered itself across the orchard and approach road. The flames were so bright that Tom had to look away. The fire caught in the trees and grass, fuel spilling and sending rivers of flame to carve their course.

"Holy fucking shit," Tom muttered.

"One down," Lane said. He stood, threw aside the SAM launcher and ran to the car, leaning in past Tom as if he were not there, searching for Natasha. He pulled the blanket aside and laughed. "There you are!" he said. "Christ, take a look at you! Sophia, have you seen this?"

The female berserker barely glanced at Tom as she looked into the car. Then she smiled. "You look well, Natasha," she said.

"She's been buried for ten years, how the hell do you expect her to look!" Tom said.

Lane, leaning into the car, looked at Tom for the first time. Their faces were barely six inches apart. He glanced up and down and seemed to take in everything about Tom in a second. "And what the fuck do you know about it?" he said.

Lane seemed like a normal man. Strong, large, capable of protecting himself, but normal. Tom saw no changes, none of the strange mutations he had seen in Natasha's memories of her own family. Perhaps the berserkers were enjoying this. Or maybe Natasha's recollections were . . . skewed. Tom did not like that doubt, but he could not help entertaining it. He had not been expecting them to be carrying weapons—in the girl's memories they had killed with tooth and claw—but he realised quickly how foolish that assumption had been. As deadly as they were when the rage was upon them, tooth and claw would be little protection against modern military hardware.

He wondered whether the army had made that same foolish mistake.

"Here comes the other one!" Sophia said.

Lane withdrew from the car. Tom opened the door, grabbed Natasha and climbed out, standing beside the two berserkers. *They're so strong!* Natasha said in his mind. *So adapted! So powerful! I never knew, in the few hours I've been speaking with them I even guessed—*

Will they still help us? Tom asked in his mind.

Oh yes, Natasha said, and her voice was soothed by a mental smile. *They may mock me and discount you, but I still have something they want.*

"What?" Tom asked, but the girl fell silent.

The second Chinook roared over the blazing remains of the first, turning hard left and heading away, spitting bullets behind it. The aim was bad, and they rattled against the industrial units and the parking bays before them.

Sophia looked at Tom curiously, then down at Natasha where she lay in his arms. "Come with me," she said. "If you want to stay alive you do what I say when I say it, even if you think I'm wrong. Understand?"

"How can I trust you?" Tom shouted.

"We promised the girl we'd look after you."

"That doesn't mean—"

"We keep our promises," Sophia said, and her cool stare forbade him from answering back again. He nodded and followed as she ran for the open unit. Lane came along behind.

Tom could hear the tone of the Chinook's rotors changing as it landed somewhere out of view. He guessed there could be twenty or more battle-ready soldiers in there, ready to pour out, encircle the units, and take revenge for their many dead comrades.

He followed Sophia into the unit, past the piece of furniture the man and woman had been working on. It was an old table, restored and polished to a brilliant sheen, reflecting fire from outside. A bullet had skimmed its surface and gouged a foot-long oak splinter. "We won't hurt you!" Sophia called. Lane's shadow fell on the table as he entered behind Tom.

The man and woman emerged from an office at the rear of the unit, arms held high, faces pale, eyes wide.

The woman looked at what Tom held in his arms and her eyes went wider.

Sophia shot her in the face, and Lane shot the man twice in the chest.

Tom gasped and dropped Natasha onto the sawdust-covered floor.

The man went down hissing, drawing in one huge final breath, blood bubbles forming on his soaked T-shirt. Sophia stepped forward and shot him in the eye.

"Head shot," she said to Lane. "*Head* shot!" Lane simply shrugged.

"What the hell?" Tom said, but the two ignored him.

Daddy! Natasha said, and Tom looked down at where he had dropped the girl. She moved feebly on the ground. He bent to pick her up, tucking his hands beneath her body—it was not so cold now, no longer carrying the chill of the grave—and heaved her back into his arms. His back hurt. He bit his lip and groaned against the pain.

Sophia smirked at him. Tom turned away.

"Back door," Lane said, and Sophia darted into the office at the rear of the unit.

Tom heard her throwing bolts and shifting furniture, and he frowned. *Barricading us in?* he thought. *We should be running! The soldiers will be here in seconds, and they'll be berserk themselves, ready for revenge. Their mates are cooking out in that orchard. There won't be time for "hands up and come out."*

You forget so quickly, Daddy, Natasha said, nestled somewhere in his panicked mind. *Trust them.*

"Trust?" he spat, unable to help himself. He looked down at the dead man and woman, tears forming however hard he tried to gulp them back.

"The next couple of minutes could be our last," Sophia said, emerging from the office. "The last thing we need is unnecessary hindrances."

"Don't try to explain murder to me!" Tom said. She looked away, sneering, and he swallowed hard.

A volley of bullets rattled into the wall beside them, spilling tools and chunks of masonry to the ground. Tom fell and crawled behind a fixed woodworking bench, dragging Natasha with him and making sure she was shielded from outside.

Lane fired several shots from his pistol, then ducked down as a sustained burst of machine gun fire slammed into the unit. The noise was tremendous. Bullets coughed gouts of concrete from the walls, tore apart the plasterboard wall of the office, struck the old oak table, ricocheted from the floor, pinged from the bulky metal woodworking tools. Tom covered his ears and waited to be shot. Natasha could not protect him from this. A ricochet would take off the top of his head, or the soldiers would get in here, blow him apart with a burst to the chest and head. He looked across at Sophia, and between them the man's body jumped and jerked as bullets struck him. Tom averted his eyes, not wishing to see the damage they caused. Even above the gunfire he heard Sophia laugh.

"What the fuck are these things?" he whispered,

and Natasha allowed him his rage, holding back any response.

The gunfire ended. Tom's ears rang with the echoes. Lane and Sophia, hunkered down behind machines, swapped glances. Lane nodded. It was as if everything were going according to plan.

Someone started shouting. "Lane! Sophia! You know there's no way out!"

Lane's eyes went wide with genuine surprise, and he coughed out a laugh. "Major Higgins, is that really you? Haven't you retired and gone to play polo into your twilight years? You old goat, I can't believe they sent you after us!"

"Come out, Lane," the man shouted.

"So where's Cole?" Lane answered.

"I have no idea!"

Lane gave the "wanker" sign to Sophia, and she laughed and nodded, returning an imitation of fellatio. "Sophia says you're a cock sucker!" Lane shouted, ducking as Sophia threw a chunk of masonry at him.

Tom could not believe the surreality of the scene. They were about to be machine-gunned to death—and he'd bet his life that these soldiers were from Porton Down, armed with silver bullets and a knowledge of what they were up against—and here were the berserkers making jokes.

Short memory, Natasha whispered. *Remember Dan and Sarah?*

Tom nodded. Yes, he remembered them. But what

could two berserkers do against twenty armed, ready and vengeful soldiers? They would take a few with them perhaps, but not all.

Another burst of gunfire continued tearing the unit apart. Tom held onto Natasha, smelling her musty odour and feeling her tiny movements against his body. Something scratched at his chest and he pulled up, disgusted and amazed. Now? She wanted feeding now? But he looked at Sophia and Lane again, saw what was happening, and he understood why.

At last they were changing. Until now they had been under control, but Sophia was shaking, her legs quivering as they seemed to stretch out behind her, and Lane's eyes were closed, jaw thickening and lips cracked and bleeding. The berserker had dropped his gun and Tom looked at it, wondering whether he could reach it without getting his arm blown off. Probably not. But still, the option was there.

Lane turned to look at him, and his eyes were red. "Hands off!" he said. Tom shrank back.

The gunfire broke off again, Higgins shouted, and that was when the first scream rose up from outside.

Tom was shaking. His toes tapped at the ground, his arms jittered where he supported himself on his elbows, and his body trembled as if in the throes of a virulent fever. He was sweating, too, dripping onto Natasha and speckling the smooth concrete floor. He tried to keep his eyes closed, but the images behind them were too painful to to keep them shut; Jo lying dead across his lap, Steven as a boy, keen to play at soldiers. So he opened his eyes to escape those images, only to give himself more terrible sights to forever remember. The dead man had been struck by several bullets, and blood and insides had splashed up onto the wall behind him. The dead woman's leg had been blown off. Lane and Sophia continued to hide behind the woodworking machinery, still changing, making light of their predicament as the screaming rose in volume from outside.

More gunfire, but this time it was not directed at them.

And Tom was *angry*. It was an anger he had never felt before, not even ten years ago when he had first been told of Steven's death. He was not even sure where it came from, but he supposed it was a combination of everything that had happened to him, a livid stew made from Jo's death, Natasha's sad history, Cole's pursuit, the bullet still lodged somewhere in his back, the two dead people splayed across the floor beside him now, their blood filling tiny cracks and scrapes in the concrete, spreading out, forming a map of their pain. Their blood. *Their blood.*

Tom stopped shaking, stared at the mess on the floor and had a sudden desire to lap it up.

The screams and gunfire outside were joined by something else—roars and screeches that he recognised from Natasha's memories.

Daddy, she said beneath him, *I still can't change.* Her voice was so wretched that it pulled Tom back from whatever precipice he was leaning over. He raised himself up and looked down at the girl. Her mouth was bloodied, his chest dripping, and her body wavered continuously as if seen through a heat haze.

"What's out there? Just those two children?"

Dan and Sarah, all grown up now. Young and powerful and angry!

An explosion complemented the gunfire. Tom risked a look around the corner of the bench, the anger rising again, ready to drown him. He gasped and swallowed, making sure he could still breathe. His legs and arms ached from supporting himself for so long, his face throbbed, and the only part of his body that seemed not to hurt was his back.

Tracer rounds tore across the car park. The stolen BMW was a mass of flames and several bodies lay around it, their uniforms simmering and catching fire in the heat. One of them crawled feebly away from the flames, hair and fatigues smoking and then igniting.

A soldier darted past the front of the unit, and for an instant Tom wanted to run him down, punch him, tear at him until he died.

A shadow followed. A shadow that growled. The soldier's scream came from out of sight, but it did not last very long.

Two soldiers backed away across the car park, heading for the ivy-covered fence from where Lane and Sophia had first emerged. They took turns firing their weapons and reloading, and though panicked they seemed to have some level of control over their fear. One of them was covered in blood; it did not seem to be his own.

Tom looked at the blood, and saliva flooded his mouth. "What's happening to me?" he said, but nobody answered. He looked at Sophia and Lane, and though the change had shifted their bodies from the norm, they seemed to have reined in their full berserker rage. Lane had picked up his pistol and inserted a new magazine, while Sophia was reloading the rifle with shells from her pocket. Neither of them looked at him or Natasha. For some reason, they seemed to have turned serious.

There was another burst of sustained gunfire and Tom glanced outside. The two soldiers were standing back to back, both shooting at things out of sight. Their magazines seemed to run out at the same instant, and a second later shapes darted in from both sides and tore into the men. Their screams were replaced by ripping sounds as the berserkers tore them limb from limb.

"Now, do you think?" Lane said.

"About now, yes," Sophia answered. She turned to Tom. "Join us?"

"Join you where, doing what?"

"We're going outside." So saying, she stood, hefted the rifle and walked toward the front of the unit. She left strange footprints in the bloody sawdust. Lane followed her, crouched low, and Tom was left hiding with Natasha still squirming beneath him.

Take me with you, Daddy, she said, never doubting that he would go.

There was still shooting going on, though not as much as before. Men shouted commands, the *crack*

301

crack of rifles was punctuated by machine gun fire, screams became less frequent, another huge explosion shook dust from the walls and ceiling and punched against Tom's hands and knees, Sophia's rifle sang out from nearby, a hail of bullets rattled through the unit and struck walls and machines, another shot from the rifle, and then one man started shouting, the same word again and again, "Lane! Lane! Lane!"

"Major!" Lane said, as if greeting an old school friend.

I think it's safe to go now, Natasha said. Tom stood, picked up the girl and walked hesitantly out of the unit. He passed the oak table that had been shot to splinters. Shame. Jo had always liked oak, and . . .

A soldier lay several feet away, his stomach torn out and his ripped throat still pulsing blood. Tom leaned his way as death exerted an unbearable gravity.

Not now, Daddy. Not yet.

Tom frowned, shook his head, and that was when he saw the man running toward them.

"You look frightened!" Sophia called out. The major came to a halt twenty feet in front of the unit. He was shaking, panting, one side of his face splashed with blood. He held a pistol in his left hand, but made no attempt to raise it.

"Lane!" the major shouted, though there was no expression on his face. He screamed the berserker's name yet again, and it was like the bark of a dog.

Tom glanced around the car park and took in the destruction. Five minutes ago the Chinook had landed and disgorged the soldiers, and now they lay dead across the concrete. Some of them were in groups of two or three, most were alone, insides steaming in the dusk. Several still moaned, hands raised to the sunset as if trying to hold it back for another day. The BMW still blazed. The first helicopter was a bonfire in the orchard, and from out of sight beyond a row of trees and shrubs another huge pall of boiling smoke and fire marked the demise of the second aircraft.

The major stared as if blinded by fear. The berserkers closed on him from two directions. They were no longer the children Tom had seen in Natasha's memories. Dan was as big as Lane and even more powerful, his naked arms and legs shimmering as muscles flexed and relaxed. Sarah was smaller but equally formidable. Her face had elongated, pulling back her eyes and hairline. It was covered in blood. Both berserkers growled and spat, and Tom could almost sense the combined thumping of their hearts, reveling in life in this place of the dead.

"Hold back," Lane said quietly, and they sank to their knees and waited. Each of them held Higgins in their glare. The girl licked her bloody lips, tongue tasting the air like a snake's.

"Lane!" Higgins shouted.

"Eloquent as ever," Lane said, and he suddenly growled and bent at the waist, stooping into an animal pose.

"Please!" Higgins said. He started shaking his head, eyes looking left and right at his dead men.

Lane straightened, his face changing. He was crying blood. He pointed his pistol at the major. "I'm giving you the choice," he growled.

"No, please Lane!" Higgins said. "I have a son, a daughter. I have grandchildren! It's Janey's birthday in three days, what will she do without her granddad? What will she do? Please, Lane. *Please.*" He was crying now, a thin, slight man whose fatigues and rank did nothing to protect him from fear.

"I'm giving you the choice," Lane said again, enunciating each word carefully through his stretching jaw, sprouting teeth.

"Sophia?" Higgins said, but there was no help there. She still held onto her rifle, but she was changing too, growling and grunting and snarling at the corpse of a soldier at her feet.

Lane pulled himself upright, seeming to exert a massive effort to do so. His arm wavered, and then lowered. He dropped the pistol. "Your . . . last . . . chance," he said, and the final word transformed into a roar.

Higgins looked at Tom for the first time, then down at Natasha nestling in his arms. "You have no idea," he said, and then he raised his pistol and shot himself through the mouth.

Lane and Sophia were upon him before his body hit the ground.

Tom retreated back into the unit as the berserkers took their fill. He carried Natasha with him and settled her in an old rocking chair, its re-upholstered seat and back torn up by bullets. The chair moved for a couple of seconds, and then kept moving. Even above the sounds of ravenous feeding from outside, Tom could hear the subtle creaks of the girl's torso bending and stretching.

Daddy, she said, her voice uneven and strained. *Daddy!*

The chair rocked.

Tom felt sick, as if he had eaten a handful of uncooked meat. The taste in his mouth was one that never should have been there. He looked at his hands, but there was no sign of blood, and for that he was relieved.

Natasha did not look as though she could be alive—her face was frozen, hair still matted with mud, limbs and body dried and stiffened by time. And yet her joints had begun to work, and every small movement in one limb seemed to encourage movement in another.

The chair rocked.

She shifted as if every bone in her body were broken, a fluid motion that seemed to feed upon itself. Tom wondered whether now that she had started, if she would ever stop.

"What is it?" he said, but he knew, and she said, *You know.* "I can't help you," he said. "I can't take you out there while they're—"

You don't need to take me out. Her mental voice was a pained whine, and her real voice came as a low rattle: "Daddy . . ."

He knew that she was right. And he knew what she was doing to him. He supposed he had known from the beginning, and as he turned from her he saw the body of the dead woman, her face ruined and her legs blown off, and he could not tear his eyes away.

"Daddy!"

His back flared with pain, and Tom could do nothing but return to Natasha. He lifted her from the chair, sat there himself and settled her in his lap. She was heavier than before, and her teeth seemed sharper, her suckling mouth more eager. He looked down at where she gnawed at his chest, saw his blood bubbling there, and closed his eyes.

In his mind he saw more murder at the hands of the berserkers. But this time the memories were his own.

CHAPTER FIFTEEN

Cole had found a navigator inside his head. As he drove, he waited for Natasha to visit him again and entice him on to whatever fate she believed awaited him. He was happy to follow. This was his life, and the lives of everyone he had ever loved, known, met, seen, heard or killed. This was history being written, being created here and now. One bullet from his pistol could change the world. All he asked for was a chance.

So he had wandered the streets of his mind, passing through sunlight and looking to the shadows. They hid many things and some of them he saw and knew—ghosts of friends, the wraiths of the people he had killed. But none of them harmed him, none of them frightened him, because they were all of his own making. Natasha did not project herself into their images and steer them to attack. The woman from the MX5 was there, but was a product of his own memory. However much he felt disturbed at her being in the dusky alleys of his mind, he knew that she was all him. He saw her black panties and pale milky thighs, and that was the final sight he'd had of her, that was all, there was nothing else in the memory. Nothing like Natasha had made for him.

He moved on, passing across intersections where his life had changed or may change in the future. He saw no street names and decided that he had to name them himself. In the next couple of hours perhaps he would make a whole new map of his life, draw it fresh purpose, a totally different emphasis. He was a murderer and that would never change, but the justification he sought lay in those blank street signs, buried at crossroads he had yet to reach.

People watched him from the buildings lining these long roads, and they were the unknowns he was trying to save. None of them knew of Natasha, or Lane, or the others; none of them were aware of the danger they were in every second of every minute of their lives. None of them realised that there really *were* monsters. The fact that they would never appreciate what Cole was about to do did not concern him in the slightest. He was not acting for fame and fortune; he would be signing no book deals, he would appear on no talk shows.

And then, driving north on the motorway, waiting for Natasha to return and tell him where she was, Cole felt a shadow beneath the streets. It moved quickly, passing under his feet as he looked up at the faceless masses staring from the skyscrapers of his soul. He looked down at the road and saw that he was standing on a manhole, edges rusted into the frame but its promise still obvious.

He did not want to go down there.

The shadow thumped away to the left, shattering windows and cracking facades, and Cole followed on the surface, turning left from the motorway and following the road in his mind's eye. He ran faster as he drove faster, keeping an eye on the road and his mind on the shadow as it thundered on ahead. It was not Natasha—he could not feel those slick fingers in his mind, and even if she were hiding down there in his darkest subconscious, he would know her—but he did not question its presence. Perhaps as she had refined her ability to communicate in those long years below the ground, maybe he had too, in that confused decade just gone by. Perhaps his hate for her was so strong that it had torn itself from him, taking on a shadow of its own true existence. The thought that he may be following his own disembodied hatred did not concern him at all.

The shadow urged him left again, and as the sun set, so the streets of his mind lost focus. *Nearing something dark*, he thought. *Closing in on the terror.*

The shadow disappeared and Cole wailed, bumping the car into an old stone wall. But then he saw light other than the setting sun, and he knew that he was there.

Down in a shallow valley, at the edge of a spread of industrial buildings, a ball of fire blossomed into the sky.

* * *

"We're leaving." Someone nudged Tom's shoulder and he jerked awake. For a second he had no idea where he was. He'd been dreaming of blood and death and the stink of bodies turned inside out. Awake now, relief washed through him, but the stench and taste returned when he remembered what had happened, and what was still happening.

He had to pull Natasha away from his chest, wincing as her teeth brought a flap of skin with them. He gasped, she sighed and turned her head to face him. *Can she really see me?* he thought.

Not yet, Natasha said, stroking smooth fingers through his mind. *But soon.* He looked away from the girl's face.

Sophia was rearranging her clothing, trying to hold it together in the places where it had stretched and torn. She wiped blood from her mouth and chin.

"Where are we going?" he asked. "Are we going home?"

Home! Natasha said, excitement lightening her voice.

Sophia frowned. Shrugged. "Just get up and come with us," she said. "This place will be swarming soon, and we're in no state for another fight."

Tom so wanted to ask about Steven, but something held him back. As he climbed from the rocking chair he saw Lane and Sophia helping their children into a Range Rover, holding Dan and Sarah beneath the arms and shoving on their rumps. Dan especially seemed to be having trouble climbing into the vehicle, and twice he slipped and tumbled back out, only to be caught by Lane. He had not reverted as fully as Lane and Sophia. His legs were still lengthened, though thin, and his head was enlarged, forehead wide and sloping. He saw Tom watching and growled at him. Lane turned also and gave Tom a withering look.

Tom looked down at Natasha, averting his eyes.

We're not immortal, she said, but Tom had his doubts. He had seen the bullet holes in Dan's naked body, still leaking blood, one or two seeming to emit small tails of smoke or steam. If all that did to him was made it difficult to climb into a Range Rover, then perhaps they really were immortal.

"You wake after ten years in your grave and tell me that?" Tom said.

"Come *on!*" Sophia called.

Tom started to carry Natasha from the wrecked business unit when the telephone rang. Normality beckoned on the end of the line, either someone with a work request, or perhaps the dead couple's child-minder, ringing to tell them that their son had just taken his very first steps or spoken his first word. Steven's first word had been "Mama." Tom paused. He had no intention of answering the phone, but for a few precious seconds it took him away, seeming to instill a sense of peace over the terrible scene.

But the call would never be answered, and sometime soon the caller would learn the truth.

As he walked across the car park Tom tried not to see the bodies. Whatever strangeness had overcome him earlier—and really he *knew* what it was—had faded into disgust. He could still hear the roar and crackle of fire as the Chinooks and the BMW burned, the flames sparking and snapping as they consumed ammunition or exploded air pockets. The stench of cooking meat hung in the air. Tom's mouth watered. He stepped on soft things but did not look down.

"They're taking us home," Natasha said, her true voice suddenly smoother than it had ever been before. In that voice Tom heard emotion that he had never suspected her of possessing. She was a child coming back to life, a child going home, and she needed him so much.

"Yes," he said. "And there I'll find my Steven."

He climbed into the Range Rover, took the cargo space with Natasha, and everyone fell silent as Lane drove them away from the cooling dead.

I don't need you any more, Mister Wolf. My new daddy has taken me to them, and you've lost, you're wasted, you're a piss in a lake. Nobody will ever know of you, Cole. Nobody will ever understand what you were doing. You're a murderer, and you'll be caught and put in prison. You'll die in there. And I wish it could be more. I wish you could meet Lane and Sophia again. And their children, remember them? Mister Wolf, I so wish you could see what has become of their children. They'd like you. Maybe raw, maybe just breathed on by a flame, blue. But they'd like you so much.

They're thriving. I hope you remember that. Living the life they were always meant to live before you bastards caught us and put us away. We're back, Mister Wolf. Back where we belong. And now we're going home.

"Stupid little bitch. *Stupid* little bitch! You think you're all there is? You think you're the centre of all this? There're too many parts, too many involvements for there to be any one centre. You've led me on for this long, do you think I'm just going to give up? Do you really, honestly think I don't have my own ways and means? Natasha, sweetheart, I've got a magazine full of bullets here for you, and now that I've found my shadow I've also found you."

There's nothing for you to find, Mister Wolf. We were always the shadows in the night. You took away our history, but we've won it back. Now fuck off, you pathetic man. Fuck off and kill some more women.

"You sound so confident, but you can't see everything, can you? Can't see past my shadow. It's hiding things from you. Hiding what I can see. I'll see you very, very soon."

Cole's shadow rose up and filled the night, and he and Natasha could talk no more.

"We *are* going home, aren't we?" Natasha said, her voice a whisper in the silence. Dan was sleeping, and Sarah leaned back in her seat as her wounds healed. In the front seats Sophia and Lane glanced at each other.

"Home?" Lane said.

"Home," Natasha said, louder this time. "The place berserkers come from. The place we were always meant to find again. You've come from there, haven't you?

That's where you've been, isn't it? And you're taking us back there now."

Back home, Tom thought. *Back to Steven. But if that's the case, why am I so terrified to say his name?*

"Oh, Natasha," Lane said, "your mother really did talk such shit."

In his arms, the girl turned to face Tom. *Daddy?* she said in his mind. And suddenly Tom knew.

"Where's my son?" he asked. Sophia turned in the passenger seat and looked back at him, and for once there was something other than dismissal in her eyes. It may have been regret.

That was when the Mondeo swerved around a bend in the road and struck the Range Rover head-on.

CHAPTER SIXTEEN

The shadow within had smothered him. Everywhere he looked, above and below, blackness held him within its grasp. He coughed and heard nothing. He sniffed and smelled nothing. The shadow had surged from his underground and flooded the byways of his consciousness, and it was only as a hazy light began to grow ahead that Cole realised he was being protected.

The shadow changed slowly from black to an oppressive, milky white, and Cole panicked. He could hardly breathe or move. If he opened his mouth he felt something trying to force its way in—not the shadow. He pushed forward, attempting to pull away from the thing's grasp, but it held him fast—again, not the shadow. He was not sure whether or not he was even conscious, but the pain suddenly bit into his thighs again, the throbbing raw and loud, and he started to find sense.

Airbag. It had been the last thing on his mind when

he swung the car around the corner and saw the Range Rover heading his way. He'd had maybe two seconds to react.

Must be them. I've got the initiative . . . I've got the surprise . . . Speedometer, forty. The Range Rover's big, heavy, but is there really another way? Is there?

Airbag.

Next had come the instant decision, and a second later the impact as he drove into the Rover.

Now, pinned back in his seat, he knew he may have a few second's grace. The berserkers had met Major Higgins, that much was obvious, and now the major was probably a wet stain somewhere down on the valley floor. And those two Chinooks he'd seen flying over the motorway, maybe forty men packing everything they'd need to take down the berserkers?

Well, there were the flames. And there was the Range Rover.

The airbag was not deflating. It turned from white to red before his face, and Cole tasted blood, and panic settled in. He reached down into his lap and found the .45 still wedged under his thigh. It took him a few seconds to work it loose, then a couple more to aim blind, hoping that the crash had not skewed his sense of direction.

He closed his eyes, opened his mouth and pulled the trigger. The blast was huge. His ears were still ringing as he opened his eyes again and watched the airbag deflating before him. He quickly took stock. His legs still hurt like fuck, which meant he probably hadn't broken his back. He jiggled his ankles and felt the insides of his shoes, so no trapped feet. He felt as though he'd been thrown against a wall and had a gang of thugs set upon him with hammers and blowtorches while he was unconscious, but right now that sort of pain was good, because it meant that he was alive and conscious and not paralysed.

The windshield had shattered, either from the impact or the gunshot. Cole popped his seatbelt and used the pistol to knock out the remaining glass. It fell into his lap in diamond chunks, and dusk poured in.

The Mondeo was buried in the front of the Range Rover. The vehicles seemed to merge, and it was difficult to tell where one began and the other ended. Something hissed, something steamed, and Cole could smell petrol, potent and rank. The Rover's windshield had shattered and Sophia hung half-out, splayed across the bonnet. Her head was ruptured and leaking. Between Sophia and Cole, twisted into the buckled bonnet of the Mondeo, Lane.

Cole gasped.

Lane opened his eyes.

Tom sat up and shook his head. He'd been thrown against the back of the middle seats, and Natasha had tumbled to the floor at his feet. She groaned in his head, mumbling words that made no sense, and if he closed his eyes he saw jumbled images of what she had called home. They were blurring now, flickering, as if delivered to him on a fifth-generation videotape and viewed on a dodgy TV set. He could almost feel her belief and hope fading away.

None of them had been wearing seatbelts. He had been holding Natasha to his side as Lane drove them up out of the valley of death. Tom's view through the rear door had been apocalyptic: the blazing wrecks of the two helicopters, the shell of the BWM still flicking with flames, the ruptured bodies scattered across the car park and piled against the front door of one of the closed units. The sun had gone down and the fires painted the ground red. Or perhaps it was blood.

And then their brief conversation that shattered hope, Steven in his mind, and the car had driven straight into them. Tom had seen Cole in the driver's seat a split second before impact. The Range Rover's headlights had turned his face white, and his eyes were wide and dilated with madness.

He hoped that Cole was dead.

Tom looked forward. Lane had been thrown straight through the windshield and now lay twisted up on the Mondeo's rippled bonnet. Sophia was halfway through, and there was a lot of blood. Dan had gone between the front seats and crashed into the dashboard. He was moving slightly, mewling like a hungry kitten, and Tom saw his wounds, some of them new, gushing fresh blood. He was impaled on the gear stick, shuddering as he tried to lift himself off. Sarah, exhausted from her recent fight, had bounced against the rear of Sophia's seat and lay crumpled across the leather. She was not moving.

"Natasha, I think this is bad," Tom said. She answered only with another moan, and more confused images of the home it seemed she would never know.

A gunshot rang out, loud and frightening in the stunned silence following the crash. Tom ducked down, looking forward at the Mondeo. The doors were still closed, the windshield was badly cracked, nobody moved. One of the vehicle's headlamps still burned, and he could make out shadows and shapes around the cars. All of them seemed to be moving, and he wondered whether all the soldiers had been on those Chinooks, or if others had been sent here by road. Maybe there would be more shooting soon and that would be it. Maybe—

A gaping hole appeared in the Mondeo's windshield, widening quickly as the shattered glass fell inward. It was Cole. His face was lit a devilish, bloody red from the bridge of the nose down. His eyes widened as saw Lane, not two feet away from him.

For a second the scene froze, and Tom thought that instant would be his last. Nobody moved or made a sound, and perhaps he'd had a heart attack, his last wretched second on this earth imprinted on his mind as his body seized and his mind prepared to fade away.

Then Cole thrust his pistol into Lane's face and fired once, twice, again, and Lane's head came apart.

Tom ducked down behind the seat and looked at Natasha.

Mister Wolf, she said, and he nodded.

"I have to get you out of here," Tom whispered. "The others are in a bad way—still healing from the fight, maybe—and if he traps us in here we're dead. I smell petrol. I'm going to open the back door and run with you. Are you ready? Maybe we can hide, or maybe we can make it back to the industrial estate. There are lots of guns down there."

You've never fired a gun.

Tom shook his head. "It can't be that hard."

Here! Natasha said. *There are guns in here! Sophia's rifle, Lane's pistol.*

Tom nodded, mind running so fast he could barely keep up. He had to distract Cole first, then scramble over the seats, find one of the guns, figure out how to use it, find out where Cole was, shoot him before he was shot himself. Easy. "Easy," Tom said. And he smiled. Because something was coursing through him and making him feel *good*. The wound in his back was a pleasant throb rather than a burning pain, as if he were having a constant massage. His fingers and toes tingled and his senses seemed sharpened as the light faded fast. Far from being terrified at what the next thirty seconds may bring, he was looking forward to them.

He smelled blood, and it was as good as wine.

More glass smashed, Cole grunted, and Sarah stirred in the seat in front of Tom. Dan was still whining as he tried to lift himself from the broken gear stick. Sophia remained still and silent.

Several more gunshots, and this time they were directed into the Range Rover. Someone gasped in pain. A bullet blasted through the seat three inches from Tom's head and shattered the rear window. Then he heard Cole's curse and the metallic *snick* of a magazine being ejected.

"Now!" Tom whispered. "We won't have long." He shunted the handle on the rear door and kicked it open. "Run!" he shouted, dipping one foot out and scraping it across loose stones on the roadside. Then he turned, waiting until he heard Cole slip from the wrecked Mondeo and sprawl to the ground.

I love you Daddy, Natasha said. Tom smiled, confused, touched, and heaved himself over the rear seat. He landed half on Sarah and she lashed out with one hand, catching him across the face. He grunted and felt blood began to ooz from the gash she had put there. Heard her low, throaty growl. He wanted to tell her what he was doing, but by the time he'd done that Cole would be behind the Rover. Then, maybe five seconds until he realised he'd been duped. Tom had created a make-or-break scenario for all of them; he could smell the petrol, and once Cole knew what was happening he could ignite the wrecked cars with one careful shot. He punched out at the girl berserker and forced his way forward between the front seats. Dan whined louder, expecting help or trying to fight. Either way, his waving hands were ineffective. He was weak, still bleeding, and one of the wounds in the side of his head leaked something that was creamy green in the subdued light.

Tom glanced at the empty driver's seat—no pistol. Sophia was hanging across the bonnet, legs still in the passenger seat. In the footwell behind her legs lay the rifle. He leaned forward, straining against the seats that held him across the hips, touched the slick metal, curled his fingers around the barrel, pulled it toward him. Dan was batting his head, fingers scraping his scalp and drawing blood. "Get off!" Tom whispered, but the berserker was mad, and Tom sensed dark, alien thoughts dancing at the fringes of his mind.

I hear Mister Wolf! Natasha said.

Tom started to panic. He pulled the rifle out between Sophia's dangling legs. She coughed, then moaned, then growled when she felt the metal batting her knees on the way past. "I'm not against you," he whispered, hoping his words would make it through. Dan still mumbled incoherently, and then Tom heard someone else muttering her way into his mind. *Lane*, the voice said, and it was Sophia. *Lane . . . Lane?*

Tom forced himself back and pulled the rifle after him.

He's past the car now, Daddy.

Seconds . . . maybe only seconds. Tom sat up, turned around and rested the rifle on the seatback. There was a scope, but he had never used a gun, and he was afraid that if he looked through it he would miss things happening at the periphery. He had not yet seen Cole.

Sarah screeched out loud and lurched up for him.

"No!" Tom whispered, and he heard someone skidding to a halt on the road.

Cole stepped into the frame of the open back door, maybe twenty feet away. He was staring into the Range Rover, his face a dark mask of blood in the dim light, the pistol glinting in his hand. "Sneaky bastard!" he said.

Tom pointed the rifle and pulled the trigger.

Nothing happened.

Cole ran at the Rover, lifting his pistol, and Tom saw the maw of its barrel growing to swallow him whole.

Daddy! Natasha said. The others were whispering at him now, pained and angry, raging, their thoughts so dark and confused that he could make no sense of them. He pulled the trigger, and nothing happened again.

"Safety," Cole said. He stood at the open door, aimed his pistol at Tom's chest and shot him for the second time that day.

Tom fell back and his vision left him with a blinding flash, like a bulb brightening before finally burning out. He could not breathe. His chest felt heavy, as if his organs had turned to lead. For some reason he thought of Steven when he was six years old, waking one morning and creeping downstairs before he and Jo heard him, cooking them toast, buttering it, making tea with cold water and picking a rose from the back garden before bringing everything up on a tray. *Happy Christmas*, he had said, and though Christmas had been weeks away they had spent that morning laughing and playing and being everything a family was meant to be.

Tom's body began to burn from the inside out. And as all senses receded to a point on the horizon of consciousness he smelled petrol and blood, heard a volley of gunshots, and then screams as flames licked at flesh.

* * *

As Roberts fell back another shape rose from the seat, grabbed the rifle, nudged the safety and fired off a shot. Cole felt the bullet singe the hairs on his left ear. He put two bullets into the shape—one of the young bastard berserkers, all grown up—and as it howled he snatched up Natasha.

So light! He almost stumbled as he picked up the berserker bitch. He'd been prepared for some weight, but there was hardly anything to her at all. It was like lifting a bundle of straw and twigs.

The shape rose again in the backseat, shaking like a wet dog, spraying the Range Rover's ceiling with a fan of blood. Cole turned and ran, expecting at any second to feel a high velocity bullet tear out his spine. He zigzagged, feet scraping on the ground, and as he looked down at the bundle in his arms he let out an involuntary laugh. He had her! After so long, the greatest mistake of his life was about to be put right.

I'm dying, she said in his mind, *I can't move, I haven't fed, I'm dying.*

"Poor girl," Cole said, laughing again. He should stop now, stand on her chest and put a bullet in her head, but he could still hear howling and commotion from the Range Rover . . . and he could still smell petrol in the air.

He turned. There were shadows dancing in and around the crashed cars. He dropped Natasha to the ground, braced himself and fired beneath the Range Rover. The third shot threw up a spark, the spark expanded into a wavering blue flame, and seconds later the vehicle's ruptured fuel leads ignited. He turned and fell to the ground as the fuel tank exploded. Natasha had rolled to the edge of the road and he scrambled after her on hands and knees, not caring about sharp stones or the burning debris falling around him, concerned only with this berserker bitch whom he had spent years regretting not killing when he had the chance.

Don't hurt me! she said, and he shouted, "You've changed your tune!" Another thumping explosion came from along the road as the Mondeo's fuel tank went up. He was sure all these fireworks must be attracting attention, but he supposed it could have been only fifteen minutes since the first shots were fired down in the valley. Whatever, he did not have long. He would shoot the berserker now and run like fuck. Because however hot that fire, however weak those others were, he did not for a minute believe he had killed them all.

The sudden sense of his life coming to an end struck him hard. If he *had* got them all—if their tainted blood were bubbling away within those flames—then once he killed Natasha, his life no longer held meaning. They would be dead, all of them, and his sense of purpose would be fulfilled. And what would he be then? Just another murderer waiting to be caught?

For reasons he could not fully comprehend, he picked up Natasha and ran.

He leaped over the ditch at the edge of the road and started climbing up out of the valley. The ground here was loosely landscaped, small trees spaced well apart with heathers and bracken growing in between. The going was quite easy, though his legs soon began to burn. His thighs felt as if they would swell and rip apart his jeans, but he had come to ignore that pain.

"Where are you?" he said. "Where are you?" But the berserker girl was a bundle of skin and bones in his arms. Whatever was left inside—her personality, her tenacious life force—had gone away once more.

Cole paused and looked back down at the flaming vehicles. The fire lit up the road in both directions, but he could not make out any bodies, inside or outside the Range Rover. If some of them had got away they were in hiding . . . or coming after him.

He continued uphill, carrying the shell of Natasha with him. Knowing he should kill her. Feeling, somehow, that the time was not yet right.

Somebody was feeding him. Tom could smell fire and cooking flesh, feel fire of a different kind coursing through his body and melting everything he had ever known, every thought that tried to surface, in its conflagration. And yet it was the hunger that brought him around, lifting him up above the surface of unconsciousness that hid only dead depths beneath.

It felt as though he had not eaten forever, and he lapped up the food, chewing, swallowing, opening his mouth and waiting for the next morsel like a fledgling bird. *There, there,* someone said, and Tom was not sure whether they had spoken out loud or in his mind. He

was uncertain of the voice. It sounded soothing but behind it lay anger, and something else. The voice
sounded hollow. *There, there.*

"What?" he asked, unable to finish. Something
crushed down on his chest and took away all his wind,
and he gasped for long seconds as he tried to draw in
another breath. One came, eventually, and he kept it
light, in and out slowly, thinking that with every breath
his insides would break.

Meat touched his lips, he opened his mouth and
gulped it down, barely chewing.

Natasha! He tried to sit up but the weight on his
chest held him down. He opened his eyes. A shadow sat
at his side, wavering as a fire cast it left and right.

"He has her," the voice said.

No! Tom could not speak, but he thought this
shadow heard him well enough.

"Sarah has gone after them, but it's down to the girl
now. She's more than you know. This could be interesting."

She's just a little girl, Tom thought, and then he found
his breath. "She's almost dead."

The shadow shook its head. "She's almost alive."
And then it fed him some more.

Cole could hear the berserker coming.

If he kept going at this pace he would reach the access road first, then he had a mile to run before he was
back onto the main road. And even then, there was no
guarantee that anyone would stop for him. Not looking

like he did, bloodied and battered and carrying a corpse.

"Where are you?" he said, and inside he wanted her back. He wanted to feel the nearly dead girl in his mind, because her voice gave him purpose. He so wished to hear her, because his aim was to silence that voice forever as he should have done ten years before.

You were too cruel then, Natasha said, surprising him. He had not sensed her creeping into his mind. Perhaps she was hiding, down in his subconscious with the living shadow of his hate. Or maybe she had always been there.

"Cruelty's childish," he said. "I'm over it."

Don't you want to know?

Behind him he heard the sounds of pursuit. Feet slapping through the knee-high ferns that smothered the hillside. Hands pushing aside branches. The noises were coming closer, however hard Cole ran. And Natasha, light as she was, was slowing him down. He should shoot her here and now, three rounds to blow off her head, and then he could leave her for them to find. The final insult. They would be free again, but Natasha would be dead.

But did he want to know? Did he really? Did he *need* to? And the answer was yes, had always been yes. That was why Sandra Francis had died at his hand, after all. There was no other reason, and he could no longer pretend that her death had been a necessity. She died because she had refused to tell him how they had made Natasha special.

"No," he said, and Natasha laughed.

Cole paused. She had *laughed!* And it had not been

down there in the darkness, where lay all the knowledge he denied and the desires he refused to acknowledge. Natasha had laughed out loud, perhaps because she had *seen* those desires.

"That was you!" he said.

"I . . . can . . ." She said no more. He looked down at the bundle in his arms. It had spoken. *Not dead, but dreaming,* she said in his mind, *and now I'm coming back again.*

"No you're not," Cole said. He ran on, holding the berserker close to his chest with one hand, grabbing at thin tree trunks and hauling himself up the slope with the other. He dug his feet in, leaned forward, ignoring the pain in his thigh that felt as if his flesh were melting and running from his leg. Soon there would be only bone left but he would push on, because his cause was inbred, it was instinct. Nothing would swerve him from the path, and—

Then why aren't I dead already? It's because you can't. It's because you need to know. Kill me now and I'll always be a mystery, and you'll never understand why you buried me alive. You killed yourself doing that, didn't you Mister Wolf? Didn't you, Cole? I know because I've been to that place in your mind, that underground. And I've talked to the shadow of you.

"What is it?" Cole shouted. He paused, shaking the girl's corpse and hearing the crackle of weak things breaking. But she did not scream. Instead she opened her mouth and whispered, something so light that it told itself only to the dark. "What?" He leaned closer.

329

The pistol in his belt was forgotten. The sound of pursuit grew louder, but he did not care. Now, here, he would discover a truth that had haunted him for a decade. "What?"

"They . . ."

Cole only caught the first word, so he brought her closer to him, turning his head so that she could whisper into his ear.

"They made me the mother of the future," Natasha said. She came to life, warm and shifting, and before Cole could let go she had buried her teeth in his throat.

Cole tried to scream, but he heard it only in his mind.

Tom was being dragged through the dark. The shadow had revealed itself as Sophia as she bent before the flames to scoop him up, but she had changed. Her face was bashed and bloody, her hair matted, one side of her scalp burned and bubbled. And her eyes had changed the most. They reflected the flames and gave back only sadness, as if the fire told her unwanted truths.

"Lane?" Tom croaked.

"He's gone," Sophia said. "What do you think you were eating?" She held him beneath the arms and he was looking up at her face, upside down. She glanced down and a tear hit his cheek. "Dan as well. My son. I heard him screaming. He couldn't escape the fire. That's no way to go, not for anyone."

"*Eating?*"

"You have silver in you. We're immune, and Lane's flesh will help you."

"But—"

"Please!" Sophia said, her voice breaking. "Please, just leave it. It's done." She grunted as she dragged him, and Tom wondered why he did not feel nauseated. Why, in fact, he still felt hungry. The red meat was heavy in his stomach, and he could sense the goodness radiating out from there.

"I was shot," Tom said. "Cole shot me again. I felt it . . . I can feel it. Heavy, like a block of ice in my chest." This fresh pain made his back feel like a tickle. "I should be dead."

"It's not easy to kill a berserker." Sophia hauled him off the road, heading down a slope into a thicket of trees and shrubs. Hidden from the road she set him down and dropped beside him.

Tom had so many questions vying for attention that for a while he could ask nothing. The tang of meat was still rich on his tongue. His muscles burned, his veins carried fire around his body, and he was sweating so much he thought he must be seeping blood. But Sophia did not spare him a glance. He saw the burning cars reflected in her eyes, as if she were imprinting the sight on her memory.

"There is no home, is there?" he said at last. In his pain, his mind was an oasis. And in his mind loose ends were coming together, and understanding bloomed like a blood-red rose.

Sophia shook her head. "Natasha's mother was always so protective," she said. "How you can protect someone by telling such lies, I never knew. We argued about it. We fought. But Natasha was her child, and really I had little say."

"Home is where Natasha said you berserkers come from."

Sophia chuckled, a surprisingly light sound against the continuing roar of flames. "Berserkers come from Porton Down," she said. Tom saw the truth in her eyes, and that truth lay in her humanity. He had seen her as a raging monster and a vicious killer, but now, eyes reflecting the fire of her son's and husband's funeral pyre, she was as human as he.

"They made you," he said.

Sophia nodded. "We were normal families. Lane was army, as was Natasha's father. They used science, and something more arcane, and they gave us our cravings. They made us monsters. And now Natasha has made you."

Tom closed his eyes. "I think she started yesterday. Cole shot me in the back. Natasha kept me alive."

"And you her."

"She wants me to be her daddy. But . . ."

Sophia stood and grabbed him beneath the arms once more. "You'll survive. Now we have to get farther away from the road. There'll be police on the way, and more army. We'll be going soon."

"Natasha?"

"She's fine," Sophia said. She glanced up at the emerging stars and smiled. "She's just given Mister Wolf his answer."

"Steven," Tom gasped. "*Steven!* If there's no home, then where's my son?"

Sophia looked over her shoulder to see where she was going, avoiding his eyes. "We buried him in a forest in Wales," she said. "He fed us for a while."

Cole looked up. Sarah, the image of her parents, stared down at him. She held Natasha in her arms, and in the darkness the little girl seemed to be still again.

Sarah was pointing his own pistol at his face.

Cole opened his mouth to speak, but could not. His throat felt cold and exposed, and raising his right hand he felt the truth of that. He touched a part of himself he should never touch, and it sent a rocket of pain into his head. His hand came away slick and bloody.

"Please, you don't have to say anything," Sarah quipped, but she was not smiling. "I'm leaving you here. You're well hidden. They won't find you straight away. Too many bodies to scoop up first. Those bastards down there, and . . ." Cole saw the glitter of tears in the berserker teenager's eyes.

The little bitch had bitten him. Torn out his throat. And now she was not only not dead, she was more alive than she had been in years. He could not see her moving, could not hear her, but he felt her, rooting around in his mind and burrowing beneath the truth of everything he believed about himself. The streets of his subconscious were growing dark, and not because he was fading away. They darkened with approaching night.

"Natasha says you might want to know a couple of things first," Sarah said. "And I agree. It'll help you in your choice."

Choice? The girl lowered the pistol. Cole reached, hand out, asking her for the gun or a shot to the head, he knew not which. *Choice?*

"They made her special," Sarah said. "That's why we had to get away, except we wanted Natasha with us. Her father had other ideas, but once we were out there was no way we could go back for her. We thought you'd killed her, Cole. We've spent ten hopeless years living between the lines, moving around, surviving. And now . . . this. Thanks to you, we berserkers have a chance again." She knelt and reached out, thrusting her fingers into Cole's torn throat.

He tried to scream, but he could only bubble blood.

"Nasty," Sarah said. "You should be dead. But lucky for you, they gave Natasha something no other berserker has. They made her fertile."

Natasha spoke up then, a hoarse whisper eased somewhat by Cole's blood in her throat. "They made me contagious."

Sarah threw the pistol at Cole's chest. He gasped, caught it, aimed it right back at her.

"There's one round in the chamber," she said. "It'll hurt, but unless you're a very good shot, it won't kill me. Silver? You're behind the times, Mister Wolf. But now you have a choice. You think you're damned. But if you don't mind knowing the true meaning of the word, maybe we'll see you again one day."

"I'll do it!" he said. "I'm not afraid of dying. I'm going to Heaven."

"Really?" Sarah asked, scoffing. "Heaven? That's as real as home." She turned and walked back down toward the burning cars, taking Natasha with her.

They left Cole out there in the night and took Tom with them, but Tom knew that they both faced the same choice. His, he supposed, was made easier, because his heart held nothing like Cole's unreasoning hatred. And he had Natasha to take care of him.

They hid in the valley for a while—the berserkers Sophia, Sarah and Natasha, and Tom, the man who should have been dead—and then when everyone else came in, they walked out. Police cars, fire engines, ambulances, army trucks, other unmarked cars, they all flooded into the shallow valley, some of them pausing by the burning cars, most continuing down to the industrial estate. The flaming wrecks of the Chinooks lit the way.

As they walked through the night, none of them heard a gunshot. But it could have been drowned in the roar of helicopters.

Sophia's revelations about the nature of the berserkers was more of a shock to Natasha than Tom. The girl became silent, shivering against him in the small car Sarah eventually stole to drive them to safety, and however hard he tried he could not find her in his mind. She had withdrawn into herself, just as the chance had come to reach out. He supposed that for her, ten years had never really passed. She was a child again, ready to live and learn and adapt to how the world truly was.

With Natasha gone his grief came in, rich and full and heavy. He cried, great shaking sobs for his dead wife and son. Jo was the love of his life. And Steven, gone for so long yet still there, a memory refreshed by the renewed hope Tom had harboured. He could not bring himself to hate Sophia and Lane for what they had done, and that felt wrong, because without that his rage had no direction.

Perhaps one day he would find one.

He cried also for what he had lost, because he had *enjoyed* life. Maybe sometimes he had thought it worthless, meaningless, vapid, but life was for living, and he missed the simplicity of that. A kiss on his wife's cheek in the morning, watching a pair of nesting birds whilst stuck in a traffic jam, the swaying of trees as a cold northerly wind brought snow, the smile on Jo's face when she came home to a meal he had cooked, the taste of wine, the feel of sunlight on his scalp, scraps of clouds catching the setting sun and promising a good day tomorrow. And that desire for a life in music, more distant than his dead son and yet haunting him with fading tunes.

"Where are we going?" he asked. "North," Sophia replied, and it hit him like the last line of a mournful song.

He had no idea what tomorrow would bring. Sunset had passed, leaving only pain and the taste of blood behind. Below all the pain he felt remarkably alive, but he sensed that life now had a whole new set of rules.

He should have been dead. But life was no longer just for living. He was with Sophia and Sarah and Natasha now—he was infected, as much a product of Porton Down as they—and he had fallen between the lines.

When she awoke, Natasha said, "Daddy?" Tom gathered her up and held her to him, and he felt warmth in her flesh, welcomed the way her child's body shaped itself to his hug. Sophia glanced at him in the mirror, and though he saw tears in her eyes for her lost husband and son, he also saw something else. Neither she nor Sarah smiled—they were too tired for that, too overwrought, too exhausted from the healing process—but still he was sure. He saw hope.

Everything Natasha's mother had told her was wrong. The berserkers had no history, other than their time at Porton Down. They had no heritage or culture, no place living alongside humanity down through the centuries, and they had no home. But now that she was with them, it seemed as though things had changed. They could create their own place in the world, living between the lines and existing in shadows, becoming a part of legend if that suited them. They had a chance to write their own history.

And it had only just begun.

TIM LEBBON

DESOLATION

Cain is eager for a new beginning. After years of virtual imprisonment by his insane father, and intense therapy following his father's death, Cain is finally ready to see the outside world. He rents an apartment and moves in with only a few meager belongings, including a very special trunk that contains his most guarded secret—something unimaginable. Something unnatural.

The outside world isn't what Cain expected. He soon discovers that many of the other tenants are *very* strange and downright terrifying. His nightmares are becoming more hideous and more frequent. The pressure is building. If it continues to build, Cain might be forced to open his trunk....

FEARS
UNNAMED
TIM LEBBON

Tim Lebbon has burst upon the scene and established himself as one of the best horror writers at work today. He is the winner of numerous awards, including a Bram Stoker Award, critics have raved about his work, and fans have eagerly embraced him as a contemporary master of the macabre.

Perhaps nowhere are the reasons for his popularity more evident than in this collection of four of his most chilling novellas. Two of these dark gems received British Fantasy Awards, and another was written specifically for this book and has never previously been published. These terrifying tales form a window into a world of horrors that, once experienced, can never be forgotten.

FACE
TIM LEBBON

When a family picks up a hitchhiker during the worst blizzard in recent memory, they think they're doing him a favor. But he becomes threatening, disturbing, and he asks them for something they cannot—or will not—give: a moment of their time. They force him from their car, but none of them believes that this is the last they will see of him. The hitchhiker begins to haunt the family in ways that don't seem quite natural. He shows them that bad things can sometimes feel very good. He infiltrates their relationships, obsesses them, seduces them and terrifies them. Bit by bit he shows them that true horror can have a very human face.

THE
BACKWOODS
EDWARD
LEE

More than memories await Patricia when she returns to the quiet backwoods town where she grew up. A woman strangled half to death and buried alive. Children who scampered off to play, never to return. Men and women strung up and butchered for sport. Corpses dug up and bodies found—with parts missing. All these greet Patricia. All these and more...

Something from the darkest heart of the night is stalking her, while the town itself seems cursed by a nameless evil. Lust-filled dreams fuel deadly obsessions, the bodies pile up, and the blood flows. Black secrets are revealed and nightmares live in...*The Backwoods*.